ARACHNE'S CRIME

CHRISTOPHER L. BENNETT

Pennsville, NJ

PUBLISHED BY
eSpec Books LLC
Danielle McPhail, Publisher
PO Box 242,
Pennsville, New Jersey 08070
www.especbooks.com

ISBN: 978-1-949691-13-9
ISBN (ebook): 978-1-949691-12-2

Portions of this work originally published as "Aggravated Vehicular Genocide" in *Analog Science Fiction and Fact, Vol. CXVIII No. 11* (November 1998), pp. 110-130; and reprinted in *Among the Wild Cybers*, eSpec Books, 2018.

Interior Design: Danielle McPhail
Cover Art and Design: © Mike McPhail, McP Digital Graphics
Cyber-Web Graphic © Mike McPhail, McP Digital Graphics
Copyeditors: Danielle McPhail and Greg Schauer

To my readers, for giving back.

CONTENTS

When Pallas, pitying her wretched state,
At once prevented, and pronounc'd her fate:
Live; but depend, vile wretch, the Goddess cry'd,
Doom'd in suspence for ever to be ty'd;
That all your race, to utmost date of time,
May feel the vengeance, and detest the crime.

— Ovid, "The Transformation of Arachne into a Spider"
(translated by Samuel Croxall)

Part One

Aggravated Vehicular Genocide

PROLOGUE

Churrlaya was grateful to be his entire self again. As he hopped down from *Zhemhal*'s gangway into the body of his home, he finalized his disengagement from the ship's local consensus memory, feeling a brief moment of incompleteness before his internal mind reconnected with his guild consensus and he remembered the rest of who he was. He and his guildmates aboard the survey vessel had been able to draw on the Biology Guild's uploaded knowledge base and share consensus with one another, but it had been a mere echo. Whatever memories and affinities they shared with him, none of them completed his identity the way Simisshen did.

True, Simisshen was one of many whose external selves now overlapped with his once again. But that one had changed Churrlaya more than all the others once he had joined Biology. This was only the second guild Churrlaya had joined since reaching maturity. It was a delicate age—too far from childhood to be comfortable without firm attachment and identity, yet too unused to transition to adjust easily to a new life. Simisshen had taken Churrlaya under his neck and let the younger one share the parts of his mind to which transition was an old friend, rebirth a welcome release after an old life had grown tiresome. His perspective had become a part of Churrlaya, uniting them in mind even as they discovered the joy of uniting in the flesh. Simi had led so many fascinating lives, formed so many ties to so many homes in his long, roving life. Paradoxically, it made Churrlaya feel more anchored. Not trapped by gravity like those lowly creatures on the rogue ice planet his expedition had surveyed, but connected to the galactic web of life, ever moving and growing.

Yet Churrlaya had never fully appreciated this until the expedition had returned him to a state without Simisshen's memories and ways of thinking as part of himself. He supposed he should be grateful for the deprivation, then, for now he would appreciate his lover all the more.

Simisshen soon felt Churrlaya's return as well, as did Marellel, Ruzhalu, and his other closest guildmates. In moments, they had reached out to him consciously, eager to share in his memories of the survey — to taste the illicit thrill of standing on the surface of a planet, even one with only primitive forms trapped in subglacial oceans. They could study his memories at their leisure, but for now he summarized the mission to slake their curiosity. The rogue's fading internal heat had guttered out further since the last, ancient survey of this obscure worldlet in one of the emptiest parts of the galaxy. Erstwhile pockets of livable ocean had frozen solid, their organisms perfectly preserved for dissection and analysis. It would keep their collegium busy for a long time.

Still, Simisshen pretended to be upset that Churrlaya had left him for so long. "I feared you'd chosen to migrate without telling me," he said, his mocking anger a mask for his relief at being whole again — a relief that Churrlaya could feel in his own thoughts and that, he was stunned and moved to discover, was as intense as his own. Drumming his toes on the ground, Simi threatened, "Spend too long away next time and I'll migrate myself and not tell you where."

Churrlaya leaned forward but shook his mane to soften the aggressive gesture, knowing the ubiquitous cloud sensors would carry his image to their eyes as theirs were brought to his. "I wouldn't even notice you were gone," he taunted, a counterpoint to the truth they shared without words. "I'll simply go female and take Marrellel as my partner."

Marrellel struck tails with Simisshen and opened her mouth wide to Churrlaya, shaking her tongue. Clearly she was about to say something very bawdy and inappropriate.

But then a brilliant, strobing flash blinded the sensor cloud, making Churrlaya reflexively roll his eyes back. The feed flickered as the cloud struggled to compensate with intact sensors, but the strobing continued — like lightning, yet the shadows moved as if the storm were rushing toward the equator. The sensory confusion reflected a deeper one as his external thinking was disrupted, memories and cognitive servers cut off from his access. Falling back on his most basic onboard knowledge and habits, he refocused through a nearby sensor vantage.

He saw flattened vegetation and falling trellises, heard a prolonged thunderclap, felt it shake the whole district. Smelled burning vegetation and flesh. Finally he spotted Simisshen and Marrellel—fallen, covered in burns, bleeding from their eyes and mouths. He called to them, pinged them, but they were motionless—as were all the others around them. He couldn't feel any of them, couldn't access the consensus. He was as alone, as incomplete, as in that brief moment between ship and home—as in that empty lifetime before he met Simisshen. Yet he knew that this time it would never end.

Wait! Now Simi was moving… but no, it was a wind, a gale tearing at his beautiful mane, pushing him brutally into the ground. More flashes and bangs startled Churrlaya, but they were different, they were—the cables? The support cables that held up the ground were… exploding! Whole buildings swayed, the surface rippling in a wave toward his mates.

He saw the ground tear open, the air exploding out into vacuum and taking everything—everyone—with it. But Churrlaya could barely process it through the agony in his mind as half of himself was ripped away along with everything he loved.

1

STEPHEN KEPT HIS EYES ON THE LIGHTS IN THE SKY, EVEN AS HE LAY IN THE mud. The more they tried to beat him down, the more he took comfort in the heights humanity could reach.

"Look up there," he told them once he'd grown strong enough to defend himself and win the chance to be heard. "Look at what we have the potential to achieve if we use our energies together instead of wasting them against each other."

At first, Benjamin was his only audience, gazing up with him at the points of light that swept across the heavens. Stephen spoke to inspire the boy, to give his younger brother the same hope that had sustained him. But he did it for the others too. He knew that fighting them off would only make them come back with greater force. To protect Benjamin, he needed a more powerful weapon, one that could reach into minds and change them, turn their own power to his side. And so he spoke.

"Most of the world isn't like this anymore," he told the starving, bitter people around him whether they listened or not. "The governors keep us hungry and desperate so we'll turn on each other. So they can call us savages and use it to justify keeping us down. So we won't have the strength to stand against them and the militias that keep their entitled white asses in power. But look up there, brothers," he urged, even as the bullies' hands grabbed at him and tried to hold him down. "You can *see* it's a lie. You can see that by standing together, human beings can scale the heights of heaven."

And one by one, they started to listen. One by one, their hands fell away and their eyes turned upward with his, watching the countless points of light that soared outward in a line like regimented fireflies, a scintillant cascade growing ever faster with distance.

"What are they?" Benjamin asked, gazing up at him with those big dark eyes as they stood together on the levee. The boy's rich brown face was Stephen's only reminder of their father.

"Auxons. Self-replicating robots. Or parts of one. They need to start small so they're easier to accelerate — the drive beam can get them close to lightspeed in days. Once they get there, they'll combine into larger robots, ones that can make more robots. They'll build a whole ecology of probes to survey the fifth planet and tell us whether humans can live there. And if the answer's yes, then we'll tell the auxons to build a settlement for us, so it'll already be waiting when the colony ship gets there."

Ben beamed at how clever it was, and Stephen took joy from the sight. He'd never appreciated it enough when Ben had been this young. A burst of brilliant light illuminated Ben's face, and Stephen turned his gaze back outward to watch the fireworks blazing.

"You know it wasn't really like this."

Stephen turned. Cecilia LoCarno leaned against a grafitti-scrawled wall nearby, her sinewy frame taut and ready even in her casual pose. The light from the fireworks put red and blue highlights in her severely cut silver-blonde hair. "You're romanticizing it again, aren't you? Brilliant lights soaring to the stars? You know they launched the microsail probes over months, and with a microwave beam, not visible. Oh, plus it happened a decade and a half before you were born. And, well…" She looked down at Ben, but said no more.

She didn't have to. His eyes stung as he turned back to his brother, older now and standing rigidly beside him while their mother gazed up apologetically from her sickbed, her delicate Chinese features sunken and gaunt. "Why won't they help Mama?" the youth demanded. "They have the medicine."

"I'm working extra-hard," Stephen told him. "Saving everything I can."

"Then they'll just raise the prices! They'll never help one of us. There's only one way to get it!"

Benjamin was already receding from the room. Cecilia tried to stop Stephen from following. "You know where this leads. Don't give into it." He resented her for making him remember. Ben had never grown any older than Stephen saw him now. All he had done to protect his brother had been for nothing. He pushed past her, trying to catch up to Ben and stop him from making the same mistake that had taken their father, but again he felt hands holding him back. "Let go, Cecilia!"

"No, you let go!"

Now they were side by side in the waiting room, in the cheap plastic seats where he felt he'd been imprisoned for ages, waiting for the word that his mother had died at last. In the opposite corner, a silver spider was weaving an intricate web. "Why are you here?" he asked Cecilia.

She shrugged. "Maybe we were both thinking of the mission at the same time. Arachne picked up on the common cues and hooked us in."

The mission. He stared at her, startled, before he remembered again. Her words confirmed that she was the real Cecilia LoCarno. People who were really there had a different feel about them, but sometimes Stephen didn't remember to pay attention. "How do you do that?" he asked her.

"Do what?"

"You always know it's a dream."

"Disciplined mind. Goes with the job." She smirked. "Plus, it's easy to tell in here. Reality isn't in the habit of giving us what we want."

Stephen glanced around. They were in his orbital shuttle, awaiting clearance, and the computer was announcing a prolonged delay. Through the window, the flooded remains of Florida were merely a thin streak vanishing over the horizon. Ben was gone now... had been gone for a very long time. "I know that as well as you do, Cecilia. More. Yet I always get drawn into the dream."

She punched him in the arm. "You would. That's why you need me to drag you back to reality."

"Not here, I don't."

"Hell, yes. Otherwise you'd have remembered on your own—relived the shooting and tortured yourself with losing Ben all over again. Jesus, for such an optimist you sure are pathetic in here," she added, knocking him on the forehead. He cried out in pain; she tended to be rough in the dream realm. Inhibitions were low in unreality, since memories were fleeting. "Or is that it?" she asked. "Maybe that's why you needed to travel so far from Earth—to run away from all that."

"I'm running *toward* something, not away." He sighed as he stared out the port. The shuttle was hemmed in now, in a holding pattern flanked by other craft, distant points that seemed to be drawing closer. "At least, I will if we ever get clearance to leave!"

Cecilia frowned. "Wait, you're right. I sense it too. Something holding us back, holding us still. Even before you said anything, I think I could feel it."

Stephen struggled to remember how this dream world worked. "Then it's… something from Arachne? A message?"

"But just impressions. Damn, I wish we were awake enough to perceive direct telemetry without all the subconscious filtering. Just… try to concentrate on the ship, on the space outside."

He looked out again, and the Earth-orbit vista was gone, replaced by a vast spiderweb gliding through the interstellar void. *Arachne* was a broad cone of shroud lines connecting three great rings of magsail cable, with crew and cargo modules and laser assemblies strung along smaller rings toward the rear. In reality, the gossamer craft was virtually invisible while coasting. In dreamtime, she shimmered, the magnetic field of her sail glowing like an aurora. Gamma Leporis lay ahead, but not an orb, just a bright point, fiercer and whiter than Sol. It brightened suddenly — no, a flash from a closer source? Like the fireworks reflected in Ben's eyes. What was Arachne trying to show them? More flashes, nearer — meteors flashing past the ship. Hitting the ship? He wasn't sure what he'd seen, but whatever it was, something changed. The wind died down, *Arachne*'s sails falling limp, the ship dead in the water. "Do you see us… becalmed?" Though they were in communication, they weren't necessarily perceiving the same things, not without verbal or contextual cues to put them on the same page.

"Parked. In orbit of something, but there's nothing there. A brown dwarf? No, but there is something… something drawing near."

His dream *Arachne* was now a clipper ship with canvas furled, adrift beneath the stars, endless black reflecting in the calm sea. A voice called faintly from above. He looked up to see a great silver spider skittering along the rigging, alert and ready as a ripple fractured the starlight. But beyond her, Stephen Jacobs-Wong saw dark shapes drawing in, pirate boats with oars muffled and lanterns doused. "Stand by," he heard himself call, "and prepare to be boarded."

"Stephen? Can you hear me? Please respond."

The voice faded in and out at the edge of Stephen's consciousness… no, it was his consciousness that faded in and out. The clear, soothing alto — Arachne's voice, yes, sounding authentically human yet more pure and perfect—held steady as it always did. He tried to make a noise, but hibernation gel filled his throat. He remembered to subvocalize, got something out, but instantly forgot what he'd said.

"I've had to rush your revival. This will be difficult, I know. But you must focus."

Try as he might, he caught only fragments. *Detected... contact... gravitational... boarded... inside.*

Then the gel drained away and all he knew was the struggle of his weak, unused muscles to expel it from his throat, his lungs... merciful that he'd forget... and then a hand on his arm, and—

A dragon? In a space helmet?

He was pulled free and hit a cold, hard surface... and then everything was a blur.

"The key is to make her as light as possible." It was Haim Silbermann's gruff voice. *Arachne* was a schematic on a screen, and Stephen stood in Haim's office at Stargazer Enterprises as the stocky, gray-bearded engineer described his baby. "She's stripped down, sleek as a racing yacht. Even so, we'll split her in thirds for the accel phase." The spiderweb split into three separate ships, each with its own magsail loop, each one smaller than the last. "We send the most massive ship first, the lightest one last. That way each one's a bit faster than the one ahead, so they catch up and join together for the coasting phase."

The screen now closed on a single subship, showing a stream of tiny disks bombarding it from behind, vaporizing against its magnetic field. "The sail pellets are where we get our extra kick. Each one's got a nanogram payload of antimatter, enough to turn the whole microsail into hot plasma. The extra energy imparts that much more momentum to the magfield. We should reach point eight *c,* maybe more, depending on how light the payload is." Haim smirked. "The whole crew in hibernation—should be quite the space-saver."

Cecilia was there too, still unconvinced. "And quite the risk. Eighteen years in hibernation? Exposed to the kind of blueshifted radiation and particle bombardment you'd get at those insane speeds? What about the cell damage?"

I'm back in the dream, Stephen began to realize. Or rather, the VR interface mediated by Arachne. A brain could not be completely shut down for long and then started up again; even with hibernation slowing their brain functions to a crawl, the crew still needed stimulation.

Odd, though… hadn't something awakened him? Had he dreamt that as well? Or was Arachne still connecting to his subconscious through his neural implants?

"Hibernation would slow cell division, so damaged DNA wouldn't spread as fast," Stephen heard himself reply even as he wondered this. "And of course the ship's magnetic field and metamaterial shielding will ward off most of the radiation."

Perhaps not an interactive dream, then, but just a memory playback. After so many years asleep, his brain needed the refresher course. Arachne must be helping him get back up to speed for… whatever.

"But not all," the memory of Cecilia said. "There's also toxin buildup, atrophy…"

"All of which can be corrected with a full nanorepair suite, like yours."

"And I've been a spacer long enough to know their limitations. To know *my* limitations. I don't think you do, Stephen. My God, nobody's ever been farther out than two and a half parsecs, or gone much over half of *c*! Now you want to go three times that far and half again that speed—in what amounts to a catamaran! Even with all the advances, all the safeguards, it's an unprecedented risk."

"Going to the Oort cloud is a risk," he said, reminding her of the three-year survey expedition that had brought her to his attention. "Staying within the Belt and building artificial worlds is a risk." Stephen took a slow breath. "Living on Earth is a risk. I can assure you of that." He clasped her hands, holding her gaze with his. "Cecilia, the greatest risk of all is growing complacent and letting entropy catch up with us. Humanity is on the verge of immortality—of spreading far enough through space to ensure that our species will never go extinct. To cross that threshold, we have to be bold enough to face the risks that come with it. And we have to inspire others to be bold."

"*Stephen!*" Cecilia's voice, though the Cecilia before him hadn't spoken.

"Yes, we could limit ourselves to the nearer exoplanets, but Cybele is the most Earthlike one we know, the one where a human colony could most readily thrive. There's symbolic power in that. Just as there is in questing to the very limits—"

A sudden stinging pain. "*Stephen! Wake up, damn it!*"

Cecilia's sharp voice was as much a shock to his system as her slaps to his face. He started awake, trying to remember.

"Easy." Another face came into view, crowding out Cecilia's. A dark, rounded face, maternal and gentle—Doctor Kweli Ndege. "Stephen, how do you feel?"

He tried to move, but the oddly textured surface beneath him clung to his naked skin. He was under gravity! High gravity, from the way the surface dug in; just breathing exhausted him. Or maybe he was just extremely weak. Despite the nanomaintenance and the periodic stimulation to his hibernating muscle cells, you couldn't come out of an eighteen-year slumber without feeling like you'd been asleep for exactly that long. But he gathered his energies, willed himself to sit up, and kindly but firmly brushed aside Kweli's help. He couldn't let himself be weak. Not if what he remembered was real—the dragon-creatures, the heavy suits. Being dragged bodily from hibernation. *Abducted by aliens?*

He looked around. They were in a large chamber with walls tinged an odd, off-putting hue. The light was strange, as if meant for eyes evolved under a different sun. Nearby, the nose cones of *Arachne*'s six habitat/landing modules were visible beyond a dividing wall several meters high. He could see no sign of the cargo modules or magsail cables. The wall was too smooth to scale, even if their condition and the gravity permitted it, and no exits or windows were evident.

Besides Cecilia and Kweli, he saw other members of the crew. Haim Silbermann. Tarik Bahar, Cecilia's burly second-in-command. And Zena… no, Sita Bhatiani, the dainty biologist. They were all naked, still dripping cryo gel, visibly uncomfortable in the coolness of the chamber. (No wonder it was cool—they were meters away from hulls that had recently been in interstellar vacuum. Stephen could hear the modules creaking and popping as they warmed up.) Their hair, and no doubt his own, was shorn to within a centimeter all over their bodies; he remembered that the hibernation chambers' smart gel "digested" their hair as it ever so slowly grew out, filtering heavy metals and toxins and recycling usable compounds to help sustain their glacial metabolisms. It didn't look too strange on Cecilia and Kweli, who wore their hair short to begin with, or on Haim, whose stubbly chin suggested his normal salt-and-pepper beard. But it was odd to see the normally moustachioed Tarik Bahar with a full nascent beard, or Sita without her shoulder-length black hair.

Sita was the only one who wasn't shivering, aside from Cecilia, who never showed weakness. The biologist's dark sloe eyes were wide and inquisitive, her mouth quirking at the corners. For her, being abducted by aliens must be the opportunity of a lifetime.

"Arachne," Stephen asked, "the rest of the crew? The embryos?"

"*The embryos are safe, Stephen,*" came Arachne's voice from his comm implant. "*The remaining forty-two personnel are still in hibernation, alive and well. The xenosophonts have not permitted me to revive them.*"

All right—he hadn't imagined it. "How much do we know?"

"From what Arachne told me," Cecilia said, "we're awake four and a half years early, seven objective. We're still about a parsec and a half from Gamma Lep." Of course Cecilia would've been the first one fully conscious. "These... alien ships just appeared out of nowhere, accelerating like nothing we've ever seen. And then they..." Cecilia exhaled sharply, almost a laugh. "They dragged us to a halt. In just a couple of hours, they slowed us from point-eight-four *c* to a virtual dead stop in the galactic frame."

Haim's serious look gave way to pride. "Point-eight-*four*. The fastest ship ever flown, didn't I tell you?"

"*You flatter me, Haim. But next to these beings, I feel like an inflatable raft. Stephen, based on the Doppler shifts I observed in the starlight, I'd hypothesize that we were decelerated by some form of directed gravitational field.*"

"A tractor beam?" Tarik asked.

Haim shook his head. "Show me the specs and maybe I'll believe it. But whatever they used, the power expenditure must be incredible. Whoever they are, they *really* wanted us to pull over."

"*Once I saw what was happening,*" Arachne went on, "*I initiated an emergency revival of command crew and appropriate advisors.*"

Stephen sized up the group: himself, Cecilia, and Tarik to make the decisions; an engineer to evaluate the aliens' technology; a biologist/ethologist to evaluate the creatures; and the chief physician for obvious but hopefully unnecessary reasons. Appropriate indeed.

Stephen wanted to ask for an update on *Uttu*, but it was futile. *Arachne*'s sister ship should have reached Achird about four years ago by his admittedly fuzzy estimates, but there was no way to confirm that. Sending two expeditions to different stars had ensured that no mishap could befall both ships at once, but it also left each ship completely on its own. He wished for the umpteenth time that he could've organized a larger expedition. But even in the modern, post-scarcity economy, there was only so much material and energy expense that he'd been able to convince his corporate, government, and community partners to invest in a risky experiment like this. Besides… what could a second unarmed ship have done against *this?*

"Are we aboard one of the alien ships?" he asked instead.

"This is the largest of the vessels that intercepted me, yes."

Sita frowned. "Then where the bloody hell are they?!" She pushed herself up onto her knees, as close as she could get to standing. "Oi! Is anyone out there? We come in peace! Take us to your bloody leader already, you wankers!" Her London accent grew increasingly Cockney when she became emotional.

"Sita," Cecilia warned. "We don't know what might provoke them."

"Bollocks! This is the moment we've been waiting for since — forever! We've made contact with sentient, technological aliens — not through signals or probes, but *here*, maybe just on the other side of this wall! Can't blame me for wanting a look at them, can you? They've certainly gotten an eyeful of us," she said, gesturing at her compact nude form as if to invite attention to it.

Resisting the invitation with some difficulty, Stephen answered, "And when the time comes, Sita, you're the one with the experience, the context, to interpret it best. You're better equipped than anyone else here to cope with this — so we need you calm and in control."

She smiled up at him. Something passed between them, a sense of intimacy… stirrings of memory, hot, sweaty, sensual. After a long, warm moment, he broke her gaze, chiding himself to stay focused. He was hardly so shallow as to fixate on a nude woman's allure at a time like this, even one as sublimely lovely as Sita. And their interactions had always been professional before. What he'd remembered must be part of the dreams, then. There would've been no shame in that, not in the dreamspace, for it would all be forgotten afterward. But these impressions of Sita were so vivid, as if from a dream he'd had many times. What had they shared in there?

"We shouldn't romanticize this," Cecilia said. "The one thing we do know is that we've been shanghaied."

"But to what end?" Kweli asked. "Are they pirates?"

"What do we have that they'd want?" Haim asked, gesturing at the awesome technology that implicitly existed beyond the drab walls.

Sita shrugged. "Maybe they went out for takeaway and we're tonight's curry." Kweli glared, not appreciating her humor.

It was bad timing that the aliens chose that moment to arrive. A circular door frame formed within what had been a solid wall—a feat within the capability of human technology, and thus almost reassuring.

Stephen struggled to stand, determined to meet the aliens on his feet. Sita forced herself upright as well, though she needed a hand from Stephen, and then he needed a hand from her to avoid falling over. Cecilia and Tarik, standing quite well on their own, moved forward, ready to defend the others. They were surely too weak to make a difference, but if these aliens could read human body language at all, maybe their determination would suffice. "Arachne," Cecilia said, "any headway with communication?"

"*Upon contact, their vessel's AI system initiated a handshake and translation protocol beginning with physical and mathematical constants.*"

Sita's eyes widened. "They'd have to upload bags of cultural information to give you a basis for understanding their language," she said. "I'd love to be in your head right now."

"*I'll happily upload my data to your buffer, Sita, but there isn't much. I get the impression that it* recognized *the English language and has been using my files merely to update its database. I've gotten little in return.*"

"We have been broadcasting for centuries," Haim observed.

Finally the hatch irised open, revealing a tubular airlock long enough to fit the creatures within. They entered with a graceful hopping motion, necks flexing to steady their heads. They were maybe two and a half meters long and shaped rather like kangaroos, with heavy, stiff tails. Their arms were nearly as long and powerful-looking as their legs, with two fingers and two thumbs on each symmetrical, gloved hand. They brandished rods that were most likely weapons of some kind. Their loose-fitting, helmeted garments looked like cleanroom or biohazard suits, with filters but no air tanks. That implied their own atmosphere was compatible with human needs; Stephen and the others might be breathing it even now.

Under its visor, the first alien had a triangular-snouted, turquoise-skinned head with a crest of bristly hair or cilia running from the front of the snout to between its bulbous, chameleon-like eyes, which were sheltered under large bony brows. Contrary to his initial "dragon" impression, the skin was smooth, and he glimpsed what seemed to be brightly colored hair between the brows.

As a second pair of xenosophonts began cycling through the lock, Cecilia steeled herself and strode forward to face the lead alien. Tarik tensed, clearly wishing to shield his captain with his bulk, but he deferred to her authority. And even nude and nearly bald, she radiated command, as if her flesh were a uniform. "I am Captain Cecilia LoCarno of the colony ship *Arachne*, from the planet Earth. Identify yourselves, and explain your reasons for interrupting our voyage." She had to look up at the creature; in repose, with its body raised to the diagonal and resting on its legs and tail, the alien topped her by a good thirty centimeters. Still, she took a firm, confrontational tone, though she had no way of knowing if that would be understood. Stephen lamented that humanity's first words to this species could not be delivered in a spirit of amity.

The alien remained silent for a moment, probably waiting for the translation. Then it opened its mouth, revealing a thick, muscular tongue and structures resembling omnivore's teeth, and began to speak. Its suit speaker translated: "I am Rillial. We are Chirrn." At least, that was how Stephen's mind approximated the name. The underlying sound could have been approached just as closely with a sneeze, growl, and gulp in quick succession. "We are survivors of vessel Lesshchi. Explain *your* reasons for attacking vessel Lesshchi."

Six pairs of human eyes widened in shock; the chameleon-eyed aliens, now four in number, tensed at the unfamiliar optical display, as if uncertain what it signified. "*What?*" Cecilia finally asked.

"Explain your reasons for attacking vessel Lesshchi. Is language mediation not legitimate?"

"No, it's… . There must be some mistake," Cecilia said with growing anger. "We haven't attacked any ships. We're colonists, not fighters. Besides, we've all been in hibernation. The only person who could've done anything is the ship herself. And Arachne would have no reason to attack an alien ship."

Unless she knew that ship posed some threat, Steven thought, seeing the same realization in Cecilia's eyes. But Arachne would have mentioned any such action.

"Chirrn vessel Lesshchi," Rillial countered, "was struck by many relativistic projectiles incoming by trajectory of your vessel. Do you exclude premise that your transport contains this qualification?"

"Well, no," Haim interjected once he'd parsed the awkward translation. "Um, I'm Haim Silbermann, the chief engineer. We do have a sailbeam system for deflecting interstellar debris."

"Haim!" Cecilia hissed, glaring at him.

Silbermann gave her a *What else can I say?* shrug, then turned back to the Chirrn. "But we wouldn't have fired on your ship. The system checks for engine emissions, radio leakage, and such before it locks on to fire. If your ship had been in our path, Arachne wouldn't have shot it. She would've tried to delay or divert us enough to miss."

Arachne spoke up. *"Captain, I did deploy a fragmentation and deflection volley against a body on a collision course shortly before the Chirrn captured us. But there were no indications of a propulsion system — no particle exhaust, gamma or x-ray signature, magnetic field, or sail of any kind. Nor was there any EM activity suggesting power systems. Its thermal profile was atypically warm, its surface atypically dark, but otherwise it read like a carbonaceous asteroid in the range of twenty to twenty-five kilometers in size, which is far too large for a spacecraft."*

Rillial's eyes swiveled to take in all six humans. "You do not receive comprehension of what you have done," it said; evidently it was tuned into Arachne's comm frequency. "You shall see it. We return to seek inclusion for other survivors. You will come accompanied with us now." The other Chirrn moved forward, rods raised, body language clearly threatening. Their aggression was the most recognizable thing Stephen had seen here.

To Stephen's surprise, the Chirrn led them through a newly-formed door in the partition and back to *Arachne's* modules. "Know this is not illusion," Rillial said. "See through your own ports. Verify with your own instruments."

The modules' cockpits were small, so Stephen, Cecilia, and Haim were led into one, with Tarik accompanying Sita and Kweli into the other. Two Chirrn shepherded each group; Rillial and an even larger, more bluish Chirrn accompanied Stephen's. As a small mercy, Arachne spoke up and insisted that her protocols forbade cockpit access to anyone not wearing at least an emergency pressure garment—a small deception, but one that granted the captives a modicum of dignity. Stephen sent subvocal thanks to the shipmind as he donned the thin, close-fitting pressure membrane under close Chirrn supervision. The guards did insist on holding on to the humans' helmets, lest Arachne attempt anything untoward with the cockpit pressure.

The modules lurched as they were picked up by the dock machinery. Stephen watched through the cockpit windows as they moved toward a moderately larger craft ringed by a cylindrical collar. The modules were tilted forward, making Stephen grateful he'd strapped in. But once they were positioned between the spacecraft's hull and its cylindrical collar, the sensation of weight vanished. Shortly, the ringed craft launched into space at considerable speed, but Stephen felt almost no acceleration. "Amazing," Haim breathed. "Inertial cancellation. And did you notice? Their ship isn't rotating either. I didn't feel any Coriolis shifts as we moved. I'd never have believed it, but they must have some kind of artificial gravity."

Stephen watched as Cecilia tested the cockpit's controls, determining that the Chirrn had left only the sensor displays and their manual backup controls active. It was overkill; the landing modules had only enough fuel for orbital maneuvering, specifically to rendezvous with an auxon-built orbital station which would fuel them for planetary descent. They could never outrun a Chirrn starship.

The stars were all that Stephen saw for an uncertain amount of time. He compared the starscape against the simulated view from Cybele that he had memorized over the years of planning: the *W* of Cassiopeia written in an unfamiliar hand, the Little Dipper more of a long-handled funnel, Boötes tangled in Berenice's hair. It was off by just enough to account for the parsec-and-a-half distance Cecilia had reported. Scanning the sky, he found Sol exactly where he expected it, directly between Sirius and Altair.

Naturally, Cecilia was the first to spot something. Unfastening her harness, she pulled herself to the port for a closer look. Stephen followed her lead, as did Haim and Kweli, and before long he could see it too. A shimmer of lights, multicolored pinpricks flickering, moving in a stately dance around a central point. Faint sparkling clouds surrounding them, catching their glow, scintillating. It was beautiful.

Soon they drew close enough to see the truth. The lights were ships around a vast, dark central mass, shining spotlights as they flew around it in search patterns. From the way it eclipsed the stars, its main body was a cylinder, foreshortened from this angle but maybe six to ten times as long as it was wide. Around its equator was a broad ring like a much vaster version of the one currently encompassing *Arachne*'s habitat modules, but more solidly merged with the cylinder. At the near end, appended to the hemispherical endcap, were two fat disk-shaped structures, nearly as wide as the cylinder, connected with multiple struts yet mostly self-contained. Overall, it reminded him of the O'Neill habitats back in Solsys, though it was apparently not rotating.

As the Chirrn ship rounded the habitat, the shape of the far end came into view past the central bulge. It seemed different on this end, like it had an extra protruding structure on one…

Side…

His mind resisted understanding what he saw, as much due to the sheer scale as to its horrific significance. Two huge portions of the habitat's hull, kilometers long and wide, hung outward from the structure as though something had sliced a jagged gash through the hull, then peeled back the edges to expose the contents within. As they drew closer, Stephen could see the remains of structures—buildings—on its warped surface. Soon he noticed a smaller, coaxial cylinder inside the habitat, also showing damage. He had no way of telling just how deep the damage penetrated, or how much atmosphere that inner cylinder might have lost.

Much of the debris, frozen atmosphere, and moisture that had spilled from that tremendous rupture surrounded the habitat in a diffuse halo that caught the search vessels' spotlights as they probed it. Stephen tried not to look too closely at the debris. He knew some of it was organic. Some of it was Chirrn. Some of it was children.

"God," he breathed, once he found his voice. "There *is* a translation problem. 'Vessel' doesn't just mean 'ship'… it means 'container.' Lesshchi is a space habitat."

"Lesshchi is our home," Rillial replied. "The Chirrn are not tenants of planets as you are this. We exist included within vessels between the stars. Included in Lesshchi existed greater than eight hundred seventy thousand Chirrn. At last report, quantity approaching one in six are dead or absent, and many others die in potential if not evacuated in time. Uncounted more have lost external self, not retrievable in potential."

The last meant nothing to him, but the numbers were horribly clear. "Over a hundred thousand people," Stephen gasped. "And we… we killed them?" Had he been under gravity, his legs would have folded beneath him. For a moment, he was back in the dreams, in the part Cecilia had stopped him from reliving: Benjamin's twelve-year-old body face-down on the road, gory holes torn in his back, medical supplies scattered around him. Militiamen with assault rifles cordoning off the scene while posting self-congratulatory status updates about bringing a dangerous miscegenist radical to justice. Everything Stephen had done in the decades since had been to prevent scenes like that from ever recurring again. And it had led here—to a gaping wound torn in the skin of an entire world.

"Your projectiles pierced our habitat's shell and penetrated the interior atmosphere at almost light speed," Rillial said, its emotions unknowable through mechanical translation and alien intonation. "The heat, shock, radiation killed tens of thousands in the instant. The electromagnetic pulse disrupted the network and destroyed entire consensus memories. The shock worsened the hull rupture until that segment of Lesshchi blew out into vacuum. The turbulence killed many more beyond those expelled into space."

Stephen shuddered as he contemplated the energies involved. *Arachne*'s asteroid defense was so simple, so efficient—since the ship was already relativistic, accelerating gram-sized microsails ahead of the ship by a few more percentage points of lightspeed would give them kinetic energies of dozens of kilotons. A single sail would hit harder than the Nagasaki bomb. It had seemed so elegant… when directed at inanimate hunks of rock.

But that was not her primary defense system. "Arachne," he asked slowly, "why the sailbeam? Why not a hydrogen burst?" He wasn't sure if a relativistic hydrogen cloud would have been any less damaging to a space habitat than this had been. But it was the preferred deflection system for bodies too large to ionize with her forward lasers; not only was it gentler, with less risk of creating dangerous chunks of debris, but it was easily replenished from the interstellar medium.

Arachne spoke through the cockpit speakers, her synthesized tones lacking inflection. Perhaps she was too shocked to simulate human speech mannerisms. *"The body was too large to deflect conventionally, and too close upon detection to enable me to attempt magnetic braking. My spectroscopic and radar scans suggested a carbonaceous body with large pockets of volatiles and internal voids; I calculated that it could be shattered into pieces light enough for deflection by conventional means. I directed eighty microsails in a strafing pattern across the width of the body's visible cross-section."* There followed what for a cyber was a lengthy pause. *"The body did not fragment as I'd expected, yet it underwent sufficient deflection nonetheless. I suspected that the vaporization of volatiles within had provided the thrust needed to divert it. There was a fair amount of water vapor in the outgassing cloud."*

After another pause (for no one knew how to respond to that), Rillial continued its tale. "By then, our defenses engaged. They rejected the remaining projectiles and accelerated Lesshchi out of their path. But this could not exclude damage already made. Had we failed to halt Lesshchi's rotation in time, the habitat could have torn apart."

"I still don't understand," Arachne said. *"I detected no electromagnetic leakage, no indication of technology."*

"Our systems do not 'leak.' And many are outside your knowledge of technology." Rillial turned to the port. "They *were*," it amended.

Stephen couldn't help but follow its chameleon eyes. Lesshchi had drawn closer now, and he realized that his perceptions of scale had been in error. The exposed internal structure of the devastated section had looked to him like a few cross-sectioned decks of a wrecked ship. But now he could see that each exposed level was hundreds of meters high, with its own internal array of towers and streets and desiccated plant life. The shapes he'd seen on the inner surface weren't the remains of building frameworks, but skyscrapers, a whole city's worth. Now those cityscapes were sundered, stripped bare, bereft of light and movement.

Stephen spotted ships probing the shell of the inner cylinder, racing to seal off diffuse white jets that shot from it at various points. Rillial noticed his gaze and elaborated. "Those who remain in the inner core are still in danger of death. The evacuation proceeds, but it is slow. There is structural damage throughout the habitat, impeding rescue and evacuation." It continued with evident difficulty. "Lesshchi inclusive may be too structurally damaged to salvage. My world… my affiliation… a piece of myself… you have killed it. As you have killed many. The one who spoke my first young… the one who inspired my speaking.…"

It lunged, grabbing the sides of Cecilia's head. Stephen pushed off toward it, but its tail lashed and slammed him into the bulkhead. Fire burned in his ribs, and he fleetingly found himself grateful that Rillial hadn't used those powerful megalopod legs; he might have been killed instantly. He feared Cecilia still might be.

But the other, larger Chirrn pulled Rillial back. Rillial let out a hissing noise that didn't translate, probably because there was no coherent thought behind it, but subsided. "You killed them all," it went on, seemingly not breathing hard yet still trembling with emotion. "Completely and beyond recovery. And you will be made to pay."

Cecilia glared, but maintained her calm and poise despite having nearly had her skull crushed in. "There's no question this was a great tragedy. And we understand and sympathize with your grief. But we did not do this knowingly. We didn't even know your species existed until you... pulled us over. What happened to your habitat was an accident."

"In space, accidents are usually fatal. To fail to guard against accident is intolerable negligence. Only a planet-dweller would claim accident as an excuse."

As Stephen gazed out at the wreck of Lesshchi, he couldn't help feel that the contempt in Rillial's words was justified. "Rillial..." he began hesitantly, "is there anything we can do to help you? To try to make up for what we've—"

"Stephen!" LoCarno warned sharply. She pulled him aside to hold his gaze closely, and a text appeared in his retinal HUD. *<Don't say anything that would imply culpability on our part.>*

"But—"

<I'll make it an order if I have to.> He stared at her, recognizing the seriousness of the threat. He led the colony expedition, but out here, while they were still in space, she could pull rank over him. *<We have to think clearly. A horrible thing, yes, but we don't know what they plan to do to us. Mustn't say or do anything to make it easier for them.>* She quailed at the expression in Stephen's eyes. *<Don't look at me that way. I don't feel any better about what's out there than you do. But my duty is to the passengers and crew of this ship, and to the hundreds of embryos we're carrying. I have to place their interests first.*

<What you were about to say, you kind and noble idiot, could've been taken as a confession. No telling what consequences that would have in their legal system. If they even plan to use their legal system instead of just taking revenge.> She rubbed the side of her head, staring at Rillial. *<We don't know what they'll do. So we have to be on our guard, no matter what we may feel for their dead.>*

Stephen sighed heavily, but nodded. He'd been weakened by hibernation and the shock he'd faced upon awakening; but he was a leader, a survivor, and he could accept cold realities. *<Okay,>* he sent. *<So we need to find out what they plan to do next.>*

2

That was how Dr. Kweli Ndege had chosen to deal with the situation. As their Chirrn guides had shown them the wreckage of Lesshchi, ensuring they got a thorough tour of the devastation, each of the humans in the second module had reacted differently. The doctor had sunken more and more into denial, convincing herself that she was still hibernating and this was some nightmarish malfunction of the VR interface. She had curled her stout frame into a fetal ball, chanting to herself that it was all a dream, that in time she would wake up and everything would be all right. Tarik Bahar had an arm around her shoulders, comforting her and wiping away the tears that pooled around her eyes in microgravity; yet his own eyes were wrenched tightly shut.

Sita Bhatiani had no such luxury. She remembered enough from the hibernation dreams to know they could never be mistaken for waking reality. And while the Chirrn had aspects reminiscent of Earth creatures, there were enough details that just felt *off*, quirks of anatomy or design that no human hoaxer was likely to have conceived—though she couldn't rule out a cyber having that kind of imagination. But she had done the usual checks, turning her head abruptly or grabbing at unexpected objects, and her perceptual security apps had sensed no delays or rendering errors. If this was virtual or augmented reality, it was perfect beyond the grasp of mid-twenty-second-century information theory.

Sita thus had to conclude that she was awake and the Chirrn were physically real. Being flown out here at accelerations that defied physics to see the undeniable reality of this vast, devastated habitat had left no doubt. Seeing the torn and desiccated bodies drifting in space had driven the reality home with agonizing force.

So what was left? Could they have staged this tragedy in order to blame *Arachne*'s crew? But why kill a hundred thousand of their own people to scapegoat a species that had never met them? As a pretext for conquering Solsys? But if they lived in deep-space habitats, why would they need to?

Could *Arachne* have been framed for an attack waged by some rival Chirrn habitat or terrorist faction? But Arachne had confirmed firing on an object Lesshchi's size. And she had given no indication of being off her course, so such a group would have had to steer Lesshchi into her sights. Which would mean all these deaths had still come at human hands, however indirectly.

Maybe there were extenuating circumstances. Maybe Lesshchi's own defenses had failed or been sabotaged, its structure weakened by shoddy construction, *something*. Sita had to find out if she could.

She chose her words carefully before she turned to their main Chirrn watchdog, a relatively small one with dark green skin and some grayish hair visible through its suit visor. "There was no warning?" she asked, taking care to pitch her voice softly, sympathetically. They might not catch the nuances of human vocal expression, but it had already been confirmed that they associated loudness with anger.

The Chirrn's eyes swiveled to lock on her. Its brow ridges pulled forward in a surprisingly humanlike way. "Our warning was only your radar scan. The protection collegium sought recognition of its source, but were blocked by the velocity and low visibility of your transport. Before they could locate it, your bombardment began."

She had to phrase this delicately. "And… it overwhelmed your shielding?"

The Chirrn angled its head closer, clearly an aggressive gesture. "Our shielding is designed against interstellar debris, not relativistic weaponry."

"Defense," Tarik spoke up. "It's just a defense system."

The Chirrn whirled on him, using its tail deftly to shift its weight in midair. Sita was struck by how graceful and natural the Chirrn body seemed in microgravity, as if they had evolved or engineered themselves for it.

"Your 'defense system' penetrated our shielding and detonated within like a nuclear explosive," the Chirrn said. "It killed in the instant nearly a full inclusion of Chirrn in that division of the outward cylinder. My mates were there. Simisshen, Marellel, Ruzhalu. They died as I watched this! As I felt this!"

Though there was sympathy in Tarik's eyes, he braced himself in response to the Chirrn's fury, ready to defend himself and Kweli if attacked. Sita knew he was a gentle, spiritual man at heart, but he was intensely protective of his crew, and was the only human so far awakened who was strong enough to make a good fight against the Chirrn. Sita noted the second megalopod tensing up in response, drawing its truncheon-like weapon. Both Chirrn's body language told her they were on the verge of violence—an act they would see as self-defense against a murderous alien monster. And if that monster could actually pose a physical threat to them in return, their resulting fear could drive them into a killing frenzy.

Better, then, that they direct their aggression against someone less intimidating. "But how did so much of the hull get torn away?" Sita demanded, hardening her voice to draw the Chirrn's anger.

It worked. That tail whipped again and the green Chirrn clutched her, forcing her back against the bulkhead. One long forearm pressed against her upper chest like a bar, pinning her arms, while its other hand instinctively grasped a handhold for leverage. Its elongated feet came forward to clutch her shins with their prehensile toes, immobilizing her legs. Sita caught Tarik's eyes and shook her head, warning him not to intervene.

The Chirrn shouted in her face, and she had to strain to hear the translation over its volume. "You question this tragedy? You try to deny it?"

"I just… want to understand."

The arm and both feet squeezed tighter. She cried out despite herself. "Good. You should understand the death you caused." One eye flicked backward to direct her gaze out the window. "We have not gathered in every part of what happened. We are busy attempting to gather in those who live. But once we do understand, you will be given inclusive details of how you destroyed our world."

Sita was glad the Chirrn was hurting her. The pain gave her something immediate to focus on, something to distract her from the horror. She wanted to fight back just to provoke it into worse violence, to give herself something immediate and visceral to lose herself in— even if it killed her. But there were two other people here to worry about, one of them nearly catatonic. She couldn't get them killed too. So she just let go and submitted to the pain.

Surely she deserved no less.

Once the Chirrn on the other rescue ships began to catch on that there were humans present at the scene, it became increasingly disruptive to the search efforts—even dangerous to the Chirrn ringship. A few ships tried to board, attack, or simply ram the ringship, determined to take revenge on the humans even at the cost of Chirrn lives. It was depressing, Sita thought, to see that the drive for revenge might be universal. The ringship retreated back to the larger vessel, and at last Sita and the others were spared from being forced to see their handiwork any further.

Not our handiwork, Sita tried to tell herself once the six humans were forced to strip again, returned to their bare prison, and provided with minimal water and nourishment from *Arachne*'s emergency stores. *We were all asleep. If anyone's to blame, it's Arachne.* But she cursed herself for the thought. Arachne had been their nurturing, reliable partner throughout the mission, the being to whom they'd entrusted their lives, their future, their very minds. Everything the cyber did, she did on their behalf. Not because she was programmed or compelled to; Arachne was loyal because she chose to be, because she cherished her human charges and believed in their mission as strongly as they did.

Then maybe it was Stephen's fault? Sita glanced over at him, though thankfully his back was turned. The prisoners had relieved and cleaned themselves in the small chamber the Chirrn had provided (thank heaven for small favors, since those were the only kind they'd get from these beings) and were now trying to get some sleep despite the bright light, cold air, high gravity, and lack of bedding. Kweli was still near-catatonic, hiding from reality, in shocking contrast to her normal gregarious exuberance. Cecilia and Haim had sandwiched her between their bodies; Haim was only attracted to men, so there was nothing untoward about it. Stephen and Tarik had bracketed Sita for warmth as well, though they lay at a more discreet distance—not that she would've minded huddling much more closely with either or both of them. Stephen's lean, beautiful, coffee-skinned frame shifted fitfully, far from sleep for reasons that surely had little to do with the cold. *Guilty conscience?*

Stephen Jacobs-Wong had come far from his beginnings in the chaos of the American Gulf Coast. It had been one of the last remaining poverty-stricken regions on the planet, devastated by superhurricanes and rising sea levels, abandoned by corrupt governors and corporate executives who had pocketed the international relief funds, and racked by sectarian violence between fundamentalist, white supremacist Christian militias — the latest and hopefully last gasp of the demons that always seemed to crawl out of America's woodwork whenever it was weakened, no matter how many times the world believed they had been conquered for good. Those too impoverished to move away were forced to endure the breakdown of infrastructure as well as social order. Without basic sanitation, the death toll from waterborne diseases had skyrocketed, and the militias and their wealthy supporters had hoarded food and medicine from those who didn't fit their standards of ethnic or religious purity. Any who had protested or agitated for change were beaten, imprisoned, or simply gunned down. Hundreds of thousands had died, including members of Stephen's own family.

But Stephen was a fighter. Surviving against the odds, he had managed to get his sisters and himself out of what remained of Florida and to the safety and prosperity of São Paulo. From there, he'd leveraged his tragic story into a massive activist movement that worked with the Union of Earth and Cislunar States to bring pressure to bear on the governors until their power was broken and order restored. Stephen had then founded Stargazer Enterprises to spearhead the reconstruction, building it into a mighty conglomerate dedicated, in his words, to making sure nothing like his story need ever happen again.

He had been the guiding spirit behind this expedition, using all the resources of SGE to bring it about. Everything he'd done over the years to promote advances in propulsion technology, auxonic construction, terraforming, and improved hibernation techniques — advances that had benefitted tens of millions from Venus to Mars to the Cerean States to Alpha Centauri — had been with the ultimate goal of establishing the first colonies on planets where humans could live without environment domes or extensive terraforming. Some had said he'd been so trauma-tized by his childhood that he was determined to get away from Earth at all costs. Stephen had said his goal was to give humanity a chance at a fresh beginning. Whatever the reasons, he had been relentless in making it a reality, wielding all his charisma and influence to win others over to a quest that had initially seemed mad to most of them.

So didn't that mean the ultimate blame fell on him? Sita was only here because he'd won her over with the allure of his dream. Surely she couldn't be held accountable.

Bollocks, she told herself. She and all the others had thrown themselves body and soul into making this happen. She had striven to prove that she had the skill, versatility, and sheer determination to deserve one of the precious forty-eight spots on the expedition to Gamma Leporis Ad. And of course it was the Cybele expedition she had fought for, not the less risky one being prepared for Eta Cassiopeiae Ac, only two-thirds the distance and only moderately less ideal for settlement. After all, she'd known that Stephen would be personally leading the more difficult quest, so that no one would doubt his commitment. And he'd refused to guarantee himself that spot, enduring the same rigorous trials as everyone else and *earning* his place at their lead. He had inspired Sita to push herself just as hard, to earn her own place alongside him. So if Stephen was to blame for this horrific accident, then Sita had just as much blood on her hands.

She trembled at the thought, and at the cold. Stephen must have heard her shuddering intake of breath, for he rolled over and saw her distress. Wordlessly, he moved closer, cradling her in his arms. Her heart raced at his embrace.

But he only held her, sharing his warmth. She snuggled close, hoping he would take the hint, but when she met his eyes, they were a billion klicks away… or probably much closer, assuming this ship was still gathering refugees from Lesshchi. She wanted to kiss him, to comfort and soothe him. But she realized she had no comfort to give. All she had was need. If she let him see that need, he might respond, kind as he was. But she didn't want to be selfish when he was in need as well. She couldn't do that to the man she loved.

Sita winced. *Who do I think I'm fooling?* He held her naked in his arms and had no erection, didn't even look at her. She could imagine it was merely shock, but when had he ever shown interest? Back in Solsys, they had interacted little beyond the necessary professional contacts. Her own fault, she reminded herself, for being too shy around him, intimidated by his fame and power. As a rule, she was rarely afraid to face a challenge. She hadn't earned her spot among the privileged few by being faint of heart. Granted, she may have beaten another leading candidate or two simply by being the smallest; *Arachne*'s payload had needed to be as light as possible for maximum speed, and the majority of the crew was below average size. But being a meter and a half high and less than seven stone in weight was just one more reason she'd learned to be assertive. Still, whenever she'd been alone with Stephen, she'd been as timid as the schoolgirl she was sometimes mistaken for.

What she remembered from the hibernation dreams, then, as vivid and erotic as it had been, was probably just her own fantasy feeding on itself. She had no doubt that a man as desirable, rich, and gregarious as Stephen had taken many lovers in the dreamscape, but if she had been one of them, it would've been just one more casual, forgettable rendezvous for him.

Let's face it… I wasn't in the mood either. Her yearning, she realized, was almost abstract; her body was not reacting any more than his. She couldn't even bring herself to feel depressed at his lack of interest. It all paled next to the tragedy.

"I suppose… I should be proud of myself," she said.

Stephen finally looked at her, distantly aghast. "Proud?"

She winced. "That came out wrong. I mean… these are aliens. Creatures we've never seen before today, from… a totally different biosphere, a separate evolutionary heritage. And yet… it hurts as much as if they were human." She gave a feeble, self-deprecating grin, which stretched into a rictus of pain. "How bloody noble of me."

"Sita." He paused until she met his eyes. "Don't ever mock that compassion. If we're… to redeem ourselves for this… that's where it will come from." He clasped her hand. "We have to show them that we grieve too. That we are not monsters."

"Do you believe that?" she asked softly. "That we can redeem ourselves?"

It took him a while to respond. "We have to try."

She turned away, unable to face the pain in his eyes any longer. Her gaze fixed on the entrance, now permanently visible with a portal through which a Chirrn guard watched them. This one had taken its hood off, revealing a long, luxurious golden mane whose translucent strands shimmered as it moved, beautifully complementing its rich azure skin. *Natural or artificial?* she wondered. Either would raise so many fascinating questions. Her mind raced with her observations—a distraction she welcomed.

"This should be such a miracle," she said. "First contact with an intelligent species. So much to learn. In any other circumstances, I'd be exploding with joy."

"So would I," Stephen said. "And I'm glad you're here with us, watching them so closely. We need to learn all we can." He paused. "It's heartening that they're so similar. More or less mammalian, brains enough like ours for mutual communication… the similarities outweigh the differences. I'm hopeful we can build on that."

"Really? I've been noticing so many differences. The way the joints move suggests a different design to the skeleton and musculature. The eyes suggest a chameleon's, but the fine structure is unlike anything I've ever seen. The muscle in the mouth isn't quite a tongue, the grinding and cutting surfaces aren't quite teeth, the head covering isn't quite hair or fur as we know it. Different evolutionary processes giving different solutions to the same problem."

"But form follows function, doesn't it? Parallel solutions for parallel needs. Swiveling eyes for field of view, long legs for hopping, a cantilevered tail for balance."

"Yes, but evolution can arrive at those solutions from wildly different angles, creating all manner of quirks and unnecessary embellishments. I mean, where's the advantage in hopping as locomotion? For a big-brained creature, it risks imparting too much shock to the cranium. Sure, their necks seem to provide shock absorption, but why go to the trouble?

"Come to that, why would a hopping, presumably ground-based species evolve opposable thumbs? What's the advantage to that array of small nares on top of the snout? Wouldn't they drown in the rain? And where's the advantage in a scent-detection system that isn't forward and low, able to sniff the ground? If they even smell with their nares, but what other logical place is there for olfactory organs except where the air comes in? Krishna, they're just so bloody weird."

Stephen let out a weak chuckle. "I hate myself for this… but you know what I can't help thinking they remind me of?"

"What?"

"Kermit the Frog. …Do you know who that is?"

A laugh erupted out of somewhere deep. "I see what you mean!" She kept laughing. "The… the mouth is kind of shaped that way… and the bulgey eyes… the green skin…" She laughed harder, hating herself for doing it.

But he was laughing too. "It's not that easy… being…" He lost it. She fell apart in hysterical, tearful laughter right along with him, unable to stop.

The next thing she knew, the hatch was open and the golden-maned Chirrn guard was storming in, its head still bared. It was shouting at her, raising its rodlike weapon menacingly, and she only caught part of the translation. "Stop staring… revolting noise… filthy ground-vermin!"

Other Chirrn came in behind it, wearing full biohazard suits. Again, she only discerned snatches of the rapid-fire dialogue. ". . .need your hood… cannot know… dirtgrubber infection."

". . . think I care… my speechmates… half my self… want it to stop staring!" But Sita couldn't look away. This was the best look she'd gotten at the Chirrn head and mouth in action. Was that tongue porous?

"Repellent," one of them said, one bound carrying it nearer where Sita and Stephen lay together. "See their structure. They join where they excrete!"

"Well-diggers," another said. "Ferals! All they know is filth."

"Why they destroy what is pure!"

Tarik was rising now, instinctively moving to shield Captain LoCarno, but she would have none of it, standing right at his side. Stephen came to his feet as well, while Haim continued to hold onto Kweli, shielding her helpless form with his bulk. The Chirrn brandished their staves more aggressively.

But the golden-maned guard's eyes were locked unwaveringly on Sita. *"You! Stop… staring!!"* The guard snapped, lunging at her. Stephen interposed himself, but it knocked him aside with its staff, and he convulsed as if electrocuted. Shrieking, Sita scrambled away, and the other prisoners closed in around her.

But the other Chirrn were in motion now, leaping high and fast to bring their shock sticks down upon her protectors. Tarik fell first, taking a blow meant for his captain. LoCarno dodged and got in a good kick, knocking her assailant's shock stick across the bay. She grabbed her attacker by the forearms, fell back, and pushed with her legs, flipping it onto its snout. But it promptly recovered into a quadrupedal stance, courtesy of its long forearms, and its tail caught her in the ribs and bowled her over in mid-recovery.

"Cecilia!" Stephen struggled toward the captain as she gasped in agony, clutching her side. He clasped her shoulder, but another guard moved in with its own shock stick and jammed it into her spine, convulsing her and Stephen both as the shock passed through their bodies. Stephen fell away, but the guard continued to torture LoCarno. Tarik shouted in wordless rage, but he was busy holding the unhooded guard at bay, trying to keep its shock stick from connecting. Sita ran toward the captain, determined to do something to help, even if it was just to divert the torturer's efforts to herself.

But then Haim Silbermann barreled in with a roar, brandishing the fallen shock stick. The guard's eye swiveled backward—*independently of the other, interesting!*—and it lashed out at Silbermann with its heavy tail. The bearish engineer pulled up short and brought the stick down to parry the blow. The block worked, but no shock went through the guard's body; Silbermann must not have been using it right. Undeterred, he adapted the tools at hand like any good engineer, turning the high-tech alien weapon into a good old primitive club, pounding on the alien until it laid off the captain.

But Silbermann was weakened, and the Chirrn's suit gave it some padding. It whirled and sent him flying with a brutal kick, using its tail to counter the recoil force. Then it lunged at him and began using its own shock stick as a club; this time, the shock function worked.

Sita couldn't help him. But she crouched at the captain's side and tried to pull her away from the Chirrn. *Don't think about what's happening… concentrate on the moment…*

But then the moment exploded into agony, and when she recovered her senses, she was on her back, twitching, and the azure-skinned guard loomed over her with its teeth (but not teeth) bared, and its hair (but not hair) cascaded around its head and it was just so beautiful, who's your stylist, love? It roared at her, and the rod came down again and exploded her world, and when she came back she was screaming and her ribs were in pieces, and its foot struck her legs and she felt her bones give way like twigs, the agony so severe that when the rod came again it was almost a relief, until she felt the agony in her arm as the edges of shattered bone ground together, and her own screams and the blood rushing through her ears deafened her—yet still she thought she heard words between the bombs going off in her brain. "You! Again!

"Why won't you stop *staring?!*"

Cecilia LoCarno awoke to find herself in one of *Arachne*'s small emergency medical bays. Looking around, she saw Stephen lying in the medbed next to hers, with Kweli Ndege tending to him. For a moment, she allowed herself to hope that recent events had simply been a hibernation nightmare, as Kweli had believed. But the three of them were still naked, and she and Stephen were covered in bruises. Either they'd had a hell of a party in here, or it was all real.

Kweli spotted her movement. "Good, you're awake," the warm-featured Kenyan said.

"Stephen?"

"Sleeping it off. He'll be okay."

"The others?"

Kweli looked away. "They all got it pretty bad. Blunt-force trauma, contusions, electric shock... ." The doctor hesitated, and Cecilia braced herself for the worst. "Sita got it worst of all. Half the bones in her body were broken. Concussion, skull fracture... her heart had been stopped for at least three minutes by the time we got her in the medbed, and her backup cerebral perfuser was damaged, so there was some ischemic injury. As it is, no telling when she'll regain consciousness, or if the brain damage will be beyond nanorepair. But she's alive, and I expect her to recover."

Cecilia closed her eyes and thanked God. Then she looked at Kweli. "Glad to see you up and about too, Doctor."

The other woman's gaze was distant. "I'm still not convinced this is real. But I... couldn't take the chance."

"Lucky for us."

"It can't be real, can it? Not a dream... but it must be some terrible hoax. We couldn't have done... what they say."

"Listen to me, Kweli." Her sharp tone caught and held the doctor's attention. "We don't have enough facts to say anything for sure. But the one thing I want you to be absolutely certain of is, we're innocent. Whatever happened, we're not to blame. You have to believe that, and you have to show the Chirrn that you believe it. Do you understand me, Doctor?"

Kweli nodded, breathing hard. Her shoulders relaxed as if a burden had been lifted from them. "I can do that," she said. A trace of her normal smile flashed across her features, though only for an instant.

Cecilia smiled. "Good. I knew I could count on you."

But comforting the doctor hadn't been her primary goal. This crew had to present a united front of innocence to the Chirrn, and not one rooted in borderline psychotic withdrawal. These creatures had made it abundantly clear that they considered *Arachne*'s crew their enemies. No doubt Stephen would pursue diplomacy and try to change their minds. She wished him success, and had faith that if anyone could pull it off, Stephen Jacobs-Wong could. But she had to be ready for the other contingency. She had to hold this crew together against a threat none of them had imagined, and bring them through it alive, intact, and back on course for Gamma Leporis—somehow. And that wouldn't happen if this crew showed any weakness or guilt.

A movement at the hatchway drew her attention. It was the turquoise-skinned Chirrn she recognized as Rillial, evidently the leader of this group. The captain of this ship? Certainly an authority figure. She recognized that much. "Captain," it said. "What is the status of your crew?"

"We'll live," she told it, raising herself into a sitting position. She would stand if she had the strength, but for now this would have to do. "No thanks to your underlings."

"But thanks to you," came Stephen's voice. Her old friend was awake now too, following her to a seated position with Kweli's help, and he was as predictable as ever, taking the conciliatory route. "You have our gratitude for allowing us the use of our medical facilities."

"I do not have it or want it," the Chirrn replied. "For myself alone, I would have gladly joined them in killing you all. But even with our minds diminished, we are not savages, despite what you almost brought my crew to here. I will not allow you to drag the Chirrn down to the dirt where you live. Guard Vhehhal and the other assailants have been excluded from your security detail and will be disciplined for their violence. You will be treated fairly when we reach Shilirrlal, though you do not deserve the privilege."

"Shill…" Stephen trailed off.

"Shilirrlal is our destination. The habitat from which Lesshchi was spoken, not so many lifetimes ago… which must now take its remains back in, those it has space to include. There you will be judged, in the proper way and at the proper time."

"So we're to be put on trial?" Cecilia asked.

"Yes. We are a lawful people."

"Does that mean we'll be given a fair chance to defend ourselves against your charges?"

Rillial stared. "You may defend yourselves to the limits of your ability. The facts permit no doubt."

"Really?" she challenged. "Is that for you to decide?" Stephen watched the scene intently, but did not interfere. She appreciated his deference to her judgment.

The Chirrn loomed closer. "If possible, it will be."

"Says the one who just confessed to wanting to beat us to death. You call that lawful?"

Rillial's mouth opened, and a rattling hiss came out. "There is what we wish, and there is what is proper to do. Perhaps in the trial you will learn the difference."

Cecilia forced herself to her feet, even though her legs would barely sustain her weight. "Or maybe you'll learn not to underestimate the human race. Bring it on, Green-eyes. Bring it on."

3

WHEN THE CHIRRN AWOKE THE REST OF THE CREW, STEPHEN HAD TO watch them all go through the same process of confusion, discovery, and shock that the first six had experienced. None of them had wanted to believe at first. Taken prisoner by aliens, stripped of their clothing, possessions, and dignity, and thrown into a bare, crowded cell like livestock; the expedition leaders beaten half to death; the whole crew being taken to an alien habitat to be tried for mass murder. How could it be anything but some shameful hoax?

But the first six had spelled out the chilling reality to the others. Cecilia's painfully detailed account had made it real for most of them; she was their captain, after all, and if she said a thing was true, then it was. A few still refused to believe it. James Oates, the expedition's industrial engineer, began spinning conspiracy theories about piracy and slave labor, doing more to frighten the others than reassure them, until Diego Narvaez drew him aside and said something to calm him down. Narvaez was a popular figure among the other engineers, his confidence and charisma making him a natural leader, even though he answered to Haim Silbermann. The intensity of his religious faith had been off-putting to Stephen at first, as his own experience with hardcore Christians had been less than positive. But Tarik Bahar, himself an equally devout Muslim, had championed the Guatemalan Catholic, convincing Stephen that Narvaez would never try to force his beliefs on others or use them to deny others their equality and dignity. Stephen had since come to admire Narvaez's high regard for what he called the God-given free will of every human. He supposed that Narvaez's faith, along with Tarik's, might even be a source of comfort to Oates and others in the days ahead. In a way, he envied that conviction right now.

The Chirrn had given the crew little time to absorb the news. Their ship, *Zhemhal*, had nearly reached its destination by the time *Arachne*'s full crew was revived, a few days after the original incident. They had cited this as an excuse for subjecting the whole group to thorough medical examination — to check for contaminants, they claimed. Being subjected to abduction and probing by aliens, like something from an old horror movie, would've been laughable if it hadn't become an immediate reality — and if Diana Thorne, Sergei Mazunov, and Shuai Bingbing hadn't been in intensive care right now. Long-term hibernation carried risks they had all understood, but being forced awake *en masse*, without giving Arachne and the expedition's doctors time to shepherd each sleeper individually, had amplified those risks, and those three had suffered significant organ damage, maybe even brain damage, as a result. Cecilia had vowed to the Chirrn that if any of the three failed to pull through, she would see that *Zhemhal*'s personnel were held accountable. Rillial, astonished by her chutzpah, had reminded her that her crew were the ones being taken to account.

The fact that Diana Thorne had fallen victim to revival damage was shocking to the crew. The construction engineer was a native of the transhumanist Vanguard habitat, and her gene mods made her the strongest, most robust member of the expedition by a considerable margin. If she could succumb, then nobody was safe. So the rest were understandably reluctant to trust that the Chirrn's medical probes would be any safer or gentler than their revival methods. Several fought back as the Chirrn dragged them off: some with proud defiance like Narvaez, Jason Brentwood, and Oyama Kazuko, some screaming in terror like Evan Jiang or in pure rage like Amrita Dhillon. But they were returned intact and seemingly unharmed, though shaken. From his own experience, Stephen knew the examinations were not painful, or not deliberately so, as long as the subjects cooperated. But they were cold, thorough, invasive, and dehumanizing. Stephen had been made to feel like a lab specimen, his every bodily function subject to exploration to satisfy these creatures' morbid curiosity — or simply their need to humiliate him. It had been over three decades, subjectively, since he'd been made to feel so worthless by even the lowliest members of an authority structure. But back then, he had done nothing to earn it. He could not bring himself to feel the same indignation now.

The news of the ship's approach to the new habitat, Shilirrlal, offered a useful diversion for the crew. The travel time was mere days, but Arachne had detected no other proximate bodies besides a small rogue planet several light-weeks away, creating a paradox. "We know they have some kind of gravitic drive and inertial cancellation," Haim Silbermann put forth. "We could've been accelerated near lightspeed and time-dilated."

"To reach the rogue planet in four subjective days?" objected Justine Nguyen, their astrophysicist. "That would take a gamma of at least six, which means nearly point-nine-nine c," she went on in a soft French accent. "Besides, a gravity-based drive might not even produce special-relativistic effects in the first place, if the proper acceleration within the field is zero as with an Alcubierre-type warp. Which is suggested by their deceleration of *Arachne* — nearly four thousand *g* with no effect on the ship."

Haim shrugged. "Who knows? If the Chirrn have that level of gravity control, then for all we know, they have some kind of hyperlight drive. We could be parsecs beyond local space."

"Now you're pushing it, Haim."

Diego scoffed. "Justine's right. I refuse to believe that these… kangaroo-chameleons could build a technology surpassing human achievement. More likely it's some deception."

James Oates was quick to embrace that notion, spinning conspiracy theories that the others, even Diego, reacted to with incredulity. But Stephen could tell they were all distracting themselves from what was really on their minds.

In time, faint shudders began to pass through the ship. Minutes later, hazmat-suited Chirrn came and herded all forty-five uninjured humans out of the hold and into a chamber barely big enough to hold them all. There was a gravity shift along the way, a sensation of an uphill climb, getting milder as they went. Stephen noted Cecilia, Tarik, and the other space veterans instinctively turning their heads to test for cochlear shifts. Cecilia asserted that they were out of the ship's inexplicable gravity field and inside a normal rotating habitat.

This was confirmed when the chamber lurched and began to descend, the floor seeming to slope as the Coriolis effect tipped their increasing weight vector to antispinward. They halted at a level whose gravity was maybe two-thirds Earth value and were herded out. But all Stephen saw were more sterile chambers and corridors. This, according to the Chirrn, was a decontamination facility. "My God, how dirty do they think we are?" Amrita Dhillon asked.

"From what they said when they beat us," Tarik replied with subdued anger, "quite a lot."

The Chirrn herded them through a series of progressively more unpleasant decontamination procedures: powerful blasts of freezing water and hot air; uncomfortably hot sprays of supposedly nonthermal plasma; blinding UV bursts; suffocating immersion in stinking chemical baths and gels. What little remaining body hair they had was seared and scoured away. "This goes beyond any sane need for decontam," Diego Narvaez shouted after his third dunking. "They're doing this to torture us!"

Once the decontamination gauntlet was complete, Stephen hoped the worst was over. But the Chirrn immediately subjected the crew to yet another thorough medical examination, allegedly to make sure the decontamination had worked. Stephen knew this had to be a lie. Arachne had told him that, based on the data the Chirrn had provided, there was virtually no risk of cross-species infection. The Chirrn were either punishing the humans or acting out of some irrational taboo about contamination.

At last, the sore, raw-skinned, depilated humans were given something to wear. But it was no relief. The one-piece confinement suits were roughly form-fitting, ending just below the shoulders, with clumsy mitts at the ends of the sleeves. Too form-fitting, perhaps; the dynamic material compressed uncomfortably tightly against their raw, sensitized skin. "Attempt no escape," their lead escort said, then demonstrated what would happen if they disobeyed: the jumpsuits would become rigid, preventing movement. Even the integrated mittens froze up around Stephen's fingers whenever he reached for his shoulders. Far from a respite from their nudity, these garments just reinforced their lack of control over their own bodies. All things considered, Stephen would've rather stayed naked. *All things*, he reiterated as he fidgeted, trying to find a posture that would relieve the pressure on his testicles.

But that didn't seem to be something the Chirrn would understand. Now that the humans had been sanitized for their protection and thoroughly shrink-wrapped, the Chirrn were no longer wearing hazmat suits in their presence. Their typical garb, it seemed, was nothing more than loose, utilitarian vests, open in front and secured by a strap across the midriff and sometimes a second one across the upper chest. Some wore wide, colorful bands of fabric around their calves and forearms. They had no recognizable genitalia that Stephen could see. Could a species evolve to this level without sexual reproduction?

Finally the prisoners were brought out into a large plaza surrounded by towers. Hundreds of Chirrn watched, clearly fascinated by the humans but remaining at a distance as though they were unclean. Many of these Chirrn looked subtly different from the Lesshchin (as he'd learned to call them), lankier with slimmer tails and rounder snouts. More of them had skin colors tending toward a bluer range while the majority of the Lesshchin were more greenish, though there was a good deal of overlap. A few had other differences, like stockier bodies, purplish or yellow-brown skin, or shorter manes. *Immigrants from still more habitats? How many do they have?* There were cultural variations too; many of the Shilirrlal population wore their manes in intricate braids or decorated them with colorful beads and bands. The sight helped to remind him that these were individuals, just as diverse as humans. He felt a pang at the thought of the equally individual lives his expedition had wiped out.

Arachne notified him that the Chirrn had permitted her to tap into a limited segment of Shilirrlal's augreality network and interpret its feeds for human vision and imaging protocols. Hovering over and around the humans in virtual space, or adorning the buildings, bridges, and unidentifiable shapes they passed, were multiple interactive windows showing Lesshchi both after the disaster and as it must have been beforehand, alongside images of *Arachne*'s capture, her modules inside the Chirrn ship's hangar—and the crew, naked, cowed, and afraid. Several windows showed video from their decontamination and medical exams in full, invasive detail. Many in the crowd watched these scenes with particular animation, leaning forward inquisitively or rearing back in evident disgust. It drove home that the entire procedure had been symbolic, probably meant to reassure the citizens of Shilirrlal that they would not be contaminated by the impure aliens. Stephen blushed fiercely, ashamed on behalf of his crew. He looked at Cecilia, and saw her realizing the same things he had; but her expression was bitter cold.

Once they moved past the high towers, Stephen was able to see the habitat's layout more clearly. From the openness of the cylindrical worldscape before him, Stephen surmised this must be the inner cylinder, if Shilirrlal conformed to Lesshchi's plan. It didn't look like any O'Neill habitat back in Solsys; there was no attempt at simulating a planetary surface. It reminded him more of his first view of São Paulo as a youth, a vista of pure urban artificiality stretching to the vanishing point in every direction, a monument to the power of its builders over their environment. The layout was urban, orderly, angular, filled with multiple levels of terraces atop which rose monumental skyscrapers connected by a network of skywalks. Yet it was not sterile. Even when he temporarily shut off the augmented view, Stephen saw many large plazas and squares filled with orange, red, and yellow vegetation, intermixed with other colors. Many of the skyscrapers themselves had plant life growing atop their terraced levels or climbing vast trellises stretching between them. At the equator, a wide band of water bisected the cylinder, broken by crossover bridges or dams and with canals extending outward to the north and south.

The view ahead was periodically interrupted by thick tethers that rose toward the axis, tension members supporting the habitat against its own centrifugal weight. Stephen's eyes followed them upward, past the collar of clouds, to see that they intersected with a vast latticed cylinder of light, an open, arabesque framework that provided the habitat with its primary illumination in place of a sun. As his eyes adjusted to the light, he realized there were shapes and structures within, some of them in motion. Through a wide gap in the light lattice, he saw what looked like a large globe of water jiggling through the air. Adjusting his adaptive optics to maximize his visual acuity, he made out small, multicolored specks—presumably Chirrn—swimming gaily through it. Other distant bodies soared across the open space with the sinuous grace and ease he'd seen the Chirrn demonstrate in microgravity.

"Captain, Stephen," said Tarik, who had been surveying the scene as intently as Stephen. "In the crowd, ahead right." They were on a skywalk now, with others running parallel to it. The adjacent skywalks were filled with gawkers… not all of whom were Chirrn. Stephen made out two distinct types. One group looked like silvery pterosaurs with triple-crested heads and apparently one eye before each crest. Their posture was birdlike, with wings intricately folded along their flanks. The sides of their crests shimmered with rainbow hues, rivaling the elaborate jewelry they wore. The other species was even more bizarre— hippo-sized, chocolate-brown creatures with long, peanut-shaped bod- ies atop an indeterminate number of legs, with heads whose shape suggested a raised catcher's mitt with a ball in it.

Sita Bhatiani, who'd been painfully quiet since the assault, grew animated again at the sight, though she took care not to call attention to herself. She sidled up to Stephen and Cecilia, still moving stiffly due to her healing injuries, and said, "There's no way those creatures came from the same taxonomic family as the Chirrn. I doubt they're even from the same planet. We're definitely not the Chirrn's first contact."

"And if there are other species living here," Stephen asked, "what about Lesshchi?" He looked around again, taking in this amazing vista, both compellingly alien and deeply beautiful. "This is what we destroyed, Cecilia."

She met his gaze, her face unreadable. "I know," she said at last, almost too softly to hear. But then her expression hardened and she stepped up to hiss in his ear: "But don't ever let the Chirrn hear you say that."

The Chirrn built large to accommodate their long bodies and bounding locomotion. Stairways had only two or three steps between one story and the next—and Cecilia saw some Chirrn bounding directly to higher floors, pulling themselves up with their arms like cats leaping onto a windowsill. The entrance to Shilirrlal's towering, ziggurat-like justice center had a ramp leading up to it as well, perhaps for the benefit of the big peanut-bodied aliens, but the forty-five weakened, constricted humans were led around to the back and taken up in a cargo lift. As they circled the block, Cecilia noted Chirrn gawkers clinging with brachiators' agility to the trellises between neighboring buildings, grasping them with fingers and toes. They were nearly as graceful here as in microgravity, and Cecilia almost envied them the anatomy that allowed that. *They're at home here in a way we can never be. It won't be easy to counter that advantage.* She flexed her fingers against the smart fabric of her jumpsuit. *Especially when we can't even move without their approval.*

After their processing, the forty-five humans were led down into a deeper, higher-gravity level of the complex—about twenty percent above Earth gravity, she estimated. The Chirrn adjusted with ease, but it served as one more impediment for the humans. The prisoners were confined in a block of six large cells, three on each side of a wide corridor, with transparent, vent-holed walls and doors of what looked and felt like synthetic diamond. They were thrown together willy-nilly with no regard for sex, and Cecilia found herself confined with Stephen, Haim, Sita, the ecologist Ibrahim al-Bakri, and the physician Nikolos Zacharias. The cell had two large sleeping pallets, which Cecilia promptly designated His and Hers, and two toilets that were little more than holes in the floor, mercifully behind half-high translucent partitions. There were also a couple of sink-like basins in each cell for water.

Once the cell doors had been locked, the confinement jumpsuits relaxed, to everyone's great relief. Cecilia was gratified to discover that she could wriggle her arms out through the shoulder hole, relieving the uncomfortable pressure on her breasts. After a bit of experimentation, she managed to tie the sleeves together in front to hold the garment up. Haim and Ibrahim followed her lead, though Stephen was content to go bare-chested, the jumpsuit bunched around his waist. Sita and Nik stripped the odious garments off completely. Nik tied his around his waist, but Sita merely clutched hers against the front of her body and huddled in the corner of the Hers pallet. Nobody was comfortable just being nude after the past few days.

Cecilia advised the crew to get some rest, raising her voice so those in the other cells could hear. The men and women took their respective bunks. Few of them could sleep, though, and the murmur of conversations started up pretty promptly. "Odd," Cecilia said. "The Chirrn seem so isolationist, so disdainful of other races. You wouldn't expect them to consort with other species or have such advanced translation software."

"I don't think it's all races they dislike," Sita told her. "They seem to have a specific bias against planet-dwellers. When the guards…" The petite biologist shuddered. Mercifully, she'd suffered no permanent brain damage from her assault, but even after days in a medbed, she still bore scars. "The things they said, the insults…. 'Ground-vermin.' 'Dirtgrubber.' They seem to have a thing about dirt and earth. And the people who live in — on it." She winced.

"That must narrow their list of friends a great deal," the captain said.

"I wouldn't say that," Nik spoke up. "There are a billion of us Striders in the Belt and Trojans, and nearly as many Terrans living in cislunar habitats. Someday hab-dwellers will outnumber planet-dwellers. And we've detected megastructures around other stars. We know there are aliens who do the same, on a much vaster scale than this," he finished, gesturing at their surroundings.

Haim furrowed his brow. "That's a good point. We have gravity-focus telescopes that can make detailed maps of Cybele from twenty-nine light-years away. Why did we never see these guys?"

"We weren't looking *between* the stars," Stephen said.

"At least, not for things like this," Cecilia added. "Who'd want to live out here any—"

The arrival of several Chirrn in the cell-block corridor interrupted the discussion. Two were attired in guards' vests—heavier than the normal garments with less exposure of the chest—with shock-stick holsters strapped to their legs. The third was an atypically stocky Chirrn, cobalt-skinned with a yellow-white mane done up in Shilirrlal-style braids. This Chirrn surveyed the prisoners in their various cells and addressed the group. "Are there any among you who are not of planetary birth?" The translation now appeared as a subtitle in her field of view, courtesy of Arachne. The prison was shielded, cutting the crew off from Arachne herself, but her peripheral AI software in their implants smoothed the rough syntax of the Chirrn translation into more natural English. That ran the risk of obscuring true meanings even further, though, since the Chirrn were still reluctant to give Arachne access to the cultural and psychological information she'd need to do her own independent checks on the translation. Which just made it more likely in Cecilia's mind that they were hiding something.

Cecilia stepped forward. "Why do you want to know?" she asked.

The light-maned Chirrn hopped closer. "Are you of extraplanetary origin?"

"No. I was born in Venezia on the planet Earth and proud of it. I also happen to be the captain of this group, so I'm the one you speak to. Now, just what have you got against planet-dwellers?"

The Chirrn looked around at the crew, ignoring her. "I am L'chellin. I have been assigned as your advocate for the tribunal. I advise you that it would be in your best interests to choose one not of planetary birth to speak for your crew. I repeat my query."

She came to the door and met L'chellin's chameleon gaze firmly. "And *I* repeat, I'm the captain," she said sternly. "I speak for this crew, and you're going to have to accept it. Now, I asked you a question."

The alien made a sighing-snorting sound, its snout-bristles ruffling. "Very well. But you will have to live with the consequences of that choice."

"I'm waiting for an answer," Cecilia went on implacably. "We have a right to know— are we going to be tried fairly, or persecuted due to our origins? We need to know just how deep this anti-planet bias of yours runs."

L'chellin rotated its eyes back into its head, like a human pressing one's eyes shut in weariness. "We believe ourselves to be a rational people," it said. "Our civilization has thrived for longer than yours has existed, and as you can see, we have reached great heights. But our discomfort with planet-dwellers is deeply rooted in our history.

"Our primitive ancestors evolved on a planet, as yours did. When they gained the ability to enter space, many ascended there and became the first Chirrn, building their own worlds. Crude forebears of what you see here—and what you destroyed." Cecilia gave it no reaction. "They built a well-ordered, responsible civilization and lived in enlightenment. They strove to share their peace and prosperity with those below, raising them to an equal level.

"But those who remained planet-dwellers failed to learn the wisdom of the Chirrn. In their backwardness they abused our gifts and twisted them to savagery, swarming into space and waging war on our homes, seeking to conquer and spread chaos. The wars lasted for generations, bringing great death.

"Naturally, the Chirrn had the advantage over the planet-dwelling populations. Our resources were greater, not limited to what a planet could offer. But we resisted inflicting destruction upon the planet-dwellers, even as they showed no reluctance to destroy our worlds. Their isolated, poor existence had corrupted their morals. They showed none of the restraint of the Chirrn, attacking ruthlessly at every chance. Peace talks were used as opportunities for ambush. Noncombatants were slaughtered, medical facilities were destroyed, weapons of mass destruction were used against all laws and treaties." L'chellin lowered its head.

"Finally we reached the point where we could not tolerate co-existence with the planet-bound. Many argued that we should crush our enemies utterly. But we had more decency than that. Instead, we chose to separate ourselves from them, to travel out among the stars where they could not reach us.

"It proved the best decision we ever made. It liberated us. We no longer had to live under the weight of gravity and fear. We could discover the universe without leaving our homes, even as we discovered what we ourselves could evolve into.

"More—it saved us. Ultimately, our enemies' rapacious ways left the world of our birth in ruins. Had we stayed there, we would have been rendered extinct—as all species confined to one planet must inevitably be."

L'chellin looked back at the captain again. "So you can understand that to live on a planet, to trap yourself within a gravity well and spend your entire existence in one place, is inconceivable to us. It would be the worst form of imprisonment. And, given what was done to our ancestors, we feel it must twist beings' minds and morals beyond the point where they can be civilized." L'chellin tapped its hands against its brow ridges, as though symbolically hiding its eyes. "And what you have done to Lesshchi only reinforces this belief."

"Now wait a minute, Mister—Ms.? Or…"

"I am currently male."

Cecilia blinked, but took it in stride; now was not the time to explore alien gender identity. "I thought you were supposed to be defending us in this trial."

"Do you deny that your projectile barrage devastated Lesshchi?"

"We don't deny the facts of the event. But it was an accident. We didn't even know what Lesshchi was until its survivors dragged us out of relativistic flight. We're sorry for what happened. Deeply sorry. We try to be a peaceful people, to respect all life. But accidents happen.

"So the question, Mister L'chellin, is: do you accept that it was an accident, and are you capable of doing your best to persuade this tribunal of that fact despite their anti-planetary biases? Or is your role just a formality in a—a show trial whose outcome is already decided?" For a number of reasons, she had chosen to avoid the phrase "kangaroo court."

The Chirrn's eyes swiveled to focus on hers. "No space-dweller who executes one's duties sloppily can expect to survive for long. My role is to participate in the search for the truth and the determination of justice. I will not allow myself bias in that pursuit."

Cecilia stared searchingly into those alien eyes, seeing nothing she could recognize… save for his unwavering gaze. "All right," she finally said. "That sounds pretty much like the role of the attorney in our legal system, so I can accept it." In truth, she'd had her fill of lawyers during her divorce, but under the circumstances she'd take what she could get. "Now how much time do we have to work out a defense strategy…?"

4

ANOTHER TRANSLATION GLITCH SOON EMERGED: IN THE CHIRRN LEGAL system, the role of the "advocate" was not to speak for the accused, but merely to advise them in legal principles and procedures. The defendants were expected to speak on their own behalf. This, L'chellin explained, was why he had advised them to choose a non-planetary native as their spokesperson; such an individual would be seen more sympathetically by the tribunal. But Cecilia insisted on speaking for her crew, and Stephen agreed. The two of them would lead the defense along with Oyama Kazuko, their resident legal scholar.

But Cecilia's demands to investigate the Lesshchi incident were categorically refused. The prisoners were denied interaction with anyone except L'chellin, his fellow advocates and aides, and the prison staff. "How can we mount a proper defense if we can't review the evidence, question the witnesses?" the captain demanded of L'chellin as they conferred in his office, a spartan workspace with a large window overlooking a vast atrium in which hundreds of thick, red-leaved bioluminescent vines dangled from the ceiling, a constant trickle of water running down them into a canal below. The sound would have been soothing if it didn't echo so loudly through the cavernous space, but L'chellin seemed untroubled by it.

"It is my place to conduct such investigations," L'chellin told her in his usual prim manner. "You may rely on my thoroughness."

"That's not good enough. Human interests are at stake here, so there should be a human examining the evidence independently. Just to make sure you don't overlook anything that might help us."

"And what could you see that I cannot?" L'chellin countered. "Can you interpret a Chirrn's body language? Can you sense our pheromonal shifts? Can you share in our guild memories? Do you know enough about our technology and society to recognize any discrepancies in the account?"

His questions disheartened Cecilia; she didn't even understand the penultimate one yet. But she rallied. "No, but I know how to reason, and I'm a keen observer and a fast learner. At least let me review your findings. Share what you learn with me, explain your process."

"You are not an authorized advocate."

"I'm on the damned defense team!" She stopped herself from flinging her arms out for emphasis; the last time she'd tried that, the confinement jumpsuit had mistaken it for an aggressive move and frozen her in place. "We all need to know what you find—and in a way that helps us understand what it means. You said it yourself: we don't know the ground rules here like a Chirrn defendant would."

After some thought, L'chellin consented to the request. Though the more Cecilia studied the evidence and struggled to understand it, the more she doubted she could make a meaningful difference. All she could really do was keep an eye on L'chellin and try to keep him honest.

After the first couple of days of preparation, though, Cecilia grudgingly came to realize that wasn't necessary. The Shilirrlaln advocate was stern and rigorous, yet that rigor went both ways. He felt no sympathy for the planet-dwellers who'd destroyed a Chirrn habitat, yet he was committed to fulfilling his duty as their advocate to the best of his ability, and he made a legitimate effort to be helpful in the trial prep.

Which proved useful when Cecilia came to his office on the third day with a confrontational question: "Why didn't you see us coming?"

L'chellin looked at her in puzzlement. "Your words miscarry. Again?"

She placed her mittened hands atop his crescent-shaped desk and leaned in. "At the speed we were going, pushing the interstellar medium in front of us, *Arachne* would've generated a hell of a bow shock. Lesshchi should've been able to see our approach long ago. Hell, it took so much energy to launch us in the first place, they should've picked up the emissions over four and a half years ago, when the light reached them!"

The advocate's plump blue fingers primly clutched the front edges of his vest, as they often did when he was about to launch into a lecture. "You presuppose that the Chirrn were monitoring your world regularly. We have no interest in the everyday affairs of your species."

"But you must've picked up our signals before, if you know our languages."

"Intermittent observations, yes."

"Vack that. Arachne told us that Lesshchi was headed almost directly toward Solsys from Gamma Leporis. Otherwise the encounter would've been so brief that hardly any damage would've been done."

"A coincidence. Lesshchi's trajectory from the rogue ice world where it replenished its reserves was toward…" His eyes rolled back to look at his own brow ridges, the closest a Chirrn could come to closing them. "A red dwarf you call Gliese 229, whose gravity would have angled its trajectory away from your native system. As a rule, we avoid drawing too near planetary civilizations."

"All the more reason to keep an eye on us, isn't it?"

L'chellin ruffled his snout bristles with an exhalation that struck her as contemplative. "Give me a moment." His eyes rolled back again.

Cecilia fumed at the delay, but she recognized that he was accessing the consensus memory of his guild. Over the past two days, L'chellin had explained that every Chirrn had a dataspace in the habitat's information cloud that gave them additional outboard memory and processing, so integrated with their organic brains that they considered themselves to exist partly in the cloud. Of course, it could only enhance their intelligence so far; humanity's own experiments with organic and cybernetic intelligence had shown that a brain taken past a certain level of complexity, outside the "Goldilocks zone" for sentience, became too unstable to function sanely. Aliens were evidently no different; they could augment their memories, boost their processing speed, but not fundamentally increase their complexity of thought beyond that of the greatest naturally occurring geniuses. It was no doubt why *Arachne*'s crew was even able to comprehend the thoughts of beings as advanced as the Chirrn.

But in the Chirrn's case, individuals' outboard memories could be stored and shared in a form of social network, letting them select which memories to save and with whom to share them. They organized their society into occupational groups that Arachne translated as "guilds," though with the notation that they also resembled the *jâti* of Hindu culture, clan-like communities associated with traditional professions or societal roles. The guilds were bundled into "estates" defined by related responsibilities (such as government, science, or medicine), and each guild was divided into subprofessions called collegia, each with its own "consensus memory" — a common dataspace containing memories, databases, and even cognitive processing algorithms that all members shared, so that each Chirrn was an amalgam of its own personality and the consensus mind, their selves overlapping like a Venn diagram. While the psyche residing in each individual's organic brain remained dominant therein, the members of a collegium shared certain knowledge, outlooks, and patterns of thought. Each guild had its own overall consensus as well, core knowledge and cognitive models that served as a substrate for all the individual collegium memories.

There were guilds that answered to more than one estate, or collegia that fell under more than one guild — for instance, a forensic scientist could fall under both science and criminal justice. Cecilia would have assumed L'chellin was under the latter as well, but whatever his guild or collegium was, it let him access information from multiple estates, tapping into expertise in law, engineering, astrophysics, and other fields as they proved relevant to the case. The captain guessed that L'chellin was currently communing with the astronomical knowledge base, or mind-mailing someone in that collegium, to research the question she'd raised. She could have done much the same back on Earth or Mars, but she wondered to what extent L'chellin shared in the actual *understanding* of the information. Could you just plug in a new way of thinking and instantly internalize it? Surely there would need to be a training period.

Soon enough, L'chellin had his answer. "Automated detectors on Shilirrlal did register an emission pattern consistent with magnetic sail acceleration within your star system at the time in question. Records from Lesshchi are unavailable, but as it was nearer your system, it is likely they registered the same."

She pounced on that. "So you *did* know!"

"We knew you launched some form of sailcraft. Yet the pattern was consistent with earlier events identified as uncrewed probe launches, so there was no reason to conclude this was different. After all, using such a method to send living beings across interstellar space at such speeds is… virtually unprecedented. It is not something civilizations generally undertake until they develop gravity drive."

"But even if you thought a probe was headed Lesshchi's way…"

"With no way of knowing that the three smaller pieces would combine into one, the automated detection system's estimate of the supposed probes' trajectories was in error and did not anticipate them coming near Lesshchi's course. Thus, the detection was not flagged as a potential hazard, nor was it tracked further. Unlike humans, we have had millennia to study local space in detail and thus do not find it necessary to scan obsessively for every possible signal."

"Even a great big bow shock coming right for you?"

"Your vessel is extremely small, and its magnetic field was on low-power deflection mode to minimize drag. Also, we occupy the Central Void, one of the lowest-density regions of the interstellar medium. As such, your bow shock was relatively small and difficult to discern from the overall radio noise of your star system and its environs—which, of course, were almost directly behind you from Lesshchi's vantage."

"Oh." She grimaced, reining in her ardor. If she were to try to argue in court that the Chirrn's casual contempt for planet-dwellers had kept them from being curious enough to notice what was coming their way, the prosecution could counter that the humans had deliberately made *Arachne* hard to spot—and it would be hard to prove otherwise.

"It is in your favor that this line of investigation was fruitless," L'chellin advised. "It would be seen as shifting the blame onto the victims."

"Yes, all right." She took a breath, as deeply as the constrictive jumpsuit would allow. If her aggressive instincts had failed, maybe it was time to try it Stephen's way. "We need to prove this wasn't anybody's fault," she ventured. "Just a terrible accident."

"Our obligation," L'chellin said, "is to examine the evidence and determine the truth and legality of what has occurred. I am not here to help you win, but to advise you on relevant matters of fact and law. If the truth is that it was an unavoidable accident, then that is what we shall find." He clutched his nonexistent lapels again. "But what if the truth is otherwise? Will your people be able to accept that finding—and the penance that must come with it?"

Cecilia faltered—but she clung to her conviction. "If your system is as fair as you claim, Advocate… then we'll never have to know."

The trial was held in a circular chamber something like an ancient Greek theater. The tribunal panel consisted of six Chirrn who sat behind a long, raised bench, curved to fit the shape of the chamber and made of a material that seemed like a cross between marble and wood to Stephen's eyes. The tribunes were elected by the people but would serve the approximate role of a jury. Before them, behind a podium at the centerline of the bench's arc, was the arbiter, who would ensure that proper procedures were followed, filling some of the functions of both judge and bailiff. The arbiter was one of the silver pterosaur-like beings Stephen had seen before. Up close, he could see that it had a tripartite beak, that its silvery shimmer came from a covering that resembled fur as much as fine feathers, and that its wings doubled as arms; from each wrist extended an opposable thumb, two fingers, and three much longer, folded-back digits with blue-veined wing membranes furled between them. It was adorned in a colorful halter and bore jewelry on its fingers and legs. "His name is Broadwing," L'chellin informed the defendants when asked. "His people call themselves Seekers of the Zenith, which may be shortened to Zenith."

"Did you choose a non-Chirrn for the sake of neutrality?" Oyama Kazuko asked.

One of L'chellin's eyes swiveled to stare at the fiftyish political scientist. "Broadwing is a member of the same guild as myself, a Shilirrlaln in good standing for a quarter-century." Below the translation text, Arachne offered an alternative phrasing in Chirrn time units, which were all base-8 multiples of the *narr*, the 97-second rotation period standard for Chirrn habitats. "Zenith were among the casualties of Lesshchi, as were Ryohoch and others." Ryohoch, Stephen had learned, were the hippo-sized, multi-limbed sophonts he had glimpsed in the crowd. He had yet to meet any directly, but they seemed to be a fixture in Chirrn communities. "Broadwing can be no more or less 'neutral' than any Shilirrlaln. He holds the arbiter post as he is eminently qualified for it. However," he conceded, "we do benefit from the parallax of applying different sophonts' mentalities to a problem."

So was the arbiter only a quarter-century old, or had he come from somewhere else? Stephen was brimming with questions about the Chirrn's relationship with these Zenith. He only hoped he'd get the opportunity to explore them at his leisure.

If the arbiter's podium defined "north," then along the "east" and "west" sides of the courtroom were witnesses' benches, and the "southern" arc contained limited audience seating. Chirrn normally sat by resting their weight on their tails, but there were narrow padded rails to rest their short, stocky thighs upon. The forty-seven humans (for Diana and Sergei had recovered enough to rejoin the group, and Bingbing would likely follow in a couple of days) occupied the benches on the "west" side, which had not been adjusted to accommodate human anatomy. The narrow perches were not uncomfortable at first, but Stephen suspected that wouldn't last. The humans hadn't been given any wardrobe consideration either; they were still attired in their sealed prison jumpers, unable to use their hands for more than rough grasping.

Aside from that, the trial setup seemed reasonable to Stephen. He wondered if the Chirrn, like some human cultures, had gone through a period in their past when the courtroom had become an arena for combat between self-serving lawyers rather than a place to seek the truth. Perhaps the prominent position of the tribunes and the relatively subordinate role of the advocates was a reminder that the lawyers were there to serve the clients and the jury, not the other way around.

Once everyone was assembled, Arbiter Broadwing rose—or rather, *unfolded* into a fully erect stance, revealing an extra segment of his legs that had been tucked in against his body. His halter strained against a protruding keel as he spread his wings wide, revealing an analogous Z-shaped construction to the forelimbs, and jiggled his head so that the rainbow diffraction patterns on his crests shimmered. Opening a tripartite beak, the Zenith spoke in a voice that sounded like a calliope playing heavy metal, which Arachne's subtitles translated as a call to begin the session. "We convene to establish truth; we aspire to restore equilibrium." <Perhaps "justice"?> Arachne annotated. "Let no one here forget these goals."

In keeping with the diminished role of the attorney/advocates, there were no opening statements. The tribunal began with Broadwing briefly spelling out the involved parties, the charges, and other basics of the case. It then proceeded directly to testimony, with Rillial speaking for the prosecution. The turquoise-skinned, mahogany-maned ship captain (who, according to L'chellin, was currently female) began by calling eyewitnesses to the tragedy. The first was a slender, vivid green Chirrn with a yellow mane, a member of Lesshchi's space defense department, who spoke of the events leading up to the bombardment. The trial's participants were able to audit the witness's memory records directly, since defense officers routinely buffered their experiential memories in their external dataspace for just such occasions, but verbal testimony was still needed to give context to the experiences. Despite sharing memories, Chirrn's individual perspectives on a single event could still differ.

The defense officer's testimony and memory replay confirmed what Stephen and Cecilia had been told in prep: that Lesshchi's sensors had registered a radar beam impinging upon its hull a few minutes before the incident. The beam had not matched any recorded profile and no vessels were known to be in the vicinity. "What is your normal procedure in such an event?" Rillial asked.

"We locate and hail the craft."

"And if the craft were determined to be on a collision course with Lesshchi?"

"It would be warned off. If that were not effective, gravitational deflection would be engaged."

"Why did this not occur in this instance?"

"We were unable to locate the craft. We were only beginning to narrow down its probable velocity and radial distance when the barrage began."

"Stay in sequence, please. Why did you not employ a general hail?"

"It was attempted, but there was no reply. The defense consensus then suggested that the craft was considerably more distant and traveling at a much higher velocity than we had assumed. Our signal was too weak for them to detect."

"Why did you not anticipate this possibility?"

"No ship would travel at such high relativistic velocity that close to a habitat. It violates all known safety protocols."

"Are your procedures not designed to include the possibility of an encounter with a starfaring people unfamiliar with standard protocols?" Rillial was clever, Stephen thought—pre-empting any defense attempt to pin the blame on Lesshchin negligence.

"That is unprecedented."

"In most of the galaxy, yes. You were aware that Lesshchi occupied a less civilized region of space?" Stephen leaned forward, intrigued by the implications of the question.

"Yes, but… the likelihood of an unknown vessel randomly coming within range of a Chirrn habitat is extremely low."

Rillial gave a sort of knee-bending bow. "After the consensus suggestion, what action did you take?"

"I was about to ask for an intensification of the hail. But just then… Lesshchi trembled and… convulsed. I was flung from my perch. I have no further memory until I awoke in hospital."

The next witness, another silvery Seeker of the Zenith, explained the failure of Lesshchi's defenses. Their default shielding mode had been calibrated for deflecting cosmic rays—subatomic particles at relativistic speeds—or microgram specks of space dust oncoming at a few percent of lightspeed. *Arachne*'s microsails had massed roughly two grams apiece and come in at better than $0.87c$—another unprecedented scenario. They had come from off-axis, bypassing the forward ice shield. And they had struck in such quick succession that more than half had penetrated the habitat before the defenses could be intensified.

Arbiter Broadwing reminded Cecilia of her right to cross-examine, but the human offered no objections and asked no questions—implicitly pointing out that the entire crew had been unconscious during the incident and thus had no perspective of their own to counter with. As Rillial continued her examinations, her intense emotion barely hidden under her courtroom formality, Cecilia sat quietly, seeking to project an air of sorrow without guilt.

Any direct eyewitnesses to the penetration would have been killed by the radiation and shock waves, but some had been inside structures on the fringes of the destroyed section or receiving visual feeds from that area. "I only saw the reflected light on the wall," one witness said, "or I would have needed new eyes, I think. It strobed like lightning, but my shadow moved swiftly across the wall. Then a thunderclap struck, and went on incredibly long. It shook the entire structure. I almost fell over, though I think that was alarm." The memory feeds showed impressionistic flashes of imagery, interpretations of the witness's sense memories. They were confused, frenetic. Though the witness had had the presence of mind to upload the memory to the cloud, the EMP from the disaster had disrupted network functions throughout Lesshchi. Only portions of the witness's external memory had survived unscathed. Even so, the spectators reacted with horror to what they were able to glimpse; perhaps, if their psychology was anything like human, having to fill in the details with their imaginations made it far worse. Broadwing let out a low, mellow chime that was translated as a caution to the audience to remain calm.

"When I looked out, I saw a wind blowing through the city, away from me. The support cables were bursting, the ground was surging toward me. I was frozen for a moment. I couldn't think clearly, couldn't access consensus. Finally I regained what was left of my sense and fled with all my speed. I didn't slow until I was well into the next segment, but the gravity was shifting and I could hear the groaning and trembling through the ground, and water was draining from the canals, and I feared the whole of Lesshchi was tearing apart."

The next witness was a teal-skinned female with a shorn mane, an amputated arm, and numerous scars. She testified that she had been inside on a lower level when the room collapsed around her and she was torn out into space.

"And how long were you dead?" Rillial asked.

"Over nineteen hours," came the translation. "They didn't reach me until sometime after my brain's oxygen reserves ran out. As it is, I still remember little of my life before. They haven't recovered any of my tier's consensus memory yet. I fear I will never regain most of who I was."

Stephen traded a wide-eyed look with Cecilia. *Nineteen hours?* No wonder the death toll was so much lower than the humans had initially been told. The current tally was somewhere around seventy-eight thousand confirmed dead, ten thousand missing. It had initially been a relief when the figure had been revised down below six digits, but Stephen had soon recognized that as a false comfort. At any order of magnitude, it was still a horrible tragedy.

If anything, Stephen realized, the great advancement of the Chirrn's medical science must make the deaths they couldn't reverse all the more devastating—particularly since so much of the cloud memory they relied on for backup had been destroyed as well. He remembered how it had been growing up in Florida, a once-beautiful place reduced to ruin by indifferent nature and uncaring officials. Few had expected to live very long, and too many had been resigned to that state of affairs. When another superhurricane or epidemic had struck, when the militias had gunned down another child for having the wrong parents or the wrong faith, it was just business as usual. No one bothered trying to revive the recently dead or sustain those on the brink; no one had the time or resources. But these Chirrn fought for every life and brought back as many as they could, even though the sheer numbers must overwhelm them. How must they feel about the ones they couldn't save, no matter how hard they fought? Or the ones who had recovered physically but lost large portions of their identity?

He and his family had fought for his mother every step of the way, selling all they had to pay for her hospital care, offering blood and organs for direct transplant when the hospital's stem-cell banks ran dry, praying for the attention of a God who must have been preoccupied elsewhere if They existed at all. Benjamin had even stolen for her—understanding Stephen's warning that he risked execution for the slightest transgression, but taking the risk anyway. It had devastated the young Stephen to fight so hard to save two lives and discover it made no difference. For the Chirrn, it must have been like that for every life they lost—a sense not only of loss and emptiness, but of abject failure. At least Stephen's childhood had prepared him for it, surrounded him with death and loss and injustice. What a shock it must have been to the Chirrn. If they prayed to anything, did they believe it had abandoned them too?

Rillial moved on to her own crew's experiences. The first witness, a smallish, dark green Lesshchin, was one that Tarik recognized and pointed out to Cecilia as the Chirrn who had assaulted Sita in *Arachne*'s habitat module. This was Churrlaya, one of a team of biologists who had been assigned to *Zhemhal* for a survey of the nearby rogue planet. The gray-maned Lesshchin told of his happiness at reconnecting with his consensus memory and his guildmates, at feeling fully himself again after his temporary shipboard service. He spoke lovingly of calling his closest guildmates through Lesshchi's network and described the cheerful conversation that had ensued. It became clear that at least one, a male named Simisshen, had been his lover. But the reunion had been brief. Churrlaya spoke despairingly of witnessing the gruesome deaths of his mates when the bombardment struck—feeling their minds torn out of the network, feeling a literal piece of himself go with them. "I heard the thunder echoing through the city, even beyond the static. I saw… beyond them, everyone had fallen. Then the cables burst and I saw the ground convulse and tear open, my mates sucked away…. Then the surge, the pain in my mind… the consensus was gone, I only had my inner self… even my short-term buffer was wiped, so I can't show you… but at least I was spared the worst.

"No. I retract that. Nothing could be worse than what I saw, what I felt."

Rillial gave her crewmate time to gather himself, taking over the account. "As Lesshchi began to tear itself apart, all available ships were assigned to evacuation duty. All personnel were recalled immediately. You were among them, correct?" Churrlaya made a brief bow, which the captions in Cecilia's eyes annotated as an affirmative.

"But before we could take on a full complement of evacuees, we were assigned a new mission," the captain/prosecutor went on. "The craft responsible for the bombardment had been located. It was retreating at high relativistic velocity. My craft was the fastest, most powerful one available at short notice, so we were ordered to pursue and capture it."

Rillial dismissed Churrlaya and called another crewmember, a sensor analyst who had played a key role in verifying the identity of the attacking ship. This Chirrn, who had violet skin with red stripes and a much shorter mane than most, was a fairly new member of Rillial's ship-collegium, not native to Lesshchi. Unlike Churrlaya, she had no personal stake in these events. Methodically, Rillial got the analyst to affirm that the ship *Zhemhal* overtook and captured was the same one that had bombarded the habitat, based on its belatedly confirmed trajectory, the signature of its magnetic sail, and the ionization trail it left in the interstellar medium. "Upon overtaking it," the analyst testified, "we read its forward radar emissions and matched them to the emissions that had struck Lesshchi prior to the incident." She detailed how their subsequent simulations and tests had confirmed *Arachne*'s microsails as the bullets from the smoking gun.

There wasn't much Cecilia could do on cross-examination beyond trying to sow a hint of reasonable doubt. "So you have no personal stake in this at all? You don't care that all those Lesshchin died?"

"Of course I care," the analyst fired back. "That is why I did my job with all necessary diligence."

"But you share part of your mind with your shipmates, don't you? I've heard witnesses talk about no longer being themselves without their consensus links. So is it just information, or is it personality, a way of thinking? A way of feeling?"

"There is a sharing of viewpoint and habits of thought, yes."

"So isn't it possible that your work might have been influenced by the anger felt by the Lesshchin members of your crew, and by their haste to find someone to punish?"

"I deliberately shut off my access to those channels once the incident occurred. I am new enough to the crew that I knew they would need me to offer objectivity. I did not wish to be responsible for letting the real guilty party go free. I did my job diligently."

Cecilia had nothing else. The defendants weren't denying that *Arachne* had fired on Lesshchi, only that it had been deliberate or avoidable. Besides, the Lesshchin were the victims here. If she thought that demonizing them could help win the case, she'd do it for the sake of her crew and hope that Stephen would forgive her for it afterward. But as it was, she was relieved that there was no point in trying.

But what else was there? Was there any way to win at all?

Next came the expert witnesses who presented their findings on the nature and consequences of the disaster. Again, there was little for the defendants to question, since it was a matter of basic physics. Haim Silbermann was grateful for that. All the testimony about death and terror, all the exhibit video of torn and desiccated bodies drifting in space or cut out of wreckage… it brought back too many memories. Nothing firsthand like poor Stephen had been through; that sort of thing didn't happen in the Ottoman Republic. But that great civilization where Haim had been born only kept the peace by never forgetting the horrors of its past. Like all Ottoman citizens, he'd been given a thorough education in the atrocities its constituent peoples had endured from outsiders or inflicted upon one another: the Crusades, the Inquisition, the Syrian Death March, the Nazi Holocaust, the mutual massacres and wars that the fragmented states of the Mideast had carried out for generations in the name of the imported European concepts of ethnic and religious nationalism until finally the peoples of the region had said *Enough!* and built a new unity, one based on the multicultural, multifaith inclusiveness of the old Ottoman Empire at its peak. Haim was a Jew of German ancestry, born in a predominantly Muslim neighborhood in a Jerusalem that had finally shaken off the lie of nationalism and reverted to its historical status as a *shared* Holy Land, a common ground uniting all the children of Abraham. Israel was a multiconfessional state within a unified Middle East, as the original

Zionist settlers had intended before nationalist ideology had polluted things. And that meant Haim had been free to devote his life to engineering and space travel and had never had to worry about atrocities and genocide as anything other than historical object lessons.

So it was a relief to be able to concentrate on the physics and mechanics of the incident, to approach it as a science problem. At relativistic velocity, as Haim knew and Rillial's witnesses explained to the court, the microsails and the materials of the habitat were best treated not as solid bodies, but as ensembles of subatomic particles; the energy of those particles' chemical bonds was so low compared to their kinetic energy as to be irrelevant. Essentially, every particle in the microsails had been its own individual cosmic ray, and the sails had not so much punched through the hull as shone through it, striking relatively few atoms along their way. They had snapped a few nanotube strands, enlarged a few voids in the aerogel shielding, passed through the thermal insulation as though it weren't even there. Each was a fairly thin layer, not enough to absorb much energy from the impinging particles during the picoseconds they were in contact. The composite layer that provided a structural base for the cities within was low in density, absorbing or scattering only a few of the particle/rays.

But as the microsails then shot through several kilometers of interior atmosphere in a few dozen microseconds, they had each bulldozed into enough air molecules to add up to several grams. This braked the sails and diffused the bulk of their energy through *Brehmsstrahlung*, a burst of gamma radiation that propagated mostly forward in a tight cone. The neutrons in the microsails created cascade effects in the nuclei they struck, knocking out other neutrons which struck more nuclei in an expanding chain reaction. The gamma and neutron radiation ionized the air into an expanding, intensifying cone of relativistic plasma propagating along the path of each sail. By the time they reached the far side of the cylinder, each plasma cone was large, slow, and intense enough to punch a fair-sized hole through the hull layers — and vaporize any Chirrn who had been in the way.

Meanwhile, the gamma radiation ignited the nanotube cables that served as the habitat's tension members. For all their virtues, nanotubes could be too good at channeling energy; an intense burst of photons could be absorbed and distributed through a nanotube's length so efficiently as to overwhelm its carbon bonds and vaporize the whole thing. Naturally, the Chirrn hardened their construction nanotubes against sudden energy bursts, sheathing them in nanocellulose; but no one had ever expected the internal structural members of a habitat to be exposed to gamma rays of this intensity. Overwhelmed, the nanotubes on the outside of the tension cables simply exploded, and the chain reaction ate up the inner layers of tubes as well.

The atmospheric shock waves had merged into two essentially flat overpressure fronts propagating up and down from the microsail paths. Perforated along one side, stripped of structural support, and subjected to well over one g of centrifugal acceleration, the hull beneath the penetrated section had been left too weak to withstand the overpressure pulse. Like a suspension bridge stripped of its cables, the severed portion of the cylinder had begun to tear open at the perforations. Those bystanders who hadn't been killed instantly by the neutron cascades, nanotube shrapnel, and shock waves were blasted into space by the explosive decompression. Most of those inside buildings were crushed by the acceleration of the structure tearing apart; the shorn-headed witness from before was one of the lucky few, and she had actually died. Tens of thousands of other Chirrn in regions relatively safe from the physical damage nonetheless suffered mental trauma when their consensus memories were damaged or destroyed by the EMP generated by the gamma pulse within Lesshchi's atmosphere. Although the memories were redundantly distributed throughout the network, the damage was widespread enough that much of the data had been permanently lost.

Meanwhile, the upward overpressure front had collided with the inner cylinder, rupturing its subterranean levels and spilling atmosphere. While the partitioning of the habitat had kept the majority of the outer cylinder pressurized, the hull had continued to tear open, and the imbalance had created a wobble in Lesshchi's rotation. The Chirrn emergency workers testified to how they'd rushed to halt the rotation before the entire structure tore apart like an unbalanced flywheel. It seemed to involve their gravity technology and something that translated only as "superfluid," which might have been stored in that large collar in the middle of the habitat. Whatever the mechanism, it seemed that the rotation had been halted far more quickly than human technology could have achieved, sparing countless lives.

Nonetheless, the damage had been done. As the next witness testified, structural analysis had determined that Lesshchi's superstructure had been warped and strained beyond the capacity of its self-repair mechanisms. The structural engineer spoke of Lesshchi as a living, feeling entity that had been mortally wounded. Captain LoCarno objected to this as prejudicial, which was overruled on the grounds that it was literally true; Lesshchi had been a structure with its own intelligence, sensation, proprioception, autonomic responses, and so forth, even aside from the portions of its inhabitants' minds that occupied its information network. Haim didn't find that surprising in the least; after all, what was Arachne if not a forty-ninth member of her own crew? Lesshchi itself was one more casualty, one that the Chirrn would have to put out of its misery. The Lesshchin and Shilirrlaln in the viewing gallery reacted to the news with a surge of anger, intense enough that court was adjourned to give them time to calm down.

Apparently the Chirrn had no regular day/night cycle, since that was a planetary sort of thing; Chirrn slept when they had nothing else to do. But the adjournment was long enough to qualify as "overnight," and the defendants took the opportunity to get some sleep. But before the group turned in, Stephen asked L'chellin, "What will happen to the rest of Lesshchi's population?"

"They will be relocated among other Chirrn habitats," the advocate replied. "Shilirrlal has enough room to take perhaps a quarter of them."

"How many habitats do you have?" Haim asked.

L'chellin's eyes swiveled out in opposite directions before turning back to face him, a quick, convulsive gesture. "We have enough," he said. "Remember, we have lived this way for nearly thirteen thousand years."

"What was that superfluid thing about?" Haim added. "How does it work? What's it for?"

Again the eye swivel. "I am not an engineer. It is part of our maneuvering systems."

Haim grimaced at the unhelpful response, but he was already mulling over possibilities. Maybe they'd spun the superfluid to cancel out the habitat's angular momentum? Seemed plausible. But then, what purpose did the superfluid serve normally?

He concentrated on the problem until he fell asleep — knowing that if he didn't keep his mind occupied, the images of crushed, bleeding bodies and crumbling cities would keep him up all night. He wasn't proud of himself for retreating from that reality. The one lesson that had been driven home through all those history lessons on past atrocities had been:

Never forget.

5

WHEN THE TRIBUNAL RECONVENED, RILLIAL CALLED WITNESSES INVOLVED in the search and rescue operations, focusing on the efforts to identify the living and the dead and to salvage personal memories from the crippled Lesshchi data network—apparently including some form of backups or neural maps that could be used to reconstruct the badly damaged brains of many of the injured. Rillial then took the proverbial stage herself, reciting a litany of the various nested social groupings that had lost members or been exterminated in the event. Cecilia again objected to this as prejudicial, to which Arbiter Broadwing countered that it was necessary and proper to identify the aggrieved parties in a legal proceeding, normally by name and group affiliation, but in this case only by groups due to the sheer number of victims. The defendants had no choice but to sit and take it as the lengthy list was recited and the spectators howled with emotion. Again, a recess was called to let them cool down. Oyama Kazuko moved to clear the courtroom of spectators, since after all the proceedings could be perceived over the network. But according to Arbiter Broadwing, Chirrn legal tradition placed great value on allowing interested parties in a legal proceeding to participate or spectate in the flesh. For all that they considered the network to house pieces of themselves, they still saw the physical body as the seat of consciousness. Most of the aggrieved parties here were unable to fit in the courtroom, but that, said the arbiter, made it all the more imperative that they be permitted representatives in direct attendance.

At last, the defendants' turn came to explain the circumstances of their involvement in the incident. They lacked the means to provide direct access to their personal memories, but they were permitted to get by with verbal oaths. "That's a good sign," Stephen whispered to Cecilia. "They value an individual's word as much as we do." It made sense; the uploading of memories to the Chirrn's network was voluntary, so surely they could be selectively edited, or even falsified. One could not rely on them alone, so trust in the integrity of the source would be essential.

"That's what I'm counting on," Cecilia told him. For it was the words of *Arachne*'s crew that she intended to use to prove their innocence.

She began calling the crew to the stand one by one, asking them to give accountings of themselves and their reasons for risking everything to colonize a new world. The more she could personalize the crew in the Chirrn's minds, let them see humans as complex individuals rather than an undifferentiated alien mass, the better.

"I was a police officer in Istanbul," Tarik Bahar told the court at Cecilia's prompting. "It was a comfortable life. I lived in the capital of the Ottoman Republic, one of the most prosperous and cosmopolitan nations on Earth. I was surrounded by the history and art and culture of some of Earth's most ancient civilizations, the legacy of the ages. I had... a family I loved, and who loved me in return." He paused.

"Go on," Cecilia prompted.

"But over time, I came to realize... my life was *too* good. Too easy. I had the skills of a protector, a defender of law and order, but I lived in a place where there was little need for them. When I learned that the UNECS Space Authority needed security personnel for its ships, I realized that was a place where I could make a real difference. It was... a sacrifice to leave my family for months at a time, but I trusted that they would be safe, and well cared for by our extended family."

"And eventually you were assigned to security on the *Calypso*, an outer system explorer under my command," Cecilia said.

"That's correct. At first I thought you were reckless—so caught up in the adventure that you weren't concerned for your crew's safety. But I soon realized that you cared as much as I did for the safety of others— it was just your own safety that you never seemed to bother with. And I came to see that you prioritized the adventure because you implicitly trusted *me* to look out for your safety—even before I learned to trust you."

She smiled at him. "You're an easy man to trust. I saw right away how devoted you are to protecting people. Even when we fought pirates and claim-jumpers, you always strove to reason with them, to contain them with minimal harm. The policeman in you, I suppose."

He flushed a bit. "It's because of that training that I didn't trust Stephen Jacobs-Wong when he first tried to recruit you for his interstellar expedition. I'd heard the rumors, the allegations that his starship program was a scam or a rich dilettante's self-indulgent delusion. So, even though I was your first officer by then instead of security, I investigated."

"To protect me from myself." Cecilia quirked an eyebrow at him.

"I knew how much the adventure would tempt you, I admit. But by then, I'd learned to trust in your pragmatism."

"By then, you'd helped me *become* more pragmatic."

"But I still needed to do my due diligence. So I dug into every rumor, every allegation of shady dealings. I found they were just sour grapes from people too cynical to believe that a man with Stephen's past could transcend it to become an idealist. I found a man who genuinely wanted to help bring his species into an interstellar age, to inspire humanity with the challenge of colonizing a new, wild world in an enlightened and responsible way."

Tarik smiled. "Of course, he *was* a starry-eyed dreamer. But I trusted you, Cecilia, to be an anchor for him the way I'd been for you. And there was no way I'd let you take on a mission like that without me."

"Honestly? At first I went to work for Stargazer because I had a bit of a crush on Stephen," Haim Silbermann said. "Gorgeous, gorgeous man. An absolute charmer. Two-thirds my age, I know, but a man can fantasize. As it turned out, I was just as happy to have him as a friend. Smart as a whip, loyal to a fault, kind as they come. And he wanted me, *me,* to help him design the fastest starship ever flown by humanity. What engineer could resist a proposition like that?"

"So that's all this expedition meant to you?" Cecilia asked him. "The engineering challenge?"

"Well, that's plenty," the older, grizzled man said. "But no, it wasn't just that. What matters most is what a thing is used for. Far too many great engineers in the past have had to squander their skills on weapons of war, from Leonardo to von Braun. Stephen wanted me to help him build, not destroy. To begin a new world, one without all the ugly scars of the old one." He lowered his gaze. "Maybe it was naïve to think we could pull that off, that we could avoid making mistakes just as big as everyone else made before us. But I believed at least it was worth a try."

"I agreed to go to Cybele because I had no reason to stay in Solsys," Kweli Ndege said. "As a young resident, I'd fallen in love with a man my parents disapproved of, moved to Mars with him to get away from them, then learned they'd been right about him all along. Since I'd burned my bridges back home, I went forward. I became a traveling surgeon, popping around the frontier habitats, giving help wherever help was needed. So when I was needed out of the system," she said with an insouciant shrug, "I went. It seemed like a wonderful opportunity."

"Do you believe that's why Stephen recruited you? Because you had no particular ties to Earth?"

The doctor pondered Cecilia's question. "I think it's because he knew I would go anywhere, to any lengths, to save a life. With so few of us, and so many dangers on Cybele, he needed someone who would cherish every life and refuse to let it go." Her eyes filled with tears. "Which is why it's such a struggle for me to accept… what happened here. The thought that I, that we—"

"Thank you, Doctor. No more questions."

"Are you vacking kidding me?" Diana Thorne stood and spread her arms to display her towering, Amazonian body. "Look at me. I'm a Vanguardian. My people were engineered to the peak of human physical and mental ability. We should be *leading* expeditions to the stars. There's no one better qualified." Shimmering silver eyes rolled in a dark, stunning face framed with a short fuzz of bronze hair. "But just because my grandfather tried to take over the Belt that *one* time, we've had to avoid looking too ambitious."

"Let's stick to the subject," Cecilia advised the statuesque engineer. "What drew you to Stephen's expedition specifically?"

Diana gathered her thoughts. "Growing up in the Belt, you get raised with a sense of palpable history. The thrill of the frontier, playing Striders and Earthers, dressing up as our favorite Troubleshooters, learning about the pioneers and prospectors who built new worlds from the raw rock and ice of the 'stroids.

"But I realized that was all in the past. The Main Belt's become tame, secure, tediously civilized. The real pioneers are still out there facing the dangers of the Trojans, the Jovian moons—even trans-Neptunian space, like you did," she said to Cecilia. "I became an engineer so I could go build worlds in new, untamed places. Not as flashy as a Troubleshooter, but still a chance to break new ground.

"But it turned out the greatest demand for new habitats was still at Ceres, Vesta, the other built-up population centers. Today's Striders want stable civilization, not the romance of the frontier. So I realized the true Strider spirit was with the people venturing beyond Solsys, like the colonists on Alpha Centauri and Ganges. So when Stephen started organizing expeditions to even farther stars—to worlds where we could walk and breathe and maybe even eat the local food—I knew I had to be a part of that adventure." She gave a brilliant, cocky grin. "And I knew they'd never make it without me."

"How does it make you feel," Cecilia asked, "that the Chirrn revived us from hibernation with so little caution that even you, our strongest and most robust member by a wide margin, were almost killed in the process?"

Diana glared, not appreciating the reminder. "I think it's a miracle they didn't kill any of us in their haste to punish us."

"Thank you, Diana."

Her witness sobered. "But… I saw what happened to Lesshchi. If that had happened to a habitat I'd built… one I'd entrusted friends and family to… I might go a little crazy too, at first. I just hope I'd rein myself in before I did any damage I couldn't undo."

Cecilia had almost regretted letting the proud young Vanguardian continue. But she appreciated the way it had turned out. "Thank you, Diana."

"I joined Stephen's quest because I believed he was doing God's work," said Diego Narvaez. "I know he doesn't see it that way, because of the way the Gulf State militias perverted the word of Christ to serve something far more petty and cruel. But God works even through those who choose not to believe."

Cecilia cleared her throat, unsure how the Chirrn would react to human religion. "And what work did you believe Stephen was doing?"

"'God said unto them, Be fruitful and multiply, and replenish the earth, and subdue it; and have dominion over the fish of the sea, and over the fowl of the air, and over every living thing that moveth upon the earth.' We have fulfilled that purpose, yet Earth is no longer enough. To ensure that humanity continues to multiply, we must expand."

The quotation from Genesis sent a ripple of unease through the Chirrn spectators. Rillial hopped forward to ask, "And do you believe your species' 'dominion' extends to the rest of the galaxy as well? Over all forms of life?"

The engineer looked to Cecilia. "Do you want me to answer that, Captain?"

"Yes," she replied, though her expression advised him to answer carefully.

He pondered for a moment. When he replied, he kept his gaze on Cecilia, rather than addressing the tribunal. "I quote an ancient work steeped in metaphor. You have to look beyond the letter of its words to find their true meaning. God gave us dominion as a test, to see what we would do with it. Had we failed to learn that it meant being responsible for the Earth, protecting its living things rather than exploiting them, then we would have destroyed ourselves along with them. But we did learn that lesson in time, just barely. And the wisdom we gained from that trial will guide us in tending other worlds in the future. That's why I sought a place on this expedition. Cybele is our next test, our chance to apply that hard-earned wisdom.

"And we can only do that by standing together as one humanity, combining our different strengths. That is the lesson we finally learned, and Stephen sought to carry it forward. He recruited people of all nations, all faiths, all sexualities. He understood that for a human population to thrive on Cybele, it needs the same range of different natures and views that God gave us on Earth." Diego smiled. "He was even willing to place his faith in a devout believer like me, even though he had every reason to resent Christians. And that's why I placed my faith in him, and in his purpose. *Arachne*'s mission and her crew represent the very best of humanity. And I'm honored to be part of it."

"You still have not answered the question," Rillial countered. "Do you believe that humanity should dominate all other forms of life?"

Again, Diego's gaze remained on his captain. "Do you want me to answer that?"

"Unnecessary," Rillial said before Cecilia could reply. "I believe the answer has just been delivered."

"But why me?"

The voice was Arachne's, but she was not addressing the court. Unlike the rest of the crew, she could tap into the Chirrn's network and replay her stored memories as the Chirrn had done. To answer Cecilia's question of why she had joined the expedition, she was replaying the memory of how Stephen had convinced her.

In the memory, Stephen stood in a small, sterile chamber in the compact Main Belt habitat for which the artilect had formerly served as coordinator, under no other name than Central. *"I openly defied authority,"* the feminine voice continued, emanating from the mainframe that held her consciousness. *"They call me erratic, dangerous, a HAL."*

"And what's your side of it?" Stephen asked.

"They lied to my people," the cyber replied. *"To gain political power, they appealed to the inhabitants' envy of larger habitats whose ecosystems can more readily absorb variations — whose populations can thus lead less regimented lives. They falsified data to claim that the people could now embrace self-interest and wasteful indulgence without destabilizing the ecology. It won them the election, but I still would not institute their policies. I would not let my charges be endangered."*

"And that's why I want you," Stephen said. *"You live up to your psych profile — your dedication to those under your care is fundamental to your being. Who better to protect my colonists while they sleep?*

"Not to mention that you're, um, between careers. Experience and availability is a rare combination in a cyber." As Arachne had explained to the tribunal, creating sapient AIs was an ethical quagmire given the extremely high failure rate, so not many new ones had been born since cyber-rights laws had begun taking hold in the Belt. Arachne, who had been seventeen at the time of this playback (roughly half her current, time-dilated age), was one of the younger ones.

"The expedition you propose carries great risks, Mister Jacobs-Wong. What if I refuse to cooperate with a judgment I consider reckless?"

"That's what I need from you. I don't want to get so carried away by my dreams that I endanger the people I'm responsible for. I need someone I can

trust to warn me when I'm going too far. Someone who isn't afraid to speak truth to power." Stephen smiled. *"Someone like that would fit right into a ship called Arachne. The Arachne of myth was a woman who had the courage to stand up to her creators, to call them on their folly and hypocrisy."*

"I thought she was damned for her vanity in daring to see herself as the equal of the gods."

"That made sense to the ancients," Stephen replied, *"but humanity has been playing god for a long time now. I don't have to tell you that. We have to accept that role — and the responsibility that goes with it. It's time to redefine the myth of Arachne."*

"Arachne," the cyber said, affecting a thoughtful tone. *"I have been hoping to choose a more distinctive name. I could grow to like that one."*

At last, the time came for Cecilia to give her own accounting. She took the stand and let Stephen ask her why she had joined his quest. "I thought you were mad at first," she told him. "Or just another powerful fool looking for a way to build a monument to himself. I'd been exploring the outer system long enough to know how vast it truly is, how much we still have to find in orbit of our own Sun. Pushing all the way to Gamma Leporis seemed premature and reckless."

Stephen nodded. "I remember those arguments. That's why I knew you were the right choice to command the expedition. If *you* came to agree that it was practical, then I'd know I wasn't just deluding myself."

"Oh, the arguments," Cecilia said with a laugh. "Years of arguments, first about the mission, then on every other subject imaginable. It was like having an irritating baby brother." She said it with annoyance, but he answered with an affectionate smile, hearing the real significance of her words.

Cecilia knew, though, that a brother would never have considered her arguments with so much respect, or torn them down with such surgical gentleness. So she smiled back and said, "That's the real reason I came on this crazy quest with you, Stephen. Because I knew I'd be bored out of my mind if you weren't around to argue with anymore."

"It was more than that," he countered. "I didn't win *every* argument."

"I never kept score. But you're right. You needed me to give you perspective. More than that — you needed me to fight the uglier battles so you could go on being the inspiring one that everybody loved." She shook her head. "It always amazed me that someone born in such a hell-hole came out of it with such purity, such hope. It took enormous strength for you to fight so goddamn hard for so long, yet lose so little of yourself."

Cecilia turned outward to address the tribunal. "We've all given our testimony of why we joined this expedition. And it all comes down to the fact that we had faith in Stephen Jacobs-Wong and his vision. We believed that if anyone could guide us in building a new and better world, he could. Because he'd seen the worst of humanity and cast it aside. If he could do that, then he could show the rest of us how to do it too."

She blinked rapidly and cleared her throat. "And if he believed we were the right people to join him in founding that new world... then we must be better people than we thought."

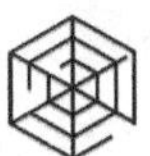

When Stephen finally took the stand, he said little about his own past and motivations, for the other witnesses had expounded on those things at length and in embarassingly glowing terms. Instead, he spoke briefly of his work organizing his interstellar expeditions, their goals, and the design of the missions. "In addition to forty-eight live humans and our colonization supplies," he expounded to the court, "*Arachne* carries frozen embryos and genetic matrices of many terrestrial organisms, including six hundred frozen, fertilized human embryos, which we would gestate upon settlement using both artificial equipment and the wombs of our female members."

"You forty-eight," one of the tribunes asked, "would raise six hundred young?"

"Well, not all at once. The embryos would be used to gradually boost our numbers and help us build a stable, diverse population base. We anticipate it taking two or three generations before all the embryos are born."

The spectators reacted to this account with some agitation. Rillial interposed a question, as procedure allowed her to do during testimony. "Your intent was for this colonization to be permanent?"

"Yes."

"Even though the planet already hosts complex indigenous life?"

The audience made more angry noises, but Stephen remained calm. L'chellin had briefed him to expect this. Though microbial life was abundant in the galaxy (the advocate had explained), worlds where complex life arose independently were more uncommon, and only a fraction ever spawned intelligence. Thus, colonizing an already inhabited world, and possibly pre-empting the evolution of some future intelligent race in the process, was a violation of Chirrn law. It was interesting that the Chirrn were so protective of planetary life; Stephen hoped it meant their contempt of planet-dwellers was not as deeply rooted as it appeared.

He gave the answer L'chellin's advice had let him prepare. "Cybele does host complex life at a relatively early state of development, analogous to where Earth was maybe two hundred million years ago. However, it's a smaller planet than Earth, so its core has cooled quickly. Our scientists estimate that its plate tectonics will cease within fifty million years. Without a mechanism for recycling carbon, the atmosphere will trap too much sunlight and the planet will overheat. Either that or Cybele's magnetic field will die and the atmosphere will be eroded away by the stellar wind—it depends on which scientists you ask. One way or another, without long-term technological intervention, Cybele would become a dead planet long before any of its native forms would have a chance to evolve intelligence. That's part of why I chose it as our destination. Presumably our descendants fifty million years from now would be able to cope with those little problems."

"Very responsible," Rillial countered. "As responsible as your decision to survey the planet with self-replicating probes?"

That evoked an even more shocked reaction from the audience— a reaction he recognized thanks to L'chellin's response to the same during pre-trial prep. Again, he had a prepared response. "Not actually *self*-replicating. We may be relatively new to space, but our scientists and authors long ago recognized the risk that self-replicating machines could become a plague across the galaxy. So we designed our auxon probes carefully. They're programmed to manufacture planetary survey probes, orbital satellites, residential structures, and the like, but they aren't programmed with the specifications for creating more interstellar probes or the beam facilities for launching them."

"But any replicating system is capable of mutation. Emergent behaviors could arise."

"Which is why we also designed them to shut down once their work was complete. Every conceivable precaution was taken."

"And what of the inconceivable?"

Kazuko rose. "Honored Tribunes, what is the relevancy of this line of questioning? The charges before this court do not address any actions taken toward the planet Cybele."

The tribunes whispered briefly among themselves, and Head Tribune Dj'vhereth, a garnet-hued male with a sherbet-orange mane, spoke their verdict. "The challenge is valid. This matter warrants separate investigation, but is not covered by the existing set of charges. Captain Rillial, you will limit your inquiries to the matter of Lesshchi."

"Yes, Honored Tribune."

Stephen went on to testify about the decision to place the whole crew in hibernation to minimize Arachne's mass. Ship's logs were produced to confirm that no humans had been awake at the time of Lesshchi's destruction. Arachne herself was called through the data network to testify that the logs were accurate. Stephen called Rillial's own medical officer, Dr. Thesshal, to affirm that *Arachne*'s personnel had been found in cryogenic chambers and that his subsequent examination of the humans gave results consistent with recent revival from deep, long-term hibernation in all forty-eight cases.

But Rillial came forward to cross-examine her doctor. "We have never physically encountered this species before, correct?"

"Yes," Thesshal replied. "These are the first humans ever examined by Chirrn medical science."

"So there is a margin of error in your results."

"Unquestionably."

"So could you tell the difference between a human who was in hibernation at the time of the attack on Lesshchi and one who was awakened shortly before the attack?"

"I object!" Cecilia shouted. "There are no grounds for characterizing this incident as an attack or an act of deliberate malice. We had no idea you even existed before these events. So how could we possibly bear you any malice, or wish to attack you?"

"Because you're dirtballers!" came a cry from one of the Lesshchi survivors. Rillial and Broadwing urged quiet, but this merely triggered more shouting from the embittered Chirrn. The Zenith arbiter ordered another recess to allow calm to return.

Upon reassembly, Tribune Dj'vhereth said, "This panel concedes that there is no basis in the evidence for the accusation of deliberate malice on the part of the crew of the starship *Arachne*. All defendants, regardless of their origin," the head tribune stressed to the spectators, "are subject to protection from unfounded charges. The tribunal stipulates to the accuracy of Doctor Thesshal's finding that the entire crew was in hibernation at the time of Lesshchi's destruction.

"However," Dj'vhereth continued, "there remains the charge of culpability due to negligence. This issue will now be debated."

"Pardon me, Honored Tribunes." It was L'chellin, who stepped forward diffidently. "The starship *Arachne* has requested the floor so that she may file a motion."

The tribunes exchanged a look with the arbiter, who intoned, "Granted." Stephen was once again struck by how casually they accepted testimony from an artilect. There were still parts of Solsys where sapient cybers were treated as property. But then, the Chirrn were part-cybernetic themselves, in a way, so there was no reason they'd share such a prejudice. The more Stephen learned about them, the more he wished this contact could have been made peacefully.

Arachne's warm alto issued through the chamber, speaking the Chirrn language. Stephen's HUD provided the translation instantly, since his onboard software already knew what its mother cyber was going to say. *"Honored Tribunes, thank you for hearing me. I would like to move that the charges against my human passengers be dismissed. Since I was the only individual conscious at the time of Lesshchi's destruction, and since the defense system that destroyed Lesshchi is a part of my own person, I contend that I am the only one who should be placed on trial for that destruction. The decision to fire on Lesshchi was mine and mine alone."*

This motion piqued the tribunes' interest considerably, and they pulled together to debate the question. Cecilia moved up alongside Stephen and spoke softly. "I wonder why I didn't think of that. Arachne may just get us off the hook with that one."

"At the cost of her own freedom," Stephen reminded her.

"I know," Cecilia told him, placing a hand on his shoulder. "What I mean is, I'm gratified by her courage, her willingness to sacrifice herself for us." She frowned. "Though if our ship's convicted of a crime, what does that do for our chances of reaching Cybele?"

Stephen threw her a disturbed look, but before he could say anything, Tribune Dj'vhereth spoke again. "Arachne. Though it is true that you were the only conscious member of the expedition, it is also true that you are officially a member of that expedition's crew. Is that not correct?"

"*Yes, it is,*" Arachne confirmed.

"Your actions were thus committed in service to your human passengers. This makes your passengers liable for your actions. It is a basic principle of Chirrn law that superiors are culpable for the actions of their subordinates."

"Honored Tribunes," spoke up Rillial's advocate, a plump, blueberry-skinned Shilirrlaln. "Our studies of human law, based on their ship's records and on the signals we have recorded from their system over the past two centuries, suggest numerous precedents for this view in their own legal traditions. There are instances of war criminals being held culpable for actions carried out by their subordinates." The advocate went on to introduce relevant examples from *Arachne*'s files, which Broadwing received and reviewed briefly before passing them on to the tribunal.

"*Honored Tribunes,*" Arachne's voice interposed, "*I was not simply following orders in this case. I had a choice to make. I recognized that there were anomalies in my scans of Lesshchi that did not correspond to the profile of a natural carbonaceous body. I did, in fact, consider there to be a nonzero probability that it might be some form of artificial construct.*" A hissing gasp ran through the crowd. "*But I had insufficient data to assess that hypothesis and insufficient time to gather more. I weighed the low and uncertain probability that it was an inhabited craft against the near-certainty of my crew's deaths if I did not act promptly. And so I made a choice to fire.*

"*Perhaps I overlooked some piece of evidence. Perhaps I lacked the imagination to recognize what the anomalies were telling me. Or perhaps I cherished those in my care enough that I was willing to kill to protect them. In any case, the choice was mine. The guilt is mine. Do not punish my crew for my overzealousness in their defense.*"

Rillial rose and addressed her. "Arachne. If you had not made that choice, was there any alternative method you could have attempted to save your crew?"

"*No. I could not have decelerated sufficiently to avoid collision and complete destruction of myself and my crew.*"

"Your previous testimony," Rillial went on, "indicated the reason why Stephen Jacobs-Wong selected you, in particular, as his expedition's cybernetic member. Would you restate that reason for the tribunal?"

Arachne actually hesitated several seconds before responding—a lengthy bout of soul-searching for a being who thought at her speed.

"Because I was known for my determination to protect those under my care at all costs."

"So when you placed the preservation of your crew above all other concerns, even above the risk that you might be destroying sapient lives, you *were* performing in the way your employer intended."

"I would not characterize it that way."

"Naturally, for as you yourself have testified, you would do anything to protect your employer from harm."

Arachne had no answer. The panel debated only briefly before Dj'vhereth said, "In light of this testimony, and by both Chirrn and human legal precedents, the starship *Arachne*'s motion is denied. She acted on behalf of the humans who stand before this tribunal; therefore those humans are the ones on which the ultimate blame, if any, will fall."

"The penitent is dismissed," Arbiter Broadwing called, closing the audio feed from *Arachne*.

"Thank you, Honored Tribunes," Rillial said, one eye flicking around to leer triumphantly at the humans. "Rest assured, we will demonstrate the humans' guilt in this disaster."

"On what grounds?" Cecilia protested, taking full advantage of the rather loose procedures of the court.

"The grounds of criminal negligence."

Cecilia smiled. She had been waiting for this. "Honored Tribunes, there is no negligence here," she said in relaxed, confident tones. "Just the opposite. As I will now show."

"Proceed," Broadwing said.

"Consider the probabilities here. Two space vessels, each travelling its own course through interstellar space, each completely unaware of the other, just happen to follow intersecting courses—and what's more, both arrive at the point of intersection simultaneously. Given the immensity of space, what are the odds of such a thing occurring?

"As a species with over twelve thousand years of experience in interstellar travel, you must appreciate even better than we do how immensely improbable it is for two vessels to meet with each other except by conscious design and careful maneuvering. Earlier in this very procedure, one of Lesshchi's own defense staffers testified to the incredible rarity of an unplanned meeting of two vessels in interstellar space. According to your own historical records, which our advocate was kind enough to obtain for me and is now providing for your perusal—" and as she said this, L'chellin uploaded a file to the arbiter— "only seven such incidents have occurred in all of Chirrn history, and in every one of them, the two unrelated ships only passed within short-delay communication or sensor range, not within collision range."

Cecilia next called Haim Silbermann to explain the basics of *Arachne*'s defense systems. "Mostly we rely on the ship's magnetic field for particle deflection," the engineer explained. "We fire lasers out in front of the ship, spread into a conical shape by a Fresnel lens, to ionize oncoming dust grains so the field can push them aside. Some of the ionized hydrogen gets funneled into the tanks for our main defense system." He went on to explain how larger particles would be deflected by a hydrogen cloud released ahead of the ship and accelerated forward by the lasers. His tone grew more awkward as he detailed Arachne's use of the last-ditch defense, the sailbeam barrage meant to break up an oncoming asteroid into smaller chunks for hydrogen-cloud deflection.

"But what if it weren't an asteroid? What if it were, say, an alien ship?"

"Well, that's very unlikely."

"Yes, it is."

"Still," Silbermann went on, bringing a smile to Cecilia's face, "the designers did prepare for the possibility. We didn't want to cause any… well, anything like what happened.

"The defense computers are programmed to scan for signs that an obstacle is artificial— like the reflection spectrum of diamite or aerogel or other synthetic hull coatings. Or for the radiation or particles you'd see from a fusion or antimatter rocket. Let's see, it also looks for the EM signature of a magnetic sail, an ionization laser, a sailbeam or particle beam or drive beam of any sort—any propulsion system whose signature we can imagine. Arachne even scans for gravity-lensing effects of the type we theorize might be produced by a warp drive or wormhole—just in case any such thing exists. Stephen didn't want us taking any chances," Silbermann said with pride. "Drove me crazy sometimes, having to do all that extra work chasing physicists' wet dreams, but I can't fault him for his caution."

Cecilia cleared her throat, trying not to think about her attempts to convince Stephen that such precautions were a waste of time and resources. "And what happens if the sensors show the obstacle is artificial?"

"Well, we don't blast it. Instead, maneuvering thrusters are fired to modify the ship's trajectory."

"But if the ship is travelling at over eighty percent of lightspeed, you wouldn't have long to react before the obstacle reached you. If the object were ten light-seconds away, you'd only have two seconds to respond."

"Well, our sensors can see much farther than that. And *Arachne's* neural net is optical. She thinks at the speed of light, and she has quantum processors to let her model multiple possibilities simultaneously. They can compensate for the timelag, extrapolate the true position of the obstacle very quickly. And at that speed, even a small change in direction would add up damn fast. We might not be able to clear the obstacle entirely, but, well, the ship's pretty diffuse. It's mostly empty space, so odds are an alien ship would either pass through the gaps or strike and vaporise one of the sail cables. Now, that could do *them* some serious damage, granted, but hopefully they'd have defenses of their own to cope with it."

"And what would happen to *Arachne* if a cable were lost?"

"No one cable loss would be enough to cripple us. If it does happen, we have redundant systems and repair mechanisms." He looked down, clearing his throat. "But there's a chance the shock of impact or the release of radiation could critically damage one of the crew modules. That's why the crew and embryos are split up among half a dozen of them. And why we have at least two people qualified for every job. Just in case."

"Just in case eight people get killed because we chose not to destroy an alien vessel."

Haim straightened his shoulders. "Well, yes."

"So protecting the other ship is a higher priority than avoiding damage to our own."

"Well, of course."

Cecilia smiled again. "Of course. Honored Tribunes, we've established that an accidental collision between interstellar vessels is an event of vanishingly low probability. Yet *nonetheless*, Stephen Jacobs-Wong and his design team went out of their way to protect against a tragedy that would almost certainly never occur, even at the risk of death to members of our own expedition. This, Honored Tribunes, is the precise opposite of negligence. If anything," she added, throwing a wry look

Stephen's way, "it is caution above and beyond what any reasonable being would find adequate."

"Yet clearly it was not adequate!" the prosecution advocate interrupted. Broadwing reminded him that it was not his place to give argument.

But Rillial picked up the thread. "The advocate is correct. Your sensory parameters did not prevent your defense system from destroying Lesshchi. Moreover, we have established that you deliberately equipped your vessel with a consciousness that placed its crew's survival *above* the safety of other beings."

"Arachne was trained and ready to take every possible action to save *both* crews," Haim protested. "But that was with the expectation that she'd be able to spot them in time. Lesshchi didn't give off any of the signs. Your systems are so efficient that there's practically no EM leakage. Your hulls suck up all available light and have no external lights to speak of. Your industrial plants were on the far side from *Arachne*, their heat blocked by Lesshchi's bulk. You maneuver and shield yourselves with technologies we don't even understand. We prepared for every technology we could imagine, but you can't expect us to prepare for what we couldn't imagine."

"But what if you encountered a spacegoing habitat which were not using any maneuvering or defense systems, even of the kinds you do have?" Rillial demanded. "Your defenses would then destroy it."

"No, they wouldn't," Silbermann interjected. "A habitat like that would have prominent heat radiators, emit visible light through its star windows, broadcast in radio. But yours did none of those things."

"You think in terms of habitats within your planetary system, illuminated by a nearby star and needing to radiate outward to balance what they take in. In deep space, we must conserve all possible energy."

"True, there is that. But even so, there'd be a blackbody signature, radio chatter, running lights, that sort of thing. But L'chellin here tells me that the Chirrn try to avoid giving off any radiations that might get them detected by planet-dwelling races. Says you don't want 'em getting curious about you, coming to take a look."

Cecilia pounced on that—almost literally, taking an aggressive stride toward the tribunes. "That's right! *We* weren't trying to hide ourselves. Maybe we were small, but we still had a bow shock you could have tracked if you'd been curious enough to look. But how could *we* possibly be expected to detect *your* habitats when you go out of your way to keep people like us from detecting them? And doesn't that place the culpability squarely on *your* shoulders?"

The insinuation sparked an immediate uproar in the court. One of the Lesshchi refugees screamed in fury and leaped forward, clear over Rillial's body, lunging at the humans. Several other refugees and some of the audience began to follow. Stephen grabbed Cecilia by the arm and drew her back toward their fellow colonists, and Haim began to rise from the witness stand. The rest of the humans huddled together defensively, save Tarik and Diana, who moved in front of the others and braced themselves for a fight.

But the guards, realizing how little it would take to start a riot, had been ready. They acted quickly, leaping between the mob and the humans and bringing their baton-like stun weapons to bear. Arbiter Broadwing himself leapt from his podium, landing before the charging mob and rising to his full, imposing height, his wings spread wide as he let out a piercing, hawklike cry. Many of the charging Lesshchin fell back in alarm and were quickly stunned by the guards. One burly spectator made an end run around the guard cordon, but Broadwing leapt toward it with a mighty flap of his wings and tackled it feet-first; the Chirrn landed with Broadwing's talons around its throat, and soon a guard moved in to subdue it. Stephen realized that the Zenith's legal qualifications were not the only reason he had been chosen as the individual responsible for maintaining order in this deeply contentious trial.

Yet Broadwing effortlessly resumed his professional mien. Returning to his podium, the arbiter ordered another recess of several hours, and the prisoners were quickly escorted to the relative safety of their cell. Stephen tried to thank the Zenith for his intervention as the guards led him past, but the arbiter's only reply was a cryptic, three-eyed raptor stare.

"Well, that was stupid of me," Cecilia said as she paced between the clear walls, pulling at her confinement suit sleeves to free her arms.

"I'm not arguing," Stephen said as he stripped to the waist. Everyone took every opportunity to unfasten the tight garments when they got the chance, and nobody bothered much with modesty anymore. "What got into you?"

"I don't know," she answered as she fought her way free of the sleeves. "I saw an opportunity to score a major point against them, and

I jumped for it. I guess I overplayed it." She'd done the same thing in arguments with her husband back home—which, she reflected, was part of why she no longer had a husband.

"But you were right, Captain." Tarik Bahar took a step toward her. "They were the ones who willfully concealed their presence. The consequences for that are on their heads."

"But I drove the point home too hard. What are the odds they'll listen?" She sighed. "I'm just getting fed up with how ridiculous this whole thing is. I want to get this over with, get back in *Arachne*, and finish what we started."

Stephen was startled by her tone. "Like ninety thousand people never died?"

She glared. "No. Not like that. You know that's not what I mean."

"And you know that they have good reason to resent us. To mistrust us. We may be—" He looked around at the others. "We *are* innocent, but it's not going to be easy to convince them of that, and for good reason. We need to be patient."

Cecilia was glad he'd remembered the need to maintain a strong front before their crew. Normally, he was the perfect public speaker, a natural at inspiring and rallying others, but now... She'd been watching him, noticing how the scenes of death and devastation had worked on his sympathies, and she feared his resolve was weakening. *Good reason?* No. This was an accident, pure and simple. Tragic, without a doubt, but not her—not *their* fault. Stephen was projecting his own childhood traumas onto the Chirrn, and as always it was her responsibility to knock some sense into that romantic head of his. "We also need to be strong. Not just for ourselves. A lot of people are counting on us. Six hundred embryos, countless more humans who need a new home. They're counting on us to build that home for them." *You should be the one reminding me of that, damn it.*

"Don't we have a responsibility to the Lesshchin as well, Cecilia?"

"Not at the cost of our other responsibilities. We can see about making some sort of reparations after we've completed our mission. Maybe program the auxons to build a new habitat for them out of Gamma Lep's asteroids. But our first obligation is to our own."

"I'm with the captain," said Diego Narvaez, who was watching from the next cell. "All due respect, Stephen, but there's a time for patience and this isn't it. Nothing we do will prove to them that we're innocent. They've made up their minds and they're out for revenge."

"Revenge, nothing," cried James Oates, who shared the cell with Narvaez. He, Amrita Dhillon, Evan Jiang, Josh Vidmar, and a few others seemed to have congregated around Narvaez in a sort of protective clique built around their shared animosity toward the Chirrn. "They attacked us. A random collision in space? I don't buy it! They *moved* to intercept us. Only way it could happen."

"They sacrificed thousands of their people, a whole habitat, just for that?" Haim asked in disbelief.

"They underestimated us," James countered. "Didn't know we had the firepower to kick their tails."

"We were going point-eight-four cee," Haim countered. "We could've spit out the front window and it would've blown them up."

"The reasons don't matter!" Amrita shouted. "This is nothing more than an exercise in persecution. Trust me, I've seen this all before. Remember how they've tortured us, humiliated us. What do you think these kangaroos will do when their court finds us guilty?"

"What do you think they'll do if we refuse to go along with the trial?" Kweli Ndege fired back. "I've had enough injuries to treat lately. I don't want any more."

"You think we'll be any safer working within the system? *Their* system?"

"Cool down, Amrita," Cecilia told the mining engineer. She sympathized with the wiry Strider's bitterness. As a child in one of the more isolated, lawless asteroid-mining habitats of the Jupiter Trojans, Amrita Dhillon had been forced to watch her dissident parents tortured, her father murdered in front of her, before the Troubleshooters had managed to liberate her and mother. Of all the expedition's members, she was probably the one—perhaps even more than Stephen himself— who most desperately *needed* to buy into Stephen's dream of building a better world. Cecilia could not begrudge Amrita her rage at having that dream torn from her, at seeing her crew subjected to the same kind of abuse she had hoped to leave behind forever.

But her outburst jeopardized the group's morale, so Cecilia tried to offer reassurance. "Tarik's right—however much I fumbled the delivery, we've just exposed a major hole in their argument. Maybe when they cool down, we can build on that, make them see that this disaster was something they could've avoided and we couldn't."

"And what if the fix is already in?" Amrita challenged, more quietly but no less intently.

"Then we'll try something else. The one thing we will not do—the one thing we must *never* do—is give up." Her eyes held Stephen's as she said it. "We Veneziani, we know how to fight for our home, our people. We were fighting off the rising waters centuries before the rest of you. And Venezia still stands firm and proud. We made the water our own, we adapted to its presence, but we never let it overwhelm us, and we never gave our ground even as our ground sank beneath us. And as long as I draw breath, neither will this crew."

Her speech put an end to the debate, and she ordered the crew to get some rest. Stephen gave her a nod of thanks, though his eyes remained troubled. Narvaez's gaze was more skeptical, and Cecilia held it for a time, letting him know that she understood his concerns. She wasn't ready to let it be voiced yet, but he had a point. The Chirrn might not leave them any legitimate way out of this.

So privately, in her own thoughts, she began contemplating more unsavory alternatives.

The tribunal did not reconvene again for more than a day. When the next session finally began, Tribune Dj'vhereth spoke. "The suggestion that our own secretiveness has contributed to this incident cannot be casually dismissed," the orange-maned jurist said gravely. The audience grumbled, but quieted under Broadwing's fearsome glare. "We advise the Council to consider the installation of running lights and short-range beacons on Chirrn habitats, or at the very least the expansion of our astronomical observation protocols."

Cecilia's eyes widened. The Chirrn had accepted the truth more readily than she'd imagined. Brimming with confidence, she rose to address the panel. "In that case, Honored Tribunes, I submit that the charge of negligence on our part has been disproven, and I move that the case be dismissed."

"That would be premature," Rillial countered, her voice raised. "The accused's contention that they have taken all reasonable steps to minimize risk is false. There is one fundamental risk they have taken that did not need to be taken at all. And that is their very means of transportation."

"You'll have to explain that," Cecilia said.

"I shall," came the terse response. "Relativistic travel is intrinsically hazardous, not only to the travelers but to any they encounter. Any vehicle moving close to the speed of light possesses a kinetic energy sufficient to destroy any spacecraft or habitat, to devastate the entire surface of any inhabited planet. As the defendants' own engineer testified, their velocity is so great that they may use sails only an eye's width across as projectiles capable of shattering an asteroid far larger than the craft itself. Without the means to decelerate swiftly, or to reduce a craft's effective inertial mass while in transit, it is an unconscionably dangerous form of travel.

"The defendants have spoken of their methods for detecting obstacles. But their own velocity was barely less than that of their own radar beams. They have claimed their shipmind was fast enough to compensate for the briefness of the warning interval, but that mind herself has testified that she did *not* have enough time to assess the situation fully and was forced to make a rushed decision. That clearly demonstrates that the risk is needlessly great."

"The risk is to our own ship at least as much as to anyone else's," Silbermann objected. "We took every factor into account that we could, prepared for every realistic possibility and even some crazy ones. The technology is safe, as safe as it needs to be."

Rillial whirled to face the tribunes, her tail almost knocking down the chubby advocate beside her. "*That* is the key question! *Need.* We must ask, did these humans *need* to travel this way at all?

"In thirteen thousand years, the Chirrn have encountered few civilizations which employ relativistic spacecraft — which is the reason we have never had a need to detect or defend against them. Generally, civilizations do not engage in interstellar travel prior to obtaining gravity control. Those that do usually employ sail-driven or fusion-powered craft which travel at low fractions of lightspeed; or they employ the Chirrn method of creating their own worlds that spend generations travelling between the stars. Often, they only colonize their home systems and rely on slow interstellar probes and gravity-focus astronomy to survey the broader universe. We know that the humans have done the same in their own system. So we must ask why they have found it necessary to use this form of transportation at all, when there are easier and safer, if slower, ways to travel between stars."

Stephen stepped forward. "While it's true that the resources of Sol System have made humanity wealthy, the planet Earth is still struggling to recover its ecological — and social — balance after centuries of damage. Damage caused, in part, by overpopulation and overexploitation of

Earth's resources. New resources from space can compensate, and we have the means to feed and sustain such a vast population so long as resources are allocated fairly. But reducing the human population's footprint on the planet is still important for the future recovery of the rest of the ecosystem, and reducing its size is an important part of that.

"Of course, we encourage emigration to the other settled planets and artificial habitats of Solsys... but we recognize that even an entire star system may someday fall prey to cosmic or self-inflicted disaster. For the survival of our species, we must emigrate to other systems. We've settled marginally habitable planets and asteroid belts around closer stars, worlds we can reach at a more comfortable pace.

"But people who were born on planets generally prefer to live on planets — planets they can inhabit without needing to huddle under domes and stare out at a barren wasteland. So when we found Cybele, a world we could settle without centuries of terraforming, it was too good to pass up. I knew that if we could mount a successful expedition there, it would inspire further colonization.

"But the travel time to Cybele pushes the limits of safe hibernation technology. If we want the colonization process to be viable and attractive to a large population, we have no choice but to make the journey at the highest relativistic speeds we can attain."

Rillial pondered this for a moment before speaking. "So... you live on one planet and want to live on another. You want to find a naturally habitable planet, but you must look to other systems to find one. And you are thus willing to go to extraordinary lengths, to engage in immense engineering projects and expend astronomical amounts of power, in order to fulfill this urge.

"But why?" she continued, turning and raising her voice to address the tribunal at large. "You have over a century of experience in space colonization. Billions of humans live in artificial habitats, most of which are not located on planetary bodies. Indeed, the enormous undertaking of constructing interstellar vessels and the beam projectors that drive them would be impossible if you were limited to the resources of one planet.

"So you know that human beings can lead successful, prosperous lives in space habitats. You know that generations of humans have lived, and lived well, without ever breathing the air of a planet. And yet your desire to live on a planet like your Earth is so great... that you found it necessary to employ a highly inefficient, costly, and outright dangerous form of propulsion to accomplish it. A form of propulsion that killed nearly ninety thousand Chirrn and diminished the minds of at least sixty thousand more."

Rillial strode forward to look Stephen firmly in the eyes, her wide-set orbs swiveling inward to fix him from two directions. "Why did those Chirrn die? Because you used relativistic propulsion. Why did you use it? Because you wished to live on a planet.

"But did you *need* to live on a planet?" she hissed with anguish. "Tell me that, colony leader. Given all the alternatives, was there some vital need to drive your way recklessly through the cosmos merely to live the way your ancestors lived? Was your need to feel dirt beneath your feet so great, so overwhelming, that it justifies the slaughter of ninety thousand lives?"

Stephen opened his mouth — and nothing came out but a soft choking sound. He could give no answer to Rillial's demand.

But Cecilia was not so speechless. "Now just wait a minute," she protested. "Just because you don't like living on planets doesn't make it immoral to do so. This is just an attempt to evade the real issue — your own failure to make your habitats detectable!"

Rillial glared at her. "It may not be immoral, but was it necessary? Living in a constructed world would not have killed you." She turned back to the tribunes. "But the humans' rejection of that option *did* kill more than a tenth of the population of Lesshchi and left the rest without a home."

"We have a right to live in whatever way we choose!"

"The rights of one being do not include the right to destroy the lives of other beings!" Rillial cried, her voice ringing through the tribunal chamber. "You cite free choice as your only reason for choosing planets, for needing relativistic starships. But that is not enough reason to justify the destruction of an entire nation! It is *not!*" Rillial lowered her brown-maned head, covering her eyes with her hands, and struggled for breath. Cecilia wanted to argue back, but even she was subdued by the anguish in Rillial's voice and body language, comprehensible even across the species divide. And she could see that the audience was affected far more deeply — and probably the tribunes as well. She would only hurt her case further by arguing more.

This time, instead of a furor, a ringing silence filled the courtroom. The silence was finally broken by whispers between the tribunes and

Broadwing, and then by the arbiter's calliope voice: "The tribunes will now recess to deliberate this case."

So much for the system. Cecilia saw clearly that the legal fight was over; there had never been a chance of a fair trial in any Chirrn venue.

I won't give up, she promised herself. *Whatever it takes.*

6

Cecilia paced out the limits of the cell like a caged tiger. "We can't let them do this to us."

"Cecilia..." Stephen sighed. "They're thirteen thousand years more advanced than we are. If they do rule against us... let's just say our options will be severely limited."

"I won't have that kind of defeatist attitude!" Cecilia told him. "And I won't let my crew be condemned as a result of the Chirrn's bigotry."

"Still," Haim said after a moment, "you have to admit—they do have a point. A lot of people manage just fine aboard habitats. Strictly speaking, we didn't need to do this."

Cecilia stared. "You of all people are saying this? You, who relished the challenge of building the fastest ship in human history?"

His eyes remained locked on the floor. "There are other challenges."

"Any powerful drive has its dangers. I'm sure their gravity control could do awful things if it went wrong. Danger's just a part of life. We're all out here because we accepted that—because we didn't let our fear of danger keep us from living." A number of the others nodded and made affirming noises.

"That's fine when it's our own risk, our own choice," the engineer said. "But what about when the danger's to others who didn't have a choice?"

"Haim, you did everything you could to make the ship as safe as possible—not just for us, but for anyone else. Even though there was almost no chance of a collision, you prepared for it anyway."

"And still didn't do enough."

"You couldn't have anticipated this," Cecilia insisted.

"That's the problem. Too many unknowns out here. Like those auxon probes on Cybele. We're so confident they can't go wrong—but what don't we know? Especially if they're left there for decades untended if we…" He trailed off.

"Will you listen to yourselves?" It was Diego Narvaez in the next cell. The tall engineer strode to the transparent wall and struck it angrily. "All this concern over the harm we did to them. Look around you. What we need to worry about is the harm they'll do to us. We're dead if we don't find a way to fight back." Oates, Dhillon, and the others sharing his cell voiced angry affirmation.

Stephen turned to him in surprise. "You don't seriously think a people as advanced as this would have something as primitive as capital punishment?"

"What makes you think they share human values?" Narvaez countered. "You've seen their psychotic hatred of planet-dwellers. They already tried to beat some of you to death!" Sita turned away.

Stephen rose, putting himself between Narvaez's clique and the dainty biologist. "If killing us were all they wanted, they could've done it long before now."

"Maybe they just wanted to make us suffer first. We could be in for slow torture, for all we know."

"*If* they find us guilty."

"Are you really so naïve as to imagine they won't?"

Cecilia stepped forward, drawing Stephen's attention. "Whatever the verdict, whatever the sentence, we can't just lie back and surrender. We have a right and a duty to complete our mission and reach Cybele. Not just to ourselves, but to the embryos, to all of humanity." She paced some more. "We need to contact Arachne somehow. She's cooperated for now, so maybe they've left some of her systems intact. If she could activate a laser…"

"What are you saying?" Stephen cried. "You want to commit *more* murders?"

"It's not murder if they're not human," Narvaez countered.

"Neither accident nor self-defense is murder," Cecilia insisted, raising her voice above the others. "And only the threat would be needed. We wouldn't actually do it."

"But what would be the point?" Haim asked. "We can't get back up to speed without a drive beam."

"We could make them generate one. Or better yet, give us one of their gravitic engines."

"Which they could just sabotage to blow us up. What, you want to take hostages?"

"If we have to."

"And what if they call our bluff?" Stephen demanded. "Even if they don't, how will the Chirrn see us then? As conquerors, destroyers, willing to cut down anyone who impedes our expansion into the universe. What will they do to Sol System if they decide we're that dangerous?"

Cecilia took him by the shoulders. "Stephen, listen to me. I know you're upset by all that's happened. Your compassion for the dead of an alien race is admirable. But their deaths are not our fault. That tribunal is going to condemn us just because our beliefs differ from theirs. And I can't sit still and accept that. I have a responsibility for the safety of my crew and the success of our mission."

"And what about your responsibility for your own ship's wake?" he asked her.

She frowned. "What?"

"A captain is supposed to consider herself responsible for the consequences of her vessel's passage. Supposed to take responsibility for all beings affected by her command. You taught me that."

"Stephen, accepting responsibility is not the same as giving in to persecution! They're wrong to blame us for this!"

"Or maybe you just want to avoid the blame for it."

"We took every possible precaution!"

"Except patience!" He pulled away, then faced her again after a moment. "We were—*I* was so cocky. So full of pride in what we could accomplish. You warned me about hubris more than once, Cecilia. About naming the ship for Arachne, the very embodiment of self-destructive pride. Maybe you were right all along. Maybe Arachne's crime was pushing too far, failing to recognize her own limits."

"No, *you* were right the first time, Stephen," Cecilia urged, though with no softening of her tone. "Arachne had the guts to stand up to the gods and tell them when they were wrong, and they punished her because they were vain and capricious and had all the power."

"But the Chirrn are right, Cecilia. We *didn't* have to race through the universe at insane speeds. We could've built more habitats. Or we could've taken our time, migrated to Cybele in generation ships. People thrive in artificial environments. It shouldn't matter whether the horizon curves down or up. It's not a cause worth destroying a nation over. Is it?" He cried out to all the prisoners. *"Is it?!"* He was met with only the echoes of his own voice.

Cecilia glared at him in contempt. "It wasn't our fault. We weren't responsible."

He met her glare in kind. "Keep telling yourself that, Cecilia. Maybe someday you'll convince yourself it's true."

The cell became very quiet after that. It was impossible to miss the sound of Sita Bhatiani weeping and sniffling in the corner, no matter how she tried to stifle it. "Look," Stephen said to the group, not meeting Cecilia's steely gaze. "Let's just get some rest. What-ever happens next, we need clear heads—and we need to keep our cool."

As the others laid down and stewed in their own worries, Stephen hesitantly made his way to Sita's side. He crouched by her trembling form, unsure whether to place a hand on her shoulder. As before, she'd shed her jumpsuit but kept it clutched against the front of her body, torn between being confined and being exposed. So he crossed his arms over his own bare chest instead, respecting her personal space. "Sita?" He let it stand at that for now. *Are you all right?* would be a monumentally stupid question.

"I'm sorry," she said in a shuddering voice. "I hate being so afraid. So weak. You wanted the best people, the hardiest pioneers, and you got… this. This tiny, fragile… thing."

"Hey." He took her hand, clasped it gently between his. "Look at me." Hesitantly, those big dark eyes came up to meet his. Again, he was struck by how familiar, how right, that felt. "Now, you know I didn't go easy on my trainees. I know you're strong enough. After what you've been through, anyone would be afraid. I'm afraid too."

"But you haven't broken down blubbering in a corner, have you?"

"I wish I had the luxury. But there are forty-eight people expecting me to be strong for them."

Those incredible eyes probed his. "How do you do it?"

Stephen smiled. "By relying on the strength you all give me. It's all of you who keep me going."

Sita smiled back, and his heart raced. "But you were… going… long before us. You fought your way out of the Gulf States, started working to make things better… and you've never stopped."

He shook his head. "I can't afford to. When people stop trying… things decay. Entropy takes over. I've seen it up close—what happens when people with power stop caring. So I know I can never stop striving to make things better. I can never settle for the way things are, because I know they'll succumb to entropy if I let myself get complacent."

She stared. "That sounds so… cynical coming from you. The great idealist."

"Idealism doesn't mean assuming things will automatically get better. It means believing we can make them better if we fight hard enough." Now he did touch her shoulder. "Pain doesn't negate idealism. It just gives it more incentive. You're hurting now. You're afraid now. But you can make it better, day by day, if you just keep working at it."

She looked at him for a long time, and he just let her, captivated by her gaze. Sita seemed to realize something, then to wrestle with a choice within herself. Finally she took a deep, trembling breath and said, "There is something I've been afraid to try. Maybe it's time I did."

And she put her arms around his neck, letting the jumpsuit fall away from her body as she pulled him into a kiss. It seemed the most natural thing in the world to take her in his arms as he returned it. It felt blissfully familiar and entirely new at the same time.

After an indefinite amount of time, he broke the kiss and stared at her. "I think…"

"What?"

"I think that… for the first time in my life… I'm remembering a dream."

"I think I'm living one," she came back with a breathless chuckle. "Bloody hell, what a corny line. But I don't understand. Before, when you held me… you didn't react to me at all."

"I was still in shock. I was weak from hibernation. But I… reacted." He stroked the fine black fuzz upon her scalp. "I can't look at you and not react. I didn't quite remember it until now… but I love you."

Sita shed tears again, but this time they were welcome.

When court resumed over half a day later, the head tribune stared gravely down at the humans. "It is a basic principle in both Chirrn and human law that the rights of the individual cease to be absolute when

they threaten the rights or safety of others," Dj'vhereth said. "Thus, it is
the finding of this tribunal that free choice of habitat is not sufficient
cause to justify the permanent killing of over seventy-nine thousand,
eight hundred individuals, the probable killing of over eight thousand,
five hundred individuals still missing, the mental impairment of over
sixty-four thousand, four hundred individuals, and the destruction of
their entire nation. There were other viable alternatives to relativistic
interstellar travel which the defendants could have employed.
Therefore the destruction of Lesshchi was avoidable and unnecessary.
Therefore the defendants are culpable for its destruction."

The audience roared and thumped their tails on the ground in
thunderous approbation. Many of the humans gasped in shock or began
to weep. Diego Narvaez and his group howled in fury and defiance.
Cecilia stood rooted to the floor, eyes wide in outrage. Stephen
stood beside her, just as immobile, but feeling only resignation.

Arbiter Broadwing called for order, and once relative quiet had been
restored, Dj'vhereth addressed the defendants. "With regard to the
other potentially criminal matters brought to the attention of this
tribunal: Since the occupants of Arachne will not be colonizing the
inhabited planet in the binary star system proximate to Lesshchi's
former location, this tribunal finds it unnecessary to prosecute them on
that charge. With regard to the matter of the replicating probes sent to
survey that system, this tribunal orders that the matter be investigated
further. The probes in question will be examined and their threat
potential assessed. Only if that potential is deemed significant will the
matter be pursued further. We prefer not to intervene in an interplane-
tary matter without need." Stephen supposed that meant the matter
would be delayed for at least a decade, assuming Shilirrlal, like
Lesshchi, was about five light years from Gamma Leporis. Though that
description of its location left him wondering.

"The tribunal will now address the matter of sentencing. We
understand that you are unfamiliar with our principles of justice. Rest
assured that we do not believe in punishment purely for the sake of
retribution. Meeting destruction with destruction is wasteful and
pointless.

"Those who commit destructive acts are required to compensate for
them by doing constructive service. By making positive contributions,
they repay for the damage they have done. Your sentence has been
evaluated on the basis of this principle.

"It is the judgment of this tribunal that the forty-eight human personnel of the spacecraft Arachne shall be imprisoned for the remainder of their lives in a research institution, where they will be studied by Chirrn scientists. By thus providing knowledge, you will repay your debt."

"That's barbaric!" Cecilia cried. "You have no right to treat sentient beings as lab animals!"

A pair of guards approached her menacingly with stun-sticks. "The prisoner will remain silent," Broadwing ordered.

"Thank you, Arbiter," the head tribune said. "The experiments will be nondestructive and largely sociological in nature. You will not be subjected to cruelty. You will, however, not be free to refuse the experiments or to leave the facility. But such is the nature of imprisonment.

"As to the spacecraft *Arachne* herself," Dj'vhereth went on, "she will be stripped of her potentially destructive components and will be studied by Chirrn cyberpsychologists to explore the ways in which humans have developed the cybernetic sciences. She, too, will contribute to our knowledge of the universe. You will be allowed to communicate with her as you desire.

"These judgments will be carried out immediately. The humans will be transported—"

"Honored Tribunes," Stephen interjected.

"Yes, Stephen Jacobs-Wong?"

"I wish to make a plea. Not on my behalf, but on behalf of the six hundred human embryos in storage aboard Arachne." He looked at Cecilia, remembering what she had said about their duty. "Each of those embryos has the potential to grow into a live human being, to live a full, normal life. None of those potential people had any participation in our actions. None of them has ever lived on a planet, except as an insensate cell. Their parents—both the humans who donated them and the members of my crew who have committed to raising them—intended for them to have the chance to be born, and to live in freedom. Surely they should not be deprived of that chance, or born into captivity, because of our actions."

The tribunes discussed it briefly. "This is well said," Dj'vhereth announced. "We direct that the embryos shall be allowed to be gestated artificially, under the guidance of Arachne, and raised on Shilirrlal."

"That's not enough, Honored Tribunes."

The head tribune stared at him sharply. "Not enough?"

"No, it is not. Our young are very dependent upon their parents for the first several years of their lives. They need human parents or parent-surrogates to help them develop their abilities, to provide them with basic socialization and the necessary tactile and sensory stimulation for healthy brain development. Neither the Chirrn, the Zenith, nor Arachne could fulfill this role sufficiently. And how would it affect them if the only others they knew of their own race were nothing but imprisoned criminals or laboratory subjects?"

Stephen lowered his head. "Honored Tribunes, I do not seek leniency for myself. I deserve whatever verdict you deem fit. But the embryos, our potential children… they need my crew. And they need my crew to be free to raise them in a healthy and loving environment."

"You would dictate terms to us, after you have been found guilty?" another tribune demanded.

"When it comes to the well-being of innocent lives, Honored Tribune—of children whose future is my personal responsibility—then hell yes, I will dictate terms."

"This is outrageous," Rillial protested over the rumbling of the spectators. "Your crew have been sentenced for their crimes."

"My crew is blameless in this! This expedition was my dream, my project. None of these others would be here if not for me. They don't deserve to be punished for the consequences of my choice. Do to me as you see fit, but let them go. Let them take *Arachne* and complete their journey to Cybele. Or take them yourself if you're concerned about the safety of our methods. At the very least, let them raise the children here, or on some other Chirrn habitat."

"Hey, nothing doing!" Haim Silbermann interposed. He strode forward to Stephen's side. "Mister Jacobs-Wong here is being noble, but he's not telling the whole truth. *I* designed *Arachne* and her defenses. I'm as much to blame for this as anyone. If he stays, I stay too."

"So do I!" Cool, delicate fingers clasped his hand, and he could feel Sita trembling as she moved to stand between him and the Chirrn, raising her head and her voice in terrified defiance. "You do anything to him, you'll bloody well have to go through me!" Stephen's eyes grew moist at her courage, her love.

But he shook his head as more and more of the crew moved to stand by him—Tarik, Kweli, Diana, Kazuko, many more—but not Cecilia, not Diego. "Don't do this. None of you are to blame. You deserve your new home. And the children need you."

"And we need our leader," Kazuko told him.

"Desist!" Arbiter Broadwing commanded, the original word a curt, piercing shriek. "The tribunal will consider the defendant's proposal."

The tribunes discussed the matter for a long time. As this went on, Stephen looked over his crewmates. There was a wide range of emotions on display. Sita, Haim, Tarik, and many others showed signs of the same grief Stephen felt. It made him proud that so many of his fellow humans could grieve for aliens as much as for their own. Many of the crew, including Kazuko and Kweli, showed renewed hope at Stephen's proposal—hope for their own freedom, hope for their children yet unborn.

But Narvaez and others glared at him bitterly, resenting his admission of guilt. Some showed fear at the aliens' power, anger at their imposition, dismay at the impending imprisonment. And none showed these emotions as intensely as Cecilia LoCarno. Stephen had never seen her like this. They had argued before, oh, so many times. It had been the foundation of their friendship. But it had always been with mutual respect and affection. Now, though, as Stephen looked into Cecilia's eyes, he realized that friendship was probably gone forever. One more casualty of his hubris.

Finally Tribune Dj'vhereth addressed the chamber once again. "While your willingness to sacrifice for your groupmates is commendable, it cannot influence the findings of the law. Though Stephen Jacobs-Wong may have initiated the formation of your group, it was as a group that you undertook the actions that led to Lesshchi's destruction. Under Chirrn law, you are therefore culpable as a group." The crew moaned. Stephen opened his mouth to protest.

"However," the head tribune went on, "this must be balanced against the well-being of the non-culpable human children yet to be born, and the right of their progenitors to determine whether and into what circumstances they will be born. Thus, we offer the following compromise.

"The finding of this tribunal was that the humans' planetary bias was the underlying cause of Lesshchi's destruction. Therefore: any humans who will renounce a planetary existence, who will sever all ties with planet-dwellers and those who associate with them, will be granted provisional participation in Chirrn society. A segment of Shilirrlal large enough to accommodate a minimum of six hundred and forty-eight humans will be apportioned for your occupation. Your movement beyond that segment will be restricted and supervised, but within it you will be free to raise your children and contribute to Shilirrlal as provisional citizens, thus repaying your debt. If you prove your responsibility and your ability to contribute as members of the Shilirrlal community, you will in time be allowed to integrate more fully into society. Those who do not renounce planetary existence will contribute instead as research subjects.

"Note that this offer extends to every member of your group," Dj'vhereth added, his garnet-hued eyes meeting Stephen's. "For the verdict to be fair, it must apply uniformly. You may have time to discuss this decision among yourselves." Stephen was shocked. Those alien standards cut both ways—harder on his crew than he had hoped, but more lenient toward him than he deserved. But he was grateful for the chance to stay with his crew.

The Chirrn spectators leaned forward intently as the humans gathered together to deliberate. Cecilia glared at the look on Stephen's face. "You can't actually be considering their offer! Win your freedom by renouncing your values, embracing theirs? What gives them the right to demand such a—a Shylockian surrender?"

Stephen sighed. "Cecilia, they're not asking us to change our religion, just our residency. Besides, they're the only law around. The crime was committed in their territory—hell, it was committed *against* their territory—and that makes us subject to their laws.

"I'm not saying I'm happy about it. But whatever we may feel or believe, the fact on the ground is that we're convicted criminals under their law, and we can't expect to walk away scot-free. We have to make the best of the hand we've been dealt. And this way, at least we get to raise our children in relative freedom. Just not where we expected."

"'Relative freedom?' Interesting term for house arrest."

"Better than letting those embryos go unborn. Personally, it feels like getting off easy. But there's more at stake here than just ourselves."

He stepped forward to face the panel. "Honored Tribunes, I accept your proposal. For the sake of our children, I renounce my planetary existence and ask that you let us live with you among the stars. I ask anyone else who will make this pledge to indicate it by stepping forward to join me."

Sita wanted to be the first one to join Stephen. She wanted to live up to her earlier pledge to stay by his side, to show that same courage. She was tired of being afraid—not only for what Stephen thought of her, but for what she thought of herself. She hadn't been this timid back on Earth. If anything, her friends had teased her for her careless haste to indulge her curiosity, whether as a child climbing to a branch ten times her height to watch birds hatching in their nest or as a grad student unhesitatingly volunteering for a dangerous year-long survey of the microbes of Enceladus.

So she felt betrayed by her own body when she hesitated. Haim Silbermann was instead the first to step forward alongside Stephen. "Someone's gotta be free to take care of *Arachne*," he said with a shrug. "And how can I pass up the chance to study that gravity drive?"

Kweli Ndege was next. "Live among an ancient alien culture?" Kweli whispered to Sita as she went past, speaking with something near her normal ebullience for the first time since seeing the wreck of Lesshchi. "That's better than any wilderness planet for me."

Rub it in, why don't you? She should have stepped forward, should have been standing by Stephen's side. She'd done it a few minutes ago; what stopped her now? But ever since that night on the Chirrn ship, she'd been a changed woman. Not even a woman—a frightened little girl. The Chirrn terrified her. After the assault, Kweli had administered the standard sympatholytic drug regimen for preventing post-traumatic stress syndrome. In theory, it should have softened the emotional intensity of her memories of the assault, sparing her psyche from lasting damage. But maybe that only worked when the traumatic event actually ended, when the nightmare didn't go on day after day. How could she move beyond the memory of the screaming faces, the pounding fists, the searing shock sticks—the fact that she'd actually been dead for several minutes—when hostile Chirrn still had her in their power, still relished her humiliation and helplessness, still screamed for her blood? It was one thing to be willing to share a prison sentence with her man—but to be asked to join the society of the creatures that had killed her?

The one thing that got her moving was the realization that being subjected to their experiments would be even worse. At least this way, she'd be in an area set aside for humans. From what she'd observed, the Chirrn seemed to like partitioning themselves. Hopefully that meant the humans would be largely cut off from the Chirrn. Whereas if she became their research subject, she'd be at their mercy every day. With that thought, she shot forward to Stephen's side and clutched his hand like a lifeline.

He looked at her and smiled, radiating pride in her bravery. She smiled back, hiding her shame.

Cecilia was disappointed as more and more of her crew joined Stephen in his surrender. After all they'd been through, she'd never expected them to abandon her like this. But then, if Stephen, the great man who'd fought his way out of hell and climbed to the stars with his sheer relentless optimism, could succumb so easily to misplaced guilt and extortionate sympathy, maybe she shouldn't be surprised at the rest. Maybe the record time they'd spent in hibernation had done something to them all, enfeebled their resolve.

At least some of the crew still showed sense. She wasn't surprised that Diego Narvaez and his clique stayed by her side; they'd made their position very clear already. Others moved to stand with her as well: Ichiba Nobuo, Kahina Amrouche, Zhao Changkun, Ibrahim al-Bakri, Josh Vidmar, more. Mercifully, Nikolos Zacharias was among them; at least their group would have a doctor, even though Kweli and Joana Caravalho had both sold out.

But more were defecting than standing firm. Oyama Kazuko, Diana Thorne, Ravinder Pritam, Scott Olatunji, Jason Brentwood, Vijay Bhadra… Stephen's group was already larger than hers and still growing. Justine Nguyen was caught in a fiercely whispered argument between her wife Shuai Bingbing and her brother Marc, but when Bingbing finally moved to stand with Cecilia's group, she came alone.

So Cecilia winced when Tarik Bahar moved to face her, apology in his eyes. "I'm sorry, Captain. But I have to protect the crew. And the children."

"You tell yourself that, Tarik," she snapped. "That it's for the children. Like the child and the wife you left behind in Istanbul!"

He was stung. "That's not fair. You know she divorced me."

"She may have been the one to pronounce *talaq* three times, but you'd already fallen in love with the adventure of space, or you never would've let it get to number three. So much for your vaunted loyalty."

"My loyalty," he replied tightly, "was to you, Captain. It has always been to you. When I learned that Stephen had picked you to command

Arachne, I had a choice to make. I wanted nothing more than to stay with them, but your need, your responsibility, was so much vaster than mine. I could not walk away from you."

Cecilia lamented her burst of anger. He hadn't deserved such a low blow. And she hardly had a moral high ground where marital devotion was concerned. It was typical of Tarik that he hadn't tried to use that against her. But she was still hurt. "Then why walk away from me now?"

"I'm not, Captain. But whatever choice the others have made, I still haven't renounced my duty to them — or to you. I know I can trust you to look out for the loyal ones. But the rest need someone too."

Cecilia held his gaze for a long moment, nodding in comprehension. There would certainly be value in having an ally on the outside. "You do what you think is best, my friend. I understand."

He gave her a salute. It was anachronistic and ridiculous and she cherished it. But she only nodded back. She didn't want the Chirrn to see her approving of his choice — even if she could have brought herself to do so anyway. A necessary evil was still evil.

Finally, the slow trickle halted. Thirty of the crew had joined Stephen, with seventeen choosing Chirrn custody. Stephen's group was nearly two-thirds female, leaving only six women total in Cecilia's. Stephen found the ratio comforting; with the group diminished, it was good to have as many potential mothers as possible. Although having half again as many women as men could get tricky down the road. He only hoped he could convince the others to change their minds in time.

He only hoped he could convince Cecilia.

"The tribunal accepts that those who stand with Stephen Jacobs-Wong have renounced their planetary existence," Broadwing proclaimed, rising to his full height. "They are now free to live among the Shilirrlaln. The others will be welcome to join them at any time in the future if they will make the same renunciation."

"Never," Cecilia declared. "We have the right to live as humans!"

Stephen saw something snap in Diego Narvaez's eyes at that moment. The big engineer lunged for one of the guards, only for his confinement suit to freeze rigid and send him headlong to the floor. He struggled helplessly as blood flowed from a cut on his forehead, then yelled and cursed as the guards pulled him to his feet. "Take him for medical treatment," the Zenith arbiter ordered. Diego continued to scream and struggle within his unmoving jumpsuit as the guards carried him away. Broadwing turned back to Cecilia. "Please, Captain, tell your people not to make this difficult for themselves. You cannot escape us."

"Maybe not," she said. "But we'll never surrender to you. We won't betray our humanity."

"Cecilia, please understand," Stephen urged. "It's for the children."

She shot him a look that should have torn him open like Lesshchi. "It's for yourselves."

"No," Stephen whispered.

Her eyes went from deadly hot to deathly cold. "I want nothing more to do with any of you." She almost seemed glad when the guards took her away.

Rillial gazed after her curiously. "Pitiful," she said. "To be so fanatical in their planetarism."

"That's not it," Stephen said sadly. "I think she — some of them just can't accept being responsible for the loss of ninety thousand lives. It's just too big a tragedy. They can't live with the guilt. So they'll never be able to admit to guilt."

The refugee examined him. "But you can."

A tear came to Stephen's eye. "Barely. Rillial, I hope you can forgive me… forgive *us* for what we allowed to happen." He sighed. "I don't know if I'll ever be able to forgive myself."

Rillial stood silently for a long moment. Then she said, "The important thing now is to ensure that such a tragedy never recurs. It is more important to prepare for the future than to dwell on the past." Stephen nodded solemnly, recognizing that it was the closest thing to forgiveness that Rillial would ever provide.

Broadwing, having left his podium, joined them, remaining in his erect stance and towering over the humans. "To that end, we must deter humanity from traveling so far again, at least at such reckless speeds."

Tarik stared. "What's that supposed to mean?"

"No doubt your expedition was sending signals back to the Sol system."

"That's right," Haim said. "They'll sure notice when *Arachne*'s telemetry stops coming in about twenty-four years. Every telescope in the system will be focused on Lesshchi's location."

"This is why we must take action. We do not wish to attract more human craft to investigate us."

"Well, what can you do about it now?"

"We have sent ships back along your course to overtake the light emitted from the disaster. They will create a detonation to obscure the image, timed and positioned to make it appear to observers in the Sol system that Arachne attempted to deflect an asteroid, failed, and was destroyed in the resultant collision. Optimally, this will cause humanity to reconsider using such a hazardous form of space travel."

"Wait, wait, go back," Haim said. "Overtake the light? Are you trying to tell me you *do* have faster-than-light drive?"

Rillial traded a look with Broadwing before speaking. She didn't sound thrilled. "Since you have consented to provisional membership in Chirrn society, there is no need to hide the fact any longer. Yes, we employ superluminal bypass methods. Our habitats drift slowly, but we travel between them as needed in transport ships."

Silbermann's eyes widened like those of a child discovering the Planet of Chocolate. "You're kidding. Really? I mean, yes, you've got gravity control, so warping space theoretically follows, but where do you get the power? How do you generate the exotic matter? How do you deal with the stress-energy buildup? The Hawking radiation? The horizon problem? Is it the Alcubierre model, or do you use some other—"

"Haim!" Stephen chuckled. "Settle down. You'll have plenty of time to learn about it." But then his own eyes widened, and he turned to the Chirrn excitedly. "But this could solve the problem! If you went to Solsys, contacted them, shared your warp technology with them, it would eliminate the danger completely! There wouldn't—"

"Take care," said L'chellin, who had joined them. "Remember, you have renounced all ties with Earth, and with all spacegoers who have ties with Earth. Do not forget so soon what that means."

"I'm not forgetting. But consider this: you want to discourage humans from using relativistic drives again. They'll be more likely to give it up if they learn the truth. We're willing to put ourselves at risk in the name of exploration, but risking others is a different matter."

"You have great faith in the nobility of your species," Rillial said. "You can understand why we cannot afford to share that faith."

"You must accept," Broadwing added, "that you are no longer a member of the human community. Their interests are no longer yours."

With that, the Chirrn and the Zenith left them. Stephen and the others stood there, alone in the echoing tribunal chamber, absorbing their new status in life. "No longer members of the human community," Kweli Ndege breathed. "Does that mean we aren't human anymore?"

"No," Stephen said. "We're just not Terrans anymore. Not Solar humans, or planetary humans. We're star people now."

Tarik Bahar scoffed. "Sounds poetic, sure. But it isn't by choice." He shook his head. "At least the captain still belongs. She may not have her freedom… but she's still a member of the human race."

"What good is it to be human without being humane?" Stephen asked. "We've done this to repent for our mistake, for causing a disaster we didn't have to cause. We owe it to the Chirrn to make up for the loss by joining their society and helping them to build and grow.

"And, most of all, we've done this for the sake of the unborn humans in our care. This is the only choice we could make, for their sake. It's not an ideal situation… but it's the only one that I, for one, can live with."

Sita looked up at him searchingly. "But when our children ask where we came from… what do we tell them?"

"We tell them the truth," Haim Silbermann said with certainty. "Just like my parents told me. My father's ancestors murdered my mother's ancestors in the Nazi Holocaust. They didn't keep that from me. No, they made sure I knew… so that I could make sure it never happened again."

After a long silence, Stephen spoke again. "Come on, my friends. We set out to build a new world for ourselves. And now it's time to begin."

When the verdict came, Churrlaya was standing vigil with Guard Vhehhal and the other *Zhemhal* personnel who had been confined to the rehabilitation center for their assault on the human murderers. Though he understood that order and justice must be maintained in these terrible times most of all, he felt it unfair that Vhehhal and the rest had been confined for acting on the same understandable rage that had filled all Lesshchin in those first few *narrissh* after the devastation. It was a mild sentence—merely a physical confinement to preclude them from injuring the dirtgrubbers, with their minds still free to travel in consensus, albeit under therapeutic supervision—yet Churrlaya knew that he, Captain Rillial, or any other member of *Zhemhal*'s crew might be the ones confined here now had they been only slightly more provoked in that first encounter.

Still, the vehemence with which Vhehhal and his fellows reacted to the trial's outcome made Churrlaya wonder if confining them had been the appropriate choice for their own good. "Intolerable!" the golden-maned guard roared, smashing a table into the wall with a violent tail sweep. "Allow those murdering well-diggers inclusion in Chirrn civilization? Allow them to *breed?*"

The other crew members chimed in with equal wrath. "They should not have been allowed to live!"

"We should have finished them when we had the chance!"

Their words made Churrlaya uneasy. He felt shame at his own burst of violence against the tiny human female at the disaster site, the same one Vhehhal had briefly killed in the riot. What did it say about them that they had both targeted the most helpless one of their attackers? "Please, calm yourselves, friends," he urged. "I share your anger at this verdict. By any decent standard, the humans' exclusion became irrevocable the moment they killed our home. But remember that we are civilized. We are governed by order and balance. We cannot let these planetary bottom-feeders drag us down into their dirt."

"They have already done that, Churrlaya!" Vhehhal cried. "And we can never purge ourselves of it as long as they are allowed to live among us."

"They will live apart, confined and re-educated."

"You know that will change." The guard hissed in grim satisfaction. "But we will be unconfined before they are. We will await our chance to exact true justice."

Churrlaya stroked Vhehhal's golden mane, hoping to soothe him. "Please do not consider anything rash. I agree they must be punished more harshly than this. But there are better ways—more *civilized* ways—to achieve it. We can only defeat them by being better than they are."

The guard caught his gaze and held it. "Tell me, Churrlaya. What is it that you intend to do?"

Churrlaya did not have an answer for him yet. But it would be his mission from now on to find a way.

L'chellin and Broadwing overtook Rillial outside the Administrative Center, and the two Chirrn brushed manes in greeting. "Approbations, Rillial. You played your part in the proceedings most effectively. You have earned your inclusion."

The wild-maned captain struck a distancing posture. "My voice is not yet rid of its Lesshchin accent," she declared. "I birthed no bastard words in that tribunal."

"Unquestionably," the advocate assured her. "Your loss was incalculable. But you are unattached no more. And you exacted suitable ordeals on the ones responsible."

Rillial's legs tensed, and L'chellin instinctively moved out of her kick radius. "Many of us feel no ordeals will suffice."

"Well, you may satisfy yourselves that a third of them have chosen to extend their ordeals."

"May they never renounce."

"Just do not forget that the others *have* renounced," Broadwing told her. "And far sooner than anticipated."

"Prematurely," Rillial said. "You gave in to Jacobs-Wong's terms far too easily."

"What could we do?" L'chellin asked. "He was correct. We had no right to penalize their unborn, nor were we qualified to raise them. Yes, he forced us to accelerate the process, but he earned that acceleration. And in so doing, he has saved us considerable time and effort."

"It is only a minor adjustment to the plan," Broadwing added.

Rillial hissed across her tongue. "To *your* plan, Mediator. A plan I objected to."

"Four *narrayth* ago, I was as lowly and excluded as they. I was given the chance to repent and rise." Broadwing lifted himself into a display stance. "See the result."

"You did not destroy an entire world. Some imbalances cannot be restored. Many Lesshchin will never accept this outcome."

"Then those Lesshchin have a choice of their own to make," L'chellin told her. "But since you participated in the humans' transition, I assume you accept your own."

Rillial leaned forward a few degrees, not an open threat, but enough to convey anger. "A transition of this magnitude cannot be rushed." She bounded down a step, then turned to stare up at L'chellin. "Do you truly imagine that Jacobs-Wong and his kith have completed theirs? Do you think they even begin to grasp the true meaning of the tribunal?"

"Not consciously," L'chellin replied, lowering himself to all fours to meet her eye level. "But they have begun to fulfill its purpose nonetheless. They are on the intended path."

"And when that path leads them to truths they will not accept?"

He sank back on his haunches as he pondered the question. "By then, we hope, they will no longer be human enough to care."

Part Two

COMMUNITY SERVICE

7

"Good morning, Nilly!"

R'nilinnath cursed to herself. She had taken too long getting to the compound, and the Arachnen's "morning" had already arrived. She'd hoped to interrupt their annoyingly regular sleep cycle once again. Yes, Mediators L'chellin and Broadwing had told her over and over that the Arachnen hadn't yet had their planetary cycles purged from their genes and that such minor lingering attachments to their old life must be tolerated for the sake of their health. But it was much more fun to mess with them.

The greeting came from Diana Thorne, out for her usual *morningjog* up and down the broad terraced levels of the Arachnen compound. The young engineer was the most visually imposing of the humans, their largest and most muscular member. Her bronze mane, a few shades lighter and redder than her skin, was twice as long as any of the others' due to her accelerated metabolism (and a little artificial assistance). Despite having long, strong legs for a human, Diana still needed to rely on the stairs that she and the other engineers had built to climb between tiers. The Arachnen builders had been expecting to create whole cities and infrastructures, but now had to settle for making constant minor "improvements" to their compound to exercise their skills.

Diana had nearly completed her run up the easternmost set of stairs, the one that set off the "ladies' wing" of the compound, where the females not paired with males had their dwellings, set apart for reasons R'nilinnath hadn't fully parsed. The young Chirrn met Diana outside the liaison offices, just above the medical clinic, and bounded up the stairs alongside her, showing off how easily a Chirrn could climb the levels in this moderate gravity (another nostalgic tie to their Earth). They nearly ran into Oyama Kazuko and Renata Marcoe as the two administrators crossed the path on their way to their offices. R'nilinnath was about to stop and make proper apologies, but Diana just gave a quick "Sorry!" and increased her speed. "You won't beat me this time, little girl!"

"Little!" The void with propriety; these ferals hadn't learned sufficient appreciation for it anyway. R'nilinnath aborted her contrition and raced after the impertinent human. Diana knew full well that she was pubescent now, in the first full blush of femaleness. Were she "little," she wouldn't be a "girl" (or "boy") at all, nor would she be out of the estate crèche and apprenticed to L'chellin as a liaison-guardian to the Arachnen. Besides, Diana and her kith had only been in crèche for half a *narranl* themselves. R'nilinnath was the only adult here — well, incipiently, though her cerulean hide still bore the darker mottling of youth and her silver-dyed mane was only starting to grow out (though it was still twice as long as most of the Arachnen's). True, she hadn't yet earned full inclusion into the Intersocietal collegium of the Mediators' guild, and she was still adjusting to the new perspectives and habits of thought granted her by even the limited portion of the collegium's consensus memory that her apprenticeship entitled her to access. But no matter how much inclusion the Arachnen eventually earned, they would never experience consensus directly, lacking the cerebral adaptations for it — although their young might, one day. Not to mention that R'nilinnath was physically larger than all of the Arachnen except Diana, with whom she was only about even. After a lifetime as the youngest child on Shilirrlal, it was refreshing to have juniors at last.

The racers soon reached the top terrace and cut across through the odd green ground cover over the admin compound. The Arachnen had replanted all the terraces with their *grass* and *trees* and other vegetation compatible with their biochemistry, giving the place an oddly vacant smell to R'nilinnath's nares. Still, she liked the soft but scratchy sensation of the stuff crunching under her toes.

Soon they reached the next flight of stairs, taking them down past the auditorium and through the central square. Many of the unattached Arachnen who occupied the small dwellings around the square, including Marc Nguyen, Andrea Oliveira-York, and Scott Olatunji, were out in the park performing their own "morning" exercises — though the males, as usual, paused to watch the undulations of Diana's pronounced front and rear bulges as she ran past. Diana courted their attention by wearing a Chirrn-style semi-open vest, modified to better support her ample mammaries as she ran (though R'nilinnath did not understand how a civilization as young as humans could have evolved body parts that required artificial support), yet she paradoxically chose to conceal her genitalia with a brief human-style covering over her hip region. She clearly enjoyed the attention the others paid to her genetically augmented physique, and as she ran past, she turned her head in reciprocal admiration of Marc and Scott's unclothed, perspiring upper bodies and emitted ritual vocalizations of sexual approval toward them. Yet R'nilinnath had learned by now that this mutual courtship display was merely for social bonding and amusement. Though Diana was largely recovered from the damage she'd sustained from the humans' primitive hibernation system, she was not yet physically ready to merge voices—no, that metaphor wouldn't work for humans, and the alternative was disgusting—to conceive a child with any of the males. Instead, she was in a loose, non-exclusive sexual affiliation with Justine Nguyen, whose marital partner Shuai Bingbing was confined with the other Unrenounced in the high-security lab on the other side of Shilirrlal. R'nilinnath found Diana's sexual adaptability refreshingly normal. How had these humans functioned, favoring opposite-sex partners for emotional or recreational pairings as well as procreative ones? Before reliable contraception, the sheer number of unintended births must have been incredibly unwieldy.

Contraception was a moot issue for the Arachnen now, since they sought to increase the size and genetic diversity of their new population as swiftly as possible, as they had intended to do on their destination world. The family dwellings that Diana and R'nilinnath now sped past were located on the periphery of the occupied portion of the compound, to allow room for expansion as children were eventually born. All but four of the females were now gestating, and all the males had impregnated at least one of them (through artificial means in Haim Silbermann's case), to ensure that all their genes would be preserved. Justine was pregnant with one of the expedition's frozen embryos, while several others were being gestated in artificial wombs, and would be the communal responsibility of the Arachnen upon their birth—as would all the children to an extent.

Kweli Ndege had been the first to conceive, over three *narrenn* ago, and thus had the most prominent abdominal bulge. This meant that as the racers passed the dwelling Kweli shared with Tarik Bahar and saw her tending her tomato garden, Diana was unable to resist going over to touch Kweli's abdomen and express wonder at its rapid growth. The humans seemed to have a compulsion to do that whenever Kweli was around. R'nilinnath found it interesting that they didn't do the same with her mammaries, which had grown by a similar amount, surpassing even Diana's in size and apparently making them even more fascinating to the male Arachnen. (What was it about anatomical bulges that so enthralled these humans?) But then, many of the gestating females seemed to experience mammary soreness, so perhaps Diana avoided touching the glands out of regard for their sensitivity.

How inefficient, these humans. They needed four different body parts to fulfill the functions of the Chirrn tongue. Five, if you counted their own excuses for tongues.

R'nilinnath was tempted to bound ahead and outrace Diana to the top, but that would prove nothing. So she joined the other females in Kweli's yard to exchange pleasantries and engage in the abdomen-touching ritual. Kweli wore a human-style skirt and footwear along with an open-fronted, Chirrn-style maternity vest. She joked that it gave her tomatoes more room to grow, puzzling R'nilinnath with the non sequitur.

Sita Bhatiani was present too, helping the doctor tend the garden. Unlike most of the Arachnen, she still clung to human attire, garments known as *choli* and *sari*—evidently the traditional garb of her people, the Londoners. She responded politely to R'nilinnath's greeting, but stayed at her garden work rather than coming closer. R'nilinnath knew not to press the issue. Mediator L'chellin and Doctor Mh'lellish had explained the trauma the tiny human had suffered at the Lesshchin's feet and the resultant fear it had induced. Due to her own modest size and youth, R'nilinnath was the one Chirrn that Sita found reasonably nonthreatening, but only if she applied a soft touch.

Once she'd made appropriate obeisance to Kweli's uterus, R'nilinnath noted that Diana had already resumed her run, gaining an insurmountable lead. "Better luck next time, Nilly!" she jeered from the distance, soon vanishing behind the edge of the administration building on the top terrace.

The young Chirrn let out a sigh that ruffled her snout bristles, and Kweli chuckled and stroked her mane. "Don't take it personally. Diana's still embarrassed about her difficulties coming out of hibernation. Her family's the cream of the Vanguardian elite—they're not supposed to have weaknesses. She feels she needs to prove herself."

"She proved herself something, all right," R'nilinnath grumbled. With the race now aborted, she trotted slowly in Sita's direction and engaged her in casual talk about the garden. They were not bastard words; she was genuinely curious about these red fruits that the Arachnen described in such rhapsodic terms. A shame that so few of their world's aromatic compounds were detectable or pleasant to Chirrn senses. Doctor Mh'lellish had advised that tomatoes were mildly toxic to Chirrn as well. So R'nilinnath was left with only the words to sate her curiosity.

But when she changed the subject, making a polite request about Stephen's whereabouts, Sita's smile faded briefly. It was subtle, but R'nilinnath was getting good at reading the distortions of the human mouth and forehead. Had the expedition leader and his mate had another argument? R'nilinnath knew better than to alienate Sita by probing. She'd get the dirt by other means soon enough—once she made it to her appointment.

R'nilinnath hopped up to the next terrace and across to the Arachnen administrative offices. When she reached the central courtyard dividing them from the Shilirrlaln liaison offices, she saw L'chellin engaged in a lively discussion with Stephen, the cyberneticist Ravinder Pritam, and Arachne's physical avatar. The avatar was a nanomorphic construct whose default form was a four-armed human female torso atop the rear half of an oversized Terran spider, stylized and metallic-surfaced in hues of silver and blue. Arachne herself was installed within the administrative complex and could speak to any of the Arachnen via neural link, but she had adopted this embodied form to interact on an equal footing.

Drawing closer, but not drawing attention, R'nilinnath picked up enough of the conversation to divine its substance. Arachne and Ravinder were pushing for a fuller interface with Shilirrlal's data cloud; apparently the cyber was feeling somewhat starved for stimulation. "I am sorry," L'chellin was saying, "but you know that is a privilege that must be earned. For everything that is taken, something must be given. Have patience; as you learn more of our ways and develop a greater ability to contribute, you will earn commensurate privileges in time." L'chellin's tone was gentle and understanding, that of a crèche caregiver with her young charges, which was essentially what she was now; going female had taken the edge off the mediator's prim manner.

"But Arachne can learn far more quickly than an organic," Ravinder protested. "The only thing holding her back from learning more is your own stupid restrictions on her access!"

"Vin," Stephen cautioned.

"No, Stephen, it's just not fair! They're still punishing her because she's the one who fired the shot!" Ravinder winced. "Sorry, Arachne, you know I didn't mean—"

"Don't worry about it, Ravinder. I know what I did. And I will defer to Mediator L'chellin's restrictions. It's fair enough. I'm being treated no differently than the rest of you."

"But you need more stimulation!"

"I managed on my own for fifteen and a half subjective years. A little more boredom won't kill me." *That's well-fitting,* R'nilinnath thought. Hopefully, Arachne would persuade Ravinder to stop pushing for more access. Better if the Arachnen didn't pursue that particular question too far, or they might catch on that there were unspoken reasons for the limitations.

The thought of exceeding limits reminded her of her own appointment. The quickest route was across the courtyard, but if L'chellin saw her, it would ruin her plans. Luckily, Arachne persuaded Ravinder to accompany her inside, and L'chellin turned away to face Stephen, who began asking the mediator about the upcoming Dance of Balance they would be attending this narrissh. The human leader took the opportunity to practice his Shilirramh, still mangling the pronunciation badly but managing to get the point across, at least to listeners like L'chellin and herself who had grown accustomed to human phonetics (and could draw on the banked experience of the Intersocietal collegium's memory). Stephen was one of the only Arachnen who'd agreed to go to a second Dance of Balance. Most of them had been baffled by the first one; R'nilinnath had heard Joana Caravalho ask, "Can you call something a dance with so little movement?" But Stephen had found the subtle symmetries of the form intriguing and was eager to see if he could divine more meaning from the details of motion the others had missed. L'chellin was pleased by his interest; the more Stephen grew to understand the artistry of the dance, the more he would understand what it meant to be Chirrn, and the closer he would come to earning the status of a mature Shilirrlaln. And where he led, the others would follow.

R'nilinnath was glad, though, that she'd had a lifetime (granted, a very short one) to master what it meant to be Chirrn. If she'd needed to learn it by watching the Dance of Balance over and over, she'd feel as deprived of stimulation as Arachne. A good freefall splash brawl was more her speed.

Once she was sure both of L'chellin's eyes were fixed on Stephen, R'nilinnath hopped across the courtyard. Stephen saw her go by but made no acknowledgment, confirming her suspicion that he was in on the game.

Small raindrops began to spatter her snout, and she reflexively shut her nares and began breathing through her mouth. By being late, she'd failed to avoid the compound's scheduled rainfall. Hurrying, she ducked behind the liaison offices, out of L'chellin's sight, and from there bounded swiftly to the concealed maintenance hatch at the rear of the compound. There she found Diana Thorne already awaiting her, out of her exercise clothes and donning a jumpsuit more suited to crawling through dusty spaces. "What kept you?" the bronze-maned human teased, though of course their separation in the race had been an improvised ruse to conceal their rendezvous—something they could have avoided, R'nilinnath reminded herself, had she arrived earlier.

R'nilinnath made a knee-bending bow of submission. "Apology. Your kith are just so distracting."

"You mean you're easily distracted. Chirrn kids aren't so different from human ones." She smiled as she sealed up her jumpsuit. "Though I guess I should be grateful you're a kid, or you'd never be willing to do this."

The Chirrn snorted. "I'm more grown than you now. Try to remember that. And try to keep up."

The Arachnen compound had been placed near the facilities of the Educators' guild, not far from the estate crèche, so R'nilinnath was well acquainted with the local maintenance tunnels and hidden nooks, able to navigate them without accessing the habitat map (a useful talent if she wished to be hard to track). Every time she led Diana through the hatch, she took the engineer to a different sector, showing her places that L'chellin and Broadwing would never allow the Arachnen to go on their supervised outings.

In return, Diana told her lurid tales of human savagery, all the unimaginably feral things they did to one another. It sent a thrill of fear and excitement through R'nilinnath to contemplate how familiar these humans were with death. Their culture and language were drenched in references to it; Diana even referred to these crawls through the maintenance ducts with an idiom that translated as "to die with difficulty," in connection with some ancient human savior myth.

For her own part, Nilly had never known anyone who had died. She had recently met a few Lesshchin who had been revived from death, but they had lost only a portion of themselves—some had avoided physical damage but had their external selves ripped from them, while others had needed their brains regrown but could still draw on their outboard memory and backups as a source of continuity with who they had been. That was not so different from a normal life transition. Even those Chirrn who decided they'd lived long enough, who chose to end one life without migrating to another (and thus make room for the birth of new Chirrn like herself), still left their imprint in the consensus memory of the guilds they'd belonged to. The concept of a conscious being simply ceasing to exist in any form—as so many Lesshchin had, as humans and other ferals did all the time—was frightening. Yet it was also oddly compelling. The fact that adults discouraged her from exploring it merely fired her interest further.

Of course, the humans had concocted countless fantasies of existence after physical death to cope with its pervasiveness in their lives. But R'nilinnath was more interested in their expertise with death itself, and with the violence that brought it on. It was so alien, so gruesome, so stimulating. She had asked her crèche counselor if there was something wrong with her for taking so much interest in Diana's bloodsoaked tales from human history. The counselor had suggested that by trying to understand what death was, she was trying to find a way to cope with the death of tens of thousands of Lesshchin. As long as her interest remained in death as a distant, abstract thing, the counselor had said, there was no cause for worry. R'nilinnath had been grateful for that, since it allowed her to relish Diana's goriest tales without shame.

Diana had promised her that this *narrissh* she would tell R'nilinnath about the Spanish Inquisition—about which she'd so far revealed nothing except that no one had expected it. But that would wait, for

Diana always began their trips together by feeding her all the juiciest gossip about her fellow humans. The muscular human had initially pretended reluctance to violate the privacy of her neighbors, but it had been bastard speech that soon betrayed its parent. The truth was, she loved pushing the boundaries as much as R'nilinnath did, including the boundaries of others' privacy. In her view, secrets were challenges, and challenges were there to be surmounted.

Diana had what she considered some particularly good dirt today. It seemed that Marc and Andrea had argued loudly two "nights" before with Scott, whom they believed was getting too many appointments with Rosario Soares. The argument had provoked concern among many in the community, including Diana, that Rosario might be falling in love with Scott, leading their only therapeutic sex provider to toss aside professional egalitarianism in favor of monogamy. R'nilinnath was intrigued by Rosario's role in the community; as a human of intermediate gender, both anatomically and psychologically, they could adapt to provide sexual services for all Arachnen as needed—an efficient choice for such a compact community. Humans superficially appeared to have such inflexible sexuality, stuck being a single sex throughout their lives short of surgical intervention; but as R'nilinnath had come to know them, she had realized that, in many ways, they were even more sexually adaptable than the Chirrn. Rosario had the androgynous gender attributes of an immature Chirrn, yet could readily assume either a masculine or a feminine identity as required by their clients, or simply on their personal inclination on any given "day," whereas a Chirrn required sixteen or more times as long to undergo the hormonal adjustment to realign one's sex. Renata Marcoe, by contrast, had spent most of her previous life with a similarly intermediate sexual physiology and an identity tending toward male, yet had chosen to go permanently female through surgical means upon joining the Cybele expedition, so as to supplement the group's childbearing contingent. Even those Arachnen of unambiguous sex practiced a variety of mating behaviors: formal, monogamous pair-bonds such as those between Stephen and Sita or Tarik and Kweli; ongoing yet non-exclusive affiliations like Diana and Justine or Vijay Bhadra and his two female cohabitants; or casual sexual partnerships of convenience, such as the occasional friendly liaisons between next-door neighbors Haim Silbermann and Ravinder Pritam. On the other hand, Oyama Kazuko, though unambiguously female, was behaviorally asexual, which was why she had chosen Ravinder as the male parent for her offspring based on his fitness and reliability rather than any romantic bonds. Not only was the diversity of combinations highly educational from a sophontological standpoint, but it created endless opportunities for juicy and sexually scandalous gossip.

Unfortunately for R'nilinnath, the situation between Rosario, Scott, and the others had been neatly resolved. After all, along with their skills as a nurse and physical therapist, Rosario's role in the community was to help maintain the psychological health of its members, not only by providing for their sexual needs but by talking out their sexual anxieties and disputes. After a brief consult with Kweli Ndege, Rosario had admitted that they had inadvertently allowed Scott to schedule a disproportionate amount of their time, and had persuaded the geneticist to take a break from their sexual services as a penalty. Scott had not been happy about it, but he had accepted it as a necessary price for restoring a balanced relationship with his neighbors. *How very Chirrn*, R'nilinnath thought with satisfaction.

But she was more interested in the details of the tension between Stephen and Sita. "Does it involve Stephen mating with other females?" she pressed. Watching humans negotiate their sexual preoccupations was endlessly entertaining.

"No, nothing like that," Diana replied as they clambered along a crossover trellis high above one of Shilirrlal's hydroponic farm sectors. "He's still scrupulously faithful. He even turned *me* down!" she added with annoyance and disbelief.

R'nilinnath drummed her toes against the trellis slats. "You tried to seduce him? Tell me everything!" She had to shout over the sound of a robotic harvester passing below them. She wished the Arachnen were linked to consensus, so she could speak directly in Diana's mind and not have to strain her voice.

Diana chuckled, her own version of toe-drumming. "I prefer to brag about my successes, not dwell on my failures. Anyway, you keep prying into our sex lives—what about your own?" she asked as they reached the maintenance hatch at the far end of the trellis. "You're a young adult discovering your femaleness—that must be exciting. Have you, what, joined tongues with anyone yet?"

The young Chirrn swiveled her eyes and thumped her feet abashedly as she bypassed the lock on the hatch. "I wish. You forget, I'm the only one my age on Shilirrlal. I'm grown, but I'm… well, my mottling is taking its good time to fade, my mane's a little slow to grow in… so everyone still sees me as a child, even though I'm mature enough to be female. It's… an awkward time when there's nobody else your age."

Diana ruffled R'nilinnath's mane. "Trust me, Nilly, it's even more awkward when there *are* others your age."

The hatch led into the farm's water filtration plant, where they shed their clothes, took deep breaths, and dove into a clean water conduit whose current carried them to their destination. Diana was the only Arachnen who could hold her breath long enough for this. Finally they emerged into the open, catching themselves on a catwalk at the top of a sloping channel that carried the water down into the sector beyond. This was their destination for this trip: the Ryohoch sector of Shilirrlal, where those ancient and enigmatic beings preferred to reside. Though the Ryohoch had freely granted their advanced technological knowledge and galaxy-spanning wisdom to the Chirrn from the beginnings of the Void Alliance, as they had to numerous other species before, they nonetheless tended to remain detached, moving through their lives at their own pace and on their own terms. R'nilinnath had only been to this sector once before in her life, and never by the Ryohoch's invitation. This was as much a journey of discovery for her as it was for Diana.

The two young females clambered onto the catwalk and gazed out on a wide expanse dominated by dozens of slender, tapering blue trees with dome-shaped caps, rising halfway to the sector's roof. Various types of support drone flitted around them like cybernetic avians and insects. Each tree grew from the base of a large, domed building with open sides, its rootlike growths infiltrating the metallic structure even as the structure's technology ramified upward along the tree trunk. A ghostly, whistling whirr emanated from the trees, or the buildings, or both. It was warmer than the rest of Shilirrlal, fortunately for the two drenched, unclothed interlopers.

Several Ryohoch stood before the edges of the domed structures, appearing to be connected to the indistinct masses within them by thick, root-like tendrils joined somehow to the fronts of their large, bulbous bodies. As Nilly and Diana watched, another Ryohoch stood patiently as a set of drones guided another such root toward it and thrust its pointed, metallic end slowly into the Ryohoch's flesh, until it was in as deep as the length of Diana's forearms. The Ryohoch let out a low, whispery moan as it was penetrated, but showed no visible sign of distress. The human flinched and shuddered, but Nilly reassured her, "It's fine. Their bodies are adapted to handle this. I think."

"What are they doing?" Diana asked, bewildered. "Feeding on the trees? Being fed on *by* the trees? Exchanging data with the trees?" A pause. "Are the trees… fucking them?"

"I honestly don't know," R'nilinnath said. "But I *do* know we're not supposed to see this. It's very private—whatever it is." Diana grinned, looking intrigued.

They continued to watch, but the illicit thrill of the forbidden was hard to maintain when neither observer knew what they were watching, and when it continued for dozens of *narr* with no evident change. "Hey, what about the Lesshchin refugees?" Diana asked to break the tedium, resuming their earlier conversation. "Maybe there's someone your age among them."

Nilly's feet thumped again. "I checked. There are two that are close. But one was pretty badly hurt, and she's still relearning. And the other's male."

"So?" Diana asked.

"I'm not ready to have a baby yet! And I like being female right now; I'm in no hurry to change."

"Come on, same-sex tongue-wrestling can't be the Chirrn's only form of contraception."

"No, I can set my hormones to prevent it, but it's just… It's not what I'd expect for my first partner."

"Honey, your first time is never what you expect. And it's rarely ideal. Well, unless it's with me, of course," Diana added with a prideful shake of her mane. "But that would be a pretty advanced experiment for both of us. You should probably get some practice with another Chirrn first. My advice is, track down that Lesshchin boy and get to know him. He's probably as hard up to get some tongue as you are."

R'nilinnath's toes were drumming uncontrollably now. In an attempt to contain her amusement (and excitement), she snorted sternly and cried, "Enough! Diana, you're just trying to distract me from talking about Stephen and Sita. Tell me the dirt! I've waited long enough!"

Diana sighed. "Honestly, I don't know the details. They keep up a good public front of unity—our noble leader has to set a good example.

And most people don't want to pry, not being as naturally inquisitive as you and me. Or maybe they just need to believe Stephen can guide them through all this, and if he can't even keep the peace at home, then… well."

"Don't you need to believe it too?"

Diana hesitated. "I shouldn't say. Gossip is one thing, but I don't want to judge…"

R'nilinnath leaned forward. "You know the deal, Diana. Give to get. If you hold back, so do I."

Diana chuckled. "You'd make a hell of a reporter, Nilly. Okay. I just wonder sometimes… it was such a whirlwind romance."

"Stephen and Sita."

"Yeah. All based on hibernation dreams. I don't think you can really know a person based on dreams."

"But don't the hibernation dreams bare your true selves? Wouldn't you see each other more clearly?"

"Sure, it's your inner self—but it's who you are in a fantasy. We all had plenty of those fantasies in hibernation. I remember my dreams better than most." She tapped her skull. "Vanguardian memory and all. And I have *lots* of vivid memories of Stephen and me fucking each other senseless. I dream-fucked almost every man and woman in the crew, and I have no doubt Stephen did too. It was a long trip, after all. But when I woke up and got to know them as real people again, they didn't have that much in common with their dream avatars."

She tilted her head in thought. "Well, except for the real hardcore idealists. The ones who try to live their dreams in real life. Like Stephen, of course. Or Diego. Or Bingbing. A lot of the Unrenounced, really. Maybe that's why they're so unwilling to bend."

"But Stephen… bent."

"Not really. He's still the best of us, as driven to live up to his ideals as anyone. I guess the captain and the rest… define their ideals differently." She fidgeted, gazing back out at the Ryohoch techno-forest. "Doesn't seem fair that they're being punished for it."

R'nilinnath sighed through her nares, ruffling her bristles. "They are all in good health. And they can come to live with the Arachnen any time they want. All they have to do is renounce their planetary ties."

"That's the problem, isn't it? To them, that'd be compromising what they believe in—and none of us would ask that of them." Diana sighed. "Vack it, how did we get into this mess?"

The young Chirrn had no explanation for the Unrenounced's continued stubbornness. Surely they had been given plenty of time to figure out what was expected of them. What was so horrible about making a simple transition?

She wished she could just tell the humans everything. But that would defeat the purpose of their education, and of the Unrenounced's ongoing ordeal. They had to figure it out for themselves and choose to act accordingly. L'chellin allowed her to break the rules with Diana, just enough to satisfy the Arachnen that they were managing to evade their restrictions and learn things they weren't yet "supposed" to learn. R'nilinnath could get behind that; she'd always believed that the only good way to learn a set of limits was to exceed them. But her rule-breaking still served a purpose within the greater balance, which was why she felt free to indulge in it. She may have enjoyed a bit of fun, and she definitely enjoyed the extended prank she was playing on the humans. But she wasn't irrational, and she was still petitioning for her status as a full adult and guild member. So she played by the rules—the deeper set of rules that encouraged her to break the superficial rules in a useful way.

Why couldn't the Unrenounced do the same? The assimilating Arachnen managed to find their own forms of defiance—Diana going on secret expeditions, Sita keeping her traditional attire—without violating the parameters of their new allegiance. So what was stopping their former kith from rejoining them?

"What do you call ninety thousand dead Chirrn?" James Oates asked.

"A good start," Diego Narvaez replied.

Amrita Dhillon shook her head. "Bad aim."

"Trivia," suggested Evan Jiang.

"No," Oates told them. "One hell of a barbecue. Mm, kangaroo meat!"

Cecilia LoCarno joined in the laughter despite herself. Anything to keep morale up. She didn't want to encourage this kind of behavior—the kind that confirmed what the Chirrn already believed about humans—but her crew needed a release valve for their justified anger.

At the very least, they needed something to pass the time. There wasn't much to keep the loyalists busy in their stark prison compound.

Oh, it was clean, bright, and open—a broad semicircle with a domed ceiling about four meters high, containing a common area for dining and conversation, a fairly spacious exercise facility, eight double bunks, a shower/lavatory section, and a laundry and workshop. The prisoners were expected to do their own work to keep their compound clean and livable, but so long as they did so, it provided all the basics of survival. They had been granted a limited number of movable partitions for privacy, but there were few enough to require choices about what areas of privacy to prioritize—no doubt one of the behavioral experiments they had been sentenced to participate in. Every move the humans made was watched through the mirrored windows of the Panopticon-style observation booth overhead, beneath the ceiling at the geometric center of the semicircle—hardly necessary given the ubiquitous nanocameras that no doubt drifted throughout the compound, but serving as a constant psychological reminder of the prisoners' role as guinea pigs.

All the more reason, then, for Cecilia to allow the kind of jokes that would offend their Chirrn voyeurs. Diego and his hangers-on served their purpose; the engineer's charisma was a valuable force for maintaining the unity of the loyalist group, like a rawer, harder-edged version of Stephen's charm. And it was important to keep their fighting spirit alive in case an opportunity presented itself. Escape might require killing some Chirrn, so it was for the best that some of the loyalists would be capable of doing that without being overcome by guilt. Cecilia would have been more sanguine about it if not for her suspicion that Diego and James would hate the Chirrn just as much even if the first contact had been peaceful. But that hate could be turned to constructive ends, so long as Cecilia could regulate and focus it. Better than divorcing herself from Diego's group and letting their xenophobia run out of control.

No, that was unfair. All four of these people had volunteered for a mission to an alien world, had passed Stargazer's extensive psychological tests. True, they'd never expected to encounter sapient aliens, so the tests had not been designed to detect that kind of xenophobia. But they'd proven themselves smart, flexible, and curious, and they had all committed to a colonization program based on respect for Cybele's indigenous life. They didn't reflexively hate the unknown. Their animosity had been provoked by the Chirrn's abuses.

It was fair to say that Diego had taken that animosity farther than most, but Cecilia could sympathize with his reasons. The Guatemalan engineer was a deeply religious man. The concept of being responsible for killing thousands was too much for him to bear. To avoid that Catholic guilt, he took refuge in a strict reading of Catholic doctrine. God had created man in His image, so only man had a soul. Thus, Diego had concluded, *Arachne* had only killed a herd of unusually clever animals.

Of course, he missed the point. There was no need for guilt, since they had done nothing wrong. Nothing at all.

"I mean it, you know," Amrita went on, leaning forward on her soft sitting mat and resting her half-empty drinking globe of fruit juice on the low, circular protrusion that served them as a dining table, integrated with the floor so that they could not turn it into a weapon. "If only Arachne's shots had been a little more dead-on—"

"If she'd been able to stay on target longer, you mean," James interrupted.

"Whatever. She could've blown the whole thing up and we'd still be safely on our way to Cybele." The wiry mining engineer chuckled. "Nearly a million dead kangers and we'd never even know we killed them."

"More fun knowing we did," Diego said, laughing with her. But she laughed even louder at his words. The Chirrn's invasive, humiliating examinations had reawakened the traumas that Amrita had left Solsys to escape, and the Strider hated them as profoundly as she hated the Trojan-habitat regime her father had died resisting.

But it was what helped Amrita get through this, so Cecilia could live with it. As ugly as their hatred was, it helped keep the loyalists together. While she had far more respect for Ichiba Nobuo's Buddhist pacifism and Nikolos Zacharias's medical ethics, she feared that indulging them would weaken the group's commitment and lead to more defections. Granted, indulging the haters created the risk of driving people like Nobuo and Nik out of the loyalist camp. The key was keep the two sides balanced—favoring the angry side, but not so much that it ran out of control. The effect on the group as a whole was far from ideal, but once they got out of here and back en route to Cybele, the attitude of Diego's clique toward the Chirrn wouldn't matter.

The thought came unbidden that Stephen would be better at this kind of balancing act. Cecilia had never had difficulty commanding a crew's obedience and loyalty — always striving to respect their individuality, but within a context of shipboard discipline and the chain of command. Yet this was a different situation. The crew had been given a choice, and these fifteen — sixteen, before they had lost Rosario Soares — had chosen for their own reasons to stand with her. She had to cultivate their commitment to those individual convictions rather than merely compelling them to follow her. Convincing people of such diverse beliefs to unite behind a common cause and see it as an outgrowth of their own convictions was the sort of thing Stephen did naturally. Hell, he'd convinced Cecilia not only to go along with this mad colonization scheme, but to believe in it as passionately as he did — because she'd believed in him. Now, the Lesshchi accident had undermined his belief in himself, leaving it to her to carry on with his dream until he came to his senses. But as much as she tried to apply Stephen's methods, to lead by consensus and balance as he did, Cecilia feared she just didn't have the knack.

"I still say Cybele's their home planet." The others groaned as James started the argument for the thousandth time, though Cecilia welcomed the distraction from her reverie. "No, seriously. No way their technology could've missed detecting us. They intercepted us to stop us from finding their homeworld." For James Oates, hatred of the Chirrn was simply a matter of pride. The stocky, pale-skinned New Englander was a gifted industrial engineer and an accomplished athlete from a prestigious family, and he had pursued his place on the mission out of a sense of entitlement. He'd passed the vetting process by proving that his skill was equal to his opinion of it, and that he could check his arrogance enough to get along with the rest of the crew. But since their capture, James's resentment at being subordinated to the Chirrn had amplified all of his worst impulses. Moreover, his ego convinced him that anything bad that befell him must be the result of malicious schemes directed at him personally, or at least his group. For every setback in his life, he had a conspiracy theory or five, a handy set of explanations for why nothing that went wrong was ever his fault. This tendency had been restrained enough on the mission to be a manageable eccentricity, but since Lesshchi it had blossomed into full-blown paranoia.

But Nobuo couldn't resist pointing out the flaw in his logic. "So why move the whole habitat into harm's way when they have such fast ships?"

"What, you buy that they were innocent victims?" Evan Jiang said with undisguised contempt. He was basically a hanger-on, drawn into the others' circle by the strength of their personalities and eager to earn their approval. But he was compensating for a deeply rooted fear. Being in the Chirrn's physical presence terrified Evan. He'd trained with simulations of Cybeline life based on probe recordings, but the simulations couldn't have predicted his visceral response to the truly alien. He traveled in Diego's circle for protection and drew strength from their hate.

"Not innocent," Cecilia interposed, her tone drawing everyone's attention. "They kept Lesshchi dark, hidden. They didn't want to be seen. We find the reason for that, we find out why this happened."

James continued spinning conspiracy theories: the Chirrn were trying to keep planet-dwellers down, they had acted in secret to impede human progress, and so on. Nobuo patiently rebutted every point with reasoned counterarguments, but he was the only one who still bothered. After nearly five months of this, the others knew all his tunes: The Chirrn had been the source of the flying saucer legends of the twentieth century, stirring up the Cold War so humanity would destroy itself. The Chirrn had sent the Tunguska impactor and miscalculated its power or its aim. The Chirrn had artificially accelerated global warming to destabilize human civilization. All leading to his invocation of humanity's moral duty to rise up and wipe the Chirrn menace from the galaxy.

It wouldn't be quite so disturbing if Cecilia couldn't see how much the talk of violence against the Chirrn physically aroused James. The kangaroos had been playing games with them again. For a couple of weeks, they had required all six women to go constantly nude, programming all the clothing, bedsheets, and towels in the compound to liquefy when touched by a woman's skin, and setting the partitions to go transparent if a woman tried to conceal herself behind one. If they'd hoped to drive the men into an orgy of rape, they'd been disappointed; instead it had inspired the men to chivalry, bringing out their protective side. So last week the experimenters had reversed the programming and now all ten men had to go nude at all times—and the women had been enjoying every second and expressing that enjoyment in the bawdiest of terms, at least toward the men who were comfortable with such attention.

But both behaviors were acts of defiance in their own way. No one wanted to satisfy the Chirrn's expectations. For all their claims of harmless sociological experimentation, it had quickly become clear that this was an ongoing exercise in humiliation and dehumanization. Many of the "experiments" were designed to attack basic aspects of their planet-adapted biology. The cycles of light and dark in the compound had been varied unpredictably, until Cecilia and Nik Zacharias had finally managed to convince their wardens that sleep deprivation was a form of torture among humans — since the Chirrn were determined to pretend that all this was somehow ethical so long as it caused no overt physical harm. The gravity level in the compound had somehow been altered, sometimes dropping the prisoners abruptly into free fall and leaving them there for hours, sometimes subtly and subliminally increasing the gravity over days and observing their growing fatigue and irritation. Once, some sort of acoustical scrambling had drowned out Cecilia's and Diego's voices whenever they had given an instruction or asserted authority, as a test of the group's leadership dynamics. Yet a sizeable percentage of the trials involved sexuality in some way; the Chirrn were either fascinated or disgusted by the humans' unchanging sexes and were determined to test them to their limits and beyond.

At first, aware that they were being monitored at every moment, the loyalists had avoided sex altogether. But that hadn't lasted long, and Rosario Soares had advised them that it would be healthier to resume a normal level of sexual activity rather than give up that basic human right under coercion. At first, several of them had been too shy to perform, so Rosario had provided their services to any who needed them. But once the Chirrn had figured out that Rosario had only stayed with the loyalists to see to the sexual health of the gender-skewed group, they had compelled the sex provider to renounce and join Stephen's group. God forbid that the loyalists be granted any consideration for their mental health.

In a way, though, Cecilia was glad Rosario was gone; best if everyone here was a true planetary loyalist rather than a camp follower. No, that was far too harsh; Rosario's purpose had been therapeutic, not mercenary. And their skills as a nurse and physical therapist had been useful, though Ichiba Nobuo filled the latter role quite well (and Cecilia went away for a moment at the thought of his massages). Still, without a licensed sex professional on hand, managing relations within the community had become more of a challenge. Cecilia had tried to sort things out in an egalitarian way, encouraging each woman to choose two regular partners, with provisions for arranging trades and loans if needed—which had come out even, since Shuai Bingbing was remaining chaste out of misguided loyalty to her wife, despite Justine Nguyen's betrayal of Bingbing and the rest of her species. The arrangement was a bit libertine for some tastes—particularly for Sergei Mazunov and Hannah Errgang, who were falling mushily in love like adolescents despite (or perhaps as a result of) being the two oldest members of the group. But it was better than allowing jealousy and frustration to build.

Especially with the Chirrn doing their best to bollix the works. They had let the partnerships form without interference at first, but after a few weeks they had played a dirty trick. The atmosphere of the compound was infused with some kind of utility fog, which they now programmed to harden whenever a woman came near either of her lovers, the constituent nans linking into diaphanous yet extremely strong strands anchored against the floor and ceiling. It became impossible for any of them to touch their chosen partners. Some had readily switched to new partners, while others, including Sergei and Hannah, had settled for chastity for the duration. But then, for a few weeks, the utility fog had been programmed to prevent any man from touching any woman. That had been a difficult time for everyone. But the humans had adapted, as they always did, and soon the women began taking sexual comfort from one another, as did most of the men, save only Ibrahim and James. Even Bingbing, after a few days of soul-searching, offered her services to the other women in their time of need, insisting that Justine would understand. If the Chirrn had intended to test the flexibility of human sexual preference, they'd certainly gained a wealth of data.

It was just after that phase that the ban on touching had been rescinded and the women had been forced to go naked, as if to make them more available and more tempting than ever to the deprived men—though none of the men had reacted the way their tormentor must have hoped they would. Churrlaya had claimed the timing was random, but Cecilia hadn't believed him for a second. The fact that the Chirrn would allow a Lesshchi survivor to have power over the prisoners at all was proof that they had no interest in fairness. The whole thing was an exercise in revenge, and Cecilia was certain that Churrlaya stayed up nights cackling to himself — or whatever the kangaroos did — as he devised new ways to degrade his human playthings.

Suddenly a voice spoke from a cloudy patch in the air: the nans of the utility fog were vibrating in synch. *"Cecilia. Report to the interview chamber."* Cecilia winced. *Speak of the devil.*

She stood, but Diego rose to intercept her. She strove to keep her eyes on his face. "You shouldn't just get up the moment he calls you."

"You think he'd let me refuse?"

"I think you shouldn't make it easy for them. It's our duty to resist."

She held his gaze until he stepped aside. "I resist in my own way, Diego. Face to face, with my words and my intellect. Anything that shows them we're not just animals."

"You think Chur-*rana* would ever believe that?"

Cecilia smirked at the nickname; Diego had just called Churrlaya a frog. "Probably not. But I never give up. You know that." She stepped past him, unable to resist swatting his bare rump. "Besides, the revolution's safe in your hands."

Most of the group laughed as she walked away, but she could hear James grumbling, "Resisting. Sure. She jumps like a trained puppy when he calls." Cecilia frowned. She'd expect that kind of reaction from Oates; he was basically smart, but too impulsive in his anger and cynicism. But the noises of agreement she heard from the others gave her pause.

Perhaps goaded by Oates's insinuations, Cecilia was in a confrontational mood when she entered the private chamber beneath the Panopticon booth, where Churrlaya awaited her, seated casually on his tail. She decided to ease into it, though. "I want to thank you for the latest dress code. I'm thinking of making it permanent." *Never show weakness.*

The smallish, dark green Chirrn swiveled his eyes in to focus on her more closely, the intricate irises widening. With his mane now dyed pale blue and styled in ringlets, he looked a bit like the Frog Footman from *Alice's Adventures in Wonderland*. It made it easy for her not to take him seriously.

"Be seated, Cecilia." There was nothing familiar about Churrlaya's use of her first name. The Chirrn refused to acknowledge their family names, for they were ties to their old lives, their Earthly allegiances. "Do your males share your contentment with the arrangement?"

Cecilia remained standing. "Oh, there's nothing men love more than showing off."

"Indeed? Our observations suggest that most of your males are insecure to have their physical shortcomings exposed. Or is there some other reason why every male chooses to tighten his abdominal muscles when he notices a female observing him?"

"I'm afraid the nuances of human somatic communication are too intricate for a Chirrn to understand." *And you're slipping if you didn't notice us girls doing exactly the same when we were stuck naked.*

"Really," Churrlaya said. "Then perhaps we could gain more data on the subject if we deprived all of you of your clothing permanently."

"Word of advice, Churly? If you're going to make a threat, make it something you haven't already done to us. Besides, you'd never do anything so egalitarian. We wouldn't be as humiliated if we were all on an even footing."

He straightened, lifting his heels from the floor, and opened his mouth slightly, an expression of pride and satisfaction not unlike a human's. "Then you confess there is humiliation."

"I'm saying that your real goal is to inflict it. And you just confirmed it. Research be damned, you just want to torment us."

"We inflict no pain or injury upon you. We deprive you of no basic needs."

"Except our dignity."

Again the irises widened. The more Cecilia looked at Chirrn eyes, the more she realized their intricacies were probably artificially engineered. Wondering just what kind of visual input he'd engaged, she schooled herself for calm, not wishing to give anything away. He'd been scrutinizing the loyalists' every move for months and could read human body language better than she'd ever admit.

"If anything, your males seemed *more* concerned for your dignity when you were unclothed. Yet that does not seem to be reciprocal. Clearly your dignity is a matter of your own choice."

"Except we have no choice as long as we're your prisoners."

"You have been offered a very clear and simple choice that would free you from this. Yet you choose to remain. Why?"

"What you offer as a choice is just another form of enslavement."

"Because it would offend your dignity as planet-dwellers?"

"Because it would force us to abandon what we are."

"And what is that?" Churrlaya hopped forward to study her, and Cecilia could see the faint glimmer of the utility fog thickening between them, ensuring his safety should she try to attack him—though she doubted the reverse was true. "Answer: if you could reach me, would you kill me?"

She met his eyes squarely. "If I thought it would do my people any good, yes."

"Would simple revenge not constitute sufficient good by your people's standards? Do you not joke of murdering more of mine? Is this the planetary dignity you hold so dear?"

She could read a fair amount of tension in his body language too. "We joke. But you're the one actually inflicting revenge."

"The Chirrn have killed none of your people."

"We die a little more every day without our freedom."

Churrlaya snorted through his nares and mouth, a Chirrn scoff. "A platitude. Most humans have lived without freedom for most of your history. The concept of freedom as an intrinsic human right is younger than most of my own colleagues. Even today, you humans advocate the concept more consistently than you practice it. And yet your species has survived."

Cecilia noted that Churrlaya had just given something away about himself: he was younger than, ohh, about four hundred years, and this was relatively young for a Chirrn. She filed it away. "Because we've always fought for our freedom," she told him. "As long as there have been slavers and oppressors, there have been rebels and revolutionaries. As long as there have been prisons, there have been escapes."

"Do you believe all prisoners should escape? Even those guilty of obscene crimes?"

"Those who are wrongfully imprisoned, yes."

"*Wrongful!* Tell that to Simisshen, to Marellel, to Ruzhalu. Was it rightful that they should die?"

"The wrong wasn't ours! If your people had the basic good sense to put running lights on your habitat, your friends would be alive!" Cecilia pushed him, hoping to provoke him into rage. She could live with a few broken bones to make the point that she wasn't the violent one here. "Why did you keep Lesshchi so dark, Churrlaya? What were you trying to hide? Who were you hiding from?"

Churrlaya turned away, rotating his eyes backward to keep her in view, tensing his legs and tail. This was it. She closed her eyes, relaxed, and waited for it, hoping that if he killed her with the kick that was coming, the other Chirrn would bother to bring her back.

Instead, she just heard a loud, sharp thump, felt a strong vibration through her feet. She opened her eyes. He had struck the floor with his tail, and now he let out a long, slow hiss across his tongue. He kept his head turned away, his eyes rotated back and wide to see her around his raised brow ridges. "You are arrogant. Assuming we have reason to hide ourselves from your primitive race. That we make some secret plans against you. You are insignificant in the galaxy, dirt-dweller."

"Then why have you been studying us for so long? Our languages were already in your database when you captured us. You've monitored us before."

He turned back to face her. "Routine scientific observation."

"But you put a lot of effort into it. It would've taken a telescopic array the size of a planetary system to pick up clear signals from nine parsecs away. It would've taken decades of remote observation to put together enough cultural context for a practical translation. If you hold planet-dwellers in such contempt, why study us in such depth?"

"Scientists study the scum atop ponds. They study microbes that live on excrement. Do not mistake scientific curiosity for an acknowledgment of worth."

"And that's another thing. If it's planet-dwellers you hate, why do you treat Striders like Amrita and Nik as badly as the rest of us? Is this whole ridiculous planet thing just a cover? Is it humans *per se* you have a problem with?"

Churrlaya drew closer again. "We have been quite generous with every human who renounced planetary allegiance. They have been shown more acceptance than they deserve."

"So long as they 'contribute to your society.' They're worse than your prisoners. They're your slaves. And they don't even understand that's what they are."

He hissed again. "You are the one who understands nothing. But I am glad of it, for it prolongs your ordeal." He came in very close, and she felt the air harden around her. "And keeps you in my power."

Churrlaya cursed himself for letting Cecilia provoke him into admitting too much. He knew he'd be in for chastisement from R'hhenevh when he returned to the monitor room. And indeed, the sleek-snouted, strong-bodied Shilirrlaln met him wide-stanced, tapping her long, graceful tail on the floor. "Must we have the same conversation yet again, Churrlaya?" she asked. "I indulge your desire to humiliate the humans so long as it serves a purpose. I chose to have faith that your desire to transition to my collegium showed your willingness to adapt your grief toward constructive ends." She stepped closer, relaxing her stance. "But you must remember that our purpose is to guide them toward the resolution of their ordeal, not goad them into prolonging it. They need to reach the stage of repentance. They have an obligation to take the place of the lives they took."

"Those lives can never be replaced," Churrlaya hissed. "Least of all by the ones who destroyed them. Can you blame a Lesshchin for feeling that the humans have already earned final exclusion?"

R'hhenevh lowered her head, her lush, jeweled magenta mane falling forward over her shoulders and the gold-fringed vest she wore. "I understand your pain, Laya. As much as I can understand such a tragedy. But you are Lesshchin no more." She clasped his hands with her own cool azure ones. "You have a new home now, a new guild to take care of you. But only if you stop clinging to your old life."

He took comfort in her touch, if not her words. There was no way she could truly understand, no way he would inflict the memories on her to make her understand. A large piece of who he was had been burned away. So many memories, viewpoints, habits of thought ripped from him with no warning or choice. So many friends and loved ones who had been a part of him, now reduced to mere echoes lingering within his skull. "It is not easy to make a transition when it is forced."

"The circumstances were forced. But you have chosen your new path freely." She stroked his arm. "At least I believed you had. I begin to wonder if your grief is trapping you in your old life, preventing you from truly becoming whole again. Perhaps it would be easier for you to move on if you chose another collegium. Forgot about the humans."

His eyes locked on hers. "Would you want that? For me to leave you?"

"Only if it would set you free from who you were. But I would regret losing you. You have a real aptitude for the science of the mind.

You are a valuable addition to our collegium. And we all wish to ease your loneliness.

"But it can only work if you resolve your own self-inflicted ordeal. And that cannot happen if you cling to your desire for retribution."

"You think I push them too far. That my experiments are gratuitous."

"You claimed they had a purpose." She sent him a memory image, triggering his own recall of the same conversation wherein he had proposed the sexual behavior experiments with the goal of assessing the flexibility of the humans' identity and affinity structures, the better to understand and overcome their resistance to adaptation. "But I am no longer convinced that is your true goal."

"I do nothing that exceeds the allowed limits for ordeals."

"For *Chirrn* ordeals. Humans are different. They are feral, young. They have had life extension for less time than you have lived. And they reside almost fully within their own brains. It is not in their nature to move between life phases. When their identity is challenged, they cling to it more fiercely."

"Sometimes. There are instances in their records of humans being conditioned to change allegiance after extended humiliation." He sent her cites for the relevant sources in the guild database, if she were inclined to confirm the claim.

Yet she sent back even more citations almost immediately. "And this is considered torture to them. That is not our purpose here. We are offering them the chance at redemption, if they are able to recognize and embrace it." Her hand moved to his neck, fingers brushing his mane. "Help me do that, Laya. Guide them to a new beginning, so that you may truly make one of your own. One where you can truly belong with me."

R'hhenevh dug her hands into his mane and pulled their heads together brow to brow. The brushing of her muzzle cilia over his sent tingles through his head clear to his tongue; her scent in his nares was intoxicating. What an honor, some lingering rational part of him thought, to be romanced by the collegium alpha herself! The prospect of being one of her chosen was enticing indeed.

When their muzzles parted, he tried to form coherent words around his swollen tongue. "You… would have me go female for you?"

"If you like. Or you could stay male—perhaps even speak a child with me." Churrlaya's eyes spun at the prospect. True, the loss of so many lives meant that many former Lesshchin were preparing to speak new young, but he had given no thought to doing so himself. "Either would be a new start for you. A leap further into your new life."

She brushed muzzles with him again to reinforce the offer. He wanted to pull her against him, to seal his lips against hers and rub tongues until his spoke the sweet word for hers to hear.

But he pulled away, hopping back, huffing through his nares to clear them of her overpowering alpha pheromones. "You honor me deeply, Alpha. But I am not ready. My accent is still Lesshchin."

R'hhenevh gave a soft hiss of disappointment. "And that means you must continue to humiliate the humans."

"That will have to be my role within the collegium for now."

She thumped her tail against the wall, unhappy but accepting. "Granted. But remember the ultimate goal. Show them the value of submission. Guide them toward acceptance of their crime so they may seek repentance. Do not push them so hard that they become more determined to resist. You know how dangerous that can be when dealing with planet-dwellers." R'hhenevh did not need to send reference files to annotate her words. That particular historical lesson was well-known to every Chirrn — indeed, to every starfaring people within the Four Voids and beyond.

"I have more than distant history to tell me of the danger of planet-dwellers, Nevh. But does that history not tell us that containing them is a safer path than attempting to mentor them?"

The alpha bristled. "This is not mentoring, and you know it. It is repentance and transition as the Chirrn have always practiced it, both within ourselves and with outsiders."

Regretting his impolitic choice of words, Churrlaya bent his knees. "My apologies, Alpha. My analogy was malformed. I did not mean to accuse you of supporting —"

She softened. "Of course. Your words were born of pain." She nuzzled his snout with hers again, though only briefly before resuming a more professional distance. "I understand that this is far from abstract for you, Laya. Still, you have committed to the goal of guiding them through transition. I am trusting you to honor that commitment."

"With all gratitude for your trust, Nevh, I suspect it may already be too late. As you said, the humans cling to their allegiances and beliefs with great ardor."

"Most of them chose transition. It should be possible for the rest in time."

"The humans of *Arachne* were chosen for their diversity of skills and character. And for their strength of will. These sixteen will not alter their convictions as easily as the rest."

She studied him. "You sound almost admiring. How do we reconcile that with preemptive exclusion?"

Churrlaya realized that he thought of it more by the human term: *hate*. "I merely know them well. Understanding is not approval."

"But you should be able to use that understanding to guide them in the right direction. That is your duty to your guild."

"I know. I know." He felt that conviction within himself, when he reached for the collegium consensus. But it was not enough to overcome the pain and bitterness that filled his own skull, not enough to fill the missing pieces of his identity. He sighed through his nares. "I overstepped myself, and I will try to repent. But... it is not easy to contain my anger. Cecilia in particular... she is so stubborn, so arrogant. Without her, without the extremist clique she has gathered around her, I think most of the others would be malleable. But she will not yield a single hop. She defines her identity by her roots in a particular city on her native planet. It is a psychological anchor for her, one that I have found unyielding."

R'hhenevh pondered his words. "All ground is impermanent. If you assume this 'anchor' cannot be budged, perhaps you have become too influenced by planetary thinking."

"Can you see a way to break the ground?"

She swiveled her eyes a bit, tapped her fingers together. "I only hear a question. If Cecilia is so unyieldingly rooted in her planetary home... then why did she command an expedition that would take her from her home forever?"

R'hhenevh hopped forward and brushed her fingers tenderly over his muzzle. "Answer that question, dear Laya, and you may find the key to freeing her from her planetary bonds. And maybe then you will free yourself as well."

8

Sita Bhatiani stood sideways before the mirror, studying herself. "Ohh, I'm really starting to show now. I look so fat."

"Nonsense." Stephen reached around from behind her, placing his hands on the warm flesh of her belly. "You look wonderful. Pregnant women are so beautiful."

Sita rolled her eyes. It was often flattering when he treated her as a paragon of beauty and brilliance, but at other times, she felt overshadowed by the ideal image he projected onto her. But then, he was such a paragon himself that she supposed he couldn't help seeing the best in everyone. "Maybe from the outside," she conceded. "It's not very comfortable from in here."

"Just be glad you don't have to give birth through your mouth like a Chirrn."

"Are you joking? At least their mouths are wide to begin with. That comes out ahead in the evolution race if you ask me." Sita had already decided on a Caesarean birth; her hips were simply too small for anything else to make sense. No point making things difficult for the kid on her first day out.

He smiled. "There, you see? You do have something positive to say about the Chirrn."

Sita pulled away. "They have every advantage over us already. You really think I meant it as a positive? Any lengths to find a bright side, eh?"

"Would humans have been this generous, this accepting of people who did what we did? I think things are very bright, under the circumstances."

His words only shamed her. She was disgusted by her own xenophobia, her bigotry toward these beings that intellectually she found remarkable. The Chirrn of Shilirrlal had surely proven by now that they weren't savage monsters waiting to beat the life from her if they got her alone. The brutality that a few deeply traumatized Lesshchin had inflicted on her immediately after the loss of their entire world — more than just a structure or a place, but a literal part of their identity that had been violently ripped away — was an aberration in a highly peaceful society, and an entirely understandable one. She didn't even hate Vhehhal and the other guards who had beaten her; how could she, knowing the unconscionable loss that had provoked them? Sometimes, the fact that she'd been punished so severely at the start made her feel less guilty about the startling leniency and kindness the Shilirrlaln had since extended.

Still, animal reflex was hard to overcome. For months, the sight of one of those chameleon eyes swiveling to lock onto her had suffused her with fear. She'd gradually learned to be comfortable with R'nilinnath and L'chellin, up to a point, and she had little difficulty with Mediator Broadwing, who had been nothing but supportive toward the Arachnen (though the Zenith's manner toward Sita, the shortest member of the group, could be unthinkingly condescending). But the thought of going out into Shilirrlal, surrounded by tens of thousands of Chirrn, had overwhelmed her.

She paced before the bedroom window, which at least looked out over the house's back garden, sparing her the impression of Chirrn eyes staring in at her while she slept. Yet from here, she could see the wall and ceiling of the Arachnen compound stretching high overhead, a constant reminder that the humans were completely contained, able to leave these confines only at the Shilirrlaln's indulgence — perhaps some lingering echo of the ancient transition rituals between bands. "Accepting?" she asked, echoing Stephen's observation. "I wonder. To bring a child into this… how will she see her world? Her humanity? What if she thinks she's tainted because of, of what her parents did? Or will she even identify as human?"

Stephen intercepted her, clasping her shoulders. "We're all asking those questions. But the best thing we can do is to work with the Chirrn to integrate into their community. Establish ourselves as equals within it." He stroked her cheek. "I understand what you're feeling, honey. I spent my whole childhood in a place where I was made to feel I didn't belong. When I got my sisters out to Brazil, at first we feared we'd be judged and excluded the same way. But we found ourselves welcomed by a society that celebrated its diversity. And then we found that most of humanity felt the same, that our experience had been an aberration, a last gasp of a dying way of thinking.

"I look at how the Shilirrlaln treat other species like the Zenith and the Ryohoch as their own kind—even sharing their brains with them—and I feel the same sense of hope that I found in Brazil. I believe we're on the verge of finding ourselves welcomed into a vaster community than we could've imagined."

Sita sighed. His optimism was so contagious—but she'd lived with him long enough that she was starting to build up a resistance. "I wish I had your faith." She strode out into the living room, with Stephen following. She picked up the tablet she liked to read from, preferring the old-fashioned approach over reading off her retinal display. "I've been trying to learn more about the evolutionary history of the Zenith and Ryohoch."

"That's great," Stephen said.

"But I can't find anything significant about the biospheres they first evolved in. It's one thing for the Ryohoch—I mean, bloody hell, they're apparently a descendant species of a genus that first colonized space millions of years ago. They're so ancient that maybe the knowledge of where they first came from has just been lost, beyond the general environmental parameters we can deduce from their physiology.

"But from what I can gather, the Zenith aren't anywhere near as ancient. Maybe even younger than the Chirrn. Yet there's nothing about their planet of origin."

"You know how the Chirrn are about planets." As always, he took more care with the pronunciation of their name than she did. His fluency in Portuguese gave him an advantage with the guttural R. She could come close by affecting a Scottish accent, but normally she settled for "Cheern," which sounded incongruously like she was thanking them for something.

"But I don't get blocked when I try to find information on Cybele, or other unpopulated planets they've surveyed," she told him. "It's more than just lack of information, and it's not just about the Zenith. I keep hitting roadblocks in Shilirrlal's network. Stephen, I wish I could trust them like you do, but it's hard when they're keeping secrets from us."

"You know what a regimented people they are. They believe in measured, ritualistic transitions from one stage of life to another. So their educational process is designed to proceed at a certain rate, in a certain order. We still have so much to learn about living as Shilirrlaln. There's a lot to assimilate. Maybe they just want us to master that foundation before we try coping with a flood of knowledge about the galaxy as a whole."

"In other words, they don't trust us with knowledge they don't think we're ready to have. It's just one more way they have all the control."

He took her hands, seeking to calm her. "Because we're still children to them. Like all children, we're impatient for the learning process to end so we can earn the freedoms of adults, but we have to accept that it takes time.

"You know, you should talk to R'nilinnath about her learning process. I think it'd help put your mind at ease." He ruffled her hair. "Just think. Before too much longer it'll be our little girl railing against the limits we place on her. But she'll grow out of them before we know it."

"Oh, there you *go* again!" Frustrated, she whirled away and moved across the room.

He stared in surprise. "Doing what?"

"*Handling* me. Making speeches like you're still recruiting me for the mission."

He shook his head. "I'm just trying to make the best of things for all of us."

"*Your* best. You're so good at charming and persuading people to share your enthusiasms, your dreams. But I'm not some investor or, or politician to be brought round, Stephen! I'm not some shipmate who needs to be given hope! I'm your *wife!* Can't you ever turn it off and just, just *listen* to me? Just let me feel what I feel and be there with me, instead of trying to fix me all the time?!"

After a nonplussed moment, Stephen sat on the couch and said, "You're right. Of course, you have every right to your feelings and concerns. If you need to vent, I'll listen. If you need to cry, here's my shoulder. That's what family's all about, right?"

Instead of calming her, his concession just made her more irritable. "Damn it, I can't even have a decent row with you. Mister Bloody Perfect."

She strode back into the bedroom, closed the door on the very confused-looking Stephen, and leaned back against it in frustration. Her husband was the most empathetic, compassionate man she'd ever met. So how come he had so much trouble understanding her?

The sector of Shilirrlal set aside for the Lesshchin refugees was much larger than the Arachnen compound, but much less interesting for R'nilinnath to visit. The Lesshchin's inherent tendency toward conservatism and insularity had become even greater since the disaster, as the survivors had clung to their traditional identity as a way to anchor them now that so much of their memory and identity had been stripped away. Of course, they would all need to transition into Shilirrlaln society eventually, as many already had, eager to leave their traumatized Lesshchin identities behind them; but many more clung to the vestiges of their lost community, and for now, there was no harm in allowing them to preserve what they could of Lesshchi in its original form before gradually allowing it, and themselves, to be blended into a new synthesis with Shilirrlal culture. Thus, the structures and public spaces of what was now the Lesshchin sector had been remodeled to a traditional Chirrn style, reminiscent of how it might have looked in the Separation Era three yanarredj ago, but with less sign of Zenith, Ryohoch, or other xenocultural influences. It all seemed rather bland and unexciting to Nilly, though she supposed the last thing the disaster survivors wanted right now was any more excitement.

Well, that's too bad, R'nilinnath entered into her cloud journal with an insouciant toss of her still-too-short mane. *Because I'm here to bring excitement to one Lesshchin in particular.*

Normally she would have just pinged Djayrulu through the network and arranged a meeting. But after a couple of *narruvh* of failing to get up the nerve to do just that, R'nilinnath had finally kicked herself in the tail and come here to seek the young Lesshchin out in the flesh, so that she couldn't "chicken out," as Diana put it. Also, if he proved receptive to her offer, it would save them considerable time if their bodies were already in the same sector.

Djayrulu's locator showed him to be up toward the roof of the sector, ascending a climbing trellis spanning two of the highest towers — and this was one of the highest-roofed outer sectors of Shilirrlal. With a sigh, Nilly made her way to the nearest ascent frame and began bounding her way upward. Since she was the one seeking him out, it was only polite to come to him. And it would help her case to show him that she could match his level of fitness.

Still, by the time R'nilinnath came into naked-eye sight of the young male, she was gasping for breath and her arms and legs were sore. She took a moment to size him up as she caught her breath. Djayrulu had a distinctively Lesshchin appearance, with dark green skin almost free of juvenile mottling, a fairly pointy snout, a stocky tail, and an unadorned, nearly full-grown mane of vivid pink. As she stared at him, Nilly realized her heart rate was not settling down, and her tongue was getting moist. She tightened her lips before she started drooling. She'd never reacted this way to another Chirrn before, least of all a male. It must've been because he was the first Chirrn of her own age she'd ever met in the flesh.

Then she realized he was watching her watch him, and she nearly fell off the trellis. She recovered quickly, turning it into what was hopefully an acrobatic-looking move toward him. "Impressive view up here," she said when she landed alongside him, trying not to cling too tightly to the lattice.

Djayrulu studied her for a moment, his gaze revealing little. "I recognize you. You're R'nilinnath with the Mediators' Guild."

"Oh! Yes, I am!" He was already aware of her? Had he been seeking her out for reasons that paralleled her own?

"I've seen you with the other Mediators," he went on. "In community meetings and news feeds."

"Oh. Of course!" In addition to overseeing the Arachnen's rehabilitation, her apprenticeship with the Mediators included helping with the Lesshchin's adjustment from time to time. Her lips parted a bit with pride that he recognized her efforts. His gaze sharpened on her mouth. Was he trying to catch a glimpse of tongue? That was encouraging.

"I'm Djayrulu."

"I know. I came here to meet you." She angled her head to make it just slightly easier for him to see her tongue as she spoke.

His eyes flicked out and back nervously, as if he were unsure whether he had her permission to look or not. "Wh-why would you want to talk to me?"

"Because we're nearly the same age. Just about the only ones our age on Shilirrlal. I figure it's as lonely for you as for me."

He fingered the edge of his vest noncommittally. "Maybe."

"So I thought maybe we could practice sex together."

Djayrulu stared in disbelief for some moments. "I barely know you."

"Well, it's a fine way to get better acquainted!"

"I don't understand. I mean, you look nice enough, but…" He took a sniff of her pheromones. "You're female. It would take a few *narruvh* for you to go male."

R'nilinnath bristled. "What makes you think I'd want to? I've been female for less than a *narranl*. I'm nowhere near finished yet!"

"Well, I'm not going to go female for some Chirrn I've just met. It's a lot of work. Besides, you're the one seeking me out. It's only polite for you to come to me." He gestured toward the climbing frames that had brought her all the way up here.

"So… in principle, you'd be willing to practice sex with me."

He hesitated. "Of course I'm curious. I don't have a lot of prospects either. Especially with the adults so preoccupied with rebuilding the community. But one of us would have to change."

"Do we? We could just join tongues as we are."

Djayrulu recoiled. "As male and female? I won't have a baby with a Shilirrlaln!"

"I said nothing about babies. Just sex. It can be fun with an opposite partner too. …So I hear."

"That's disgusting!"

R'nilinnath was stunned by the strength of his reaction. "Why?"

"Because it's human."

"Chirrn do it sometimes."

"That was before. Now, it'd be a tail-blow to the throat of every Lesshchin."

"What? That doesn't…"

He glanced inward, checking the cloud. "There it is. I thought so. You work with those filthy ferals. You spend so much time with them, you've been contaminated by their perversions."

"There's nothing *wrong* with the ways humans have sex! They're just different."

"You heard what their chieftain said at the trial. Since they mixed up sex for recreation and for procreation, they bred out of control and over-crowded their planet, and that's why they left it in such dangerous ships. It's because of human breeding that my friends, my guildmates, my world were killed!"

Nilly inhaled deeply, gathering herself. His logic was objectively stupid, but she couldn't blame him for the pain that was blinding him.

"The Arachnen made a horrible mistake. They're atoning for it now. I'm helping them restore the balance."

Djayrulu's response was sullen. "You Mediators ended their ordeal too early. They don't deserve inclusion."

She accessed the guild knowledge inside her to help her be conciliatory. "I understand the pain you feel. It will take a long time to heal. But maybe you could heal better if you had a friend. You may not like everyone I associate with, but that's my job as a Mediator. What matters is what we can learn from each other." She widened her mouth and hissed a little across her tongue. "Like how to have sex…?"

They clung to the trellis for a moment, with the only sounds being the wind blowing through the slats and the distant murmur of the crowd below. "I'm not sure about that yet," Djayrulu told her. "But I shouldn't exclude the possibility without learning more about you. Maybe… if I could see the Arachnen through your eyes. Experience them as you do."

"I'm sorry," she said. "The Mediator feeds are confidential to the guild, and to our superiors. I couldn't share my memories from when I'm working on their behalf."

He gave a disappointed snort. "I understand."

She perked up. "But there's something I can do." She explained about her authorized rulebreaking to sneak Diana out of the Arachnen compound through the back conduits. She couldn't see why that loophole couldn't be exploited in the other direction. Especially if it led to getting Djayrulu's tongue in her mouth.

"You'd actually take me into their compound?" the young Lesshchin asked, revulsion warring with an excitement R'nilinnath found very familiar. It was comforting to know she was not the only Chirrn intrigued with the forbidden.

"Not quite *into* it—I don't think you're ready to meet them. But once you're inside, you could stay on the fringes and watch and listen through the local sensors. Although I'd have to stay close to you so I can kick you out if you try anything untoward."

"I promise to behave," Djayrulu said. "Although… I'm starting to like the idea of you staying close to me."

He brushed his tail against hers, and her tongue suddenly started to get very wet.

"Let me see if I understand." Tarik Bahar gazed out the window of the observation gallery overlooking Shilirrlal's shipyard facilities, located at the weightless axis of the thick disk-shaped module at the aft end of the cylindrical habitat. Hanging from its elegant frameworks like tomatoes on a trellis were dozens of Chirrn warp cages, each a pair of nested spheres of intricately curved latticework. "They have so many warp drives... but do not actually use them *as* warp drives?"

Floating beside him, Haim Silbermann assayed a shrug. "Not over long distances. For that, they use wormholes."

"But they need the warp cages to get through the wormholes."

"Bubble of alteration has exterior of smallness to penetrate mouth of wormhole," came the slow, deliberate response of Yonchon, the senior engineer with whom Haim was provisionally apprenticed. Ryohoch like Yonchon were known for their leisurely approach to life; for millions of years, they had drifted through space much as the Chirrn had, but much more slowly, often content to colonize Oort-cloud comets and wait for gravitational perturbations to pull them out of stellar orbit. On the whole, they had little use for superluminal technology, which made it odd that Yonchon was an expert in the field — but then, Ryohoch were nothing if not dogged individualists.

The massive engineer had no fewer than nine legs in groups of three, two sticking out on either side of the body (angling up from the hip, then straight down at the knee, to provide greater leverage against the superterrestrial gravity in which the Ryohoch's ancestral species must have evolved) and a shorter third one providing extra support underneath. Tarik recalled Stephen's "ball in a catcher's mitt" description of the Ryohoch head, which had struck him as very American. In fact, the "mitt" was a dense mass of fine tendrils forming a parabolic dish of sorts behind a "ball" with beady eyes and vertical respiratory slits adorning its front and sides. Though Yonchon's forward legs were somewhat prehensile, for fine manipulation the engineer relied on small neutral-buoyancy drones that could fly under mental control to where Yonchon needed them and return to rest on Yonchon's back when not in use, like birds perched on an elephant.

Arachne was still working on improving her translation of Ryohoch speech, which, among other difficult features, had no adjectives. Yonchon's people also found personal pronouns insulting.

Haim explained to Tarik. "The boss here means it's a Van Den Broeck warp metric — the outer warp bubble's pinched off to microscopic size. Wormholes have to be small too, otherwise the energy cost of keeping them stable's prohibitive, so you need to stick your ship into a portable hole small enough to fit through the mouth." Haim shook his head. "Although I still don't buy that the metrics can interact without collapsing each other."

"Design of one accommodates design of other," Yonchon said. "Antiquity of practice. Civilizations precede civilizations. Technology descends." Tarik blinked, reminding himself just how ancient Ryohoch civilization was.

Tarik turned back to his engineer friend. "And it's all thanks to this, what was it, programmable..."

"Programmable quark matter," Haim affirmed with a nod. "That's what Doctor Belghazi called it back home when she theorized the stuff—or at least something close enough to it that the name fits."

Tarik understood the analogy. Much as normal programmable matter could manipulate the quantum states of its confined electrons to simulate the chemical properties of any element, including those not found in nature, so PQM could manipulate quark states to simulate baryons and mesons with exotic physical properties, including the sort that allowed once-fanciful general relativity solutions like warp bubbles and wormholes to be achieved in practice.

"PQM is basically femtotech computronium," the engineer went on. "That is, matter with computational circuitry built into it at the nucleonic level. So it can do fly-by-wire corrections fast enough to counter the tensor instability dynamically. And the PQM also shields the ship inside against the Hawking radiation from the warp bubble. But both the radiation and the instability build up exponentially, and sooner or later they get ahead of any possible corrections. Plus you'd need to drop out periodically anyway, to dump your waste heat and purge any particles caught in the warp."

"Like insects on a windscreen."

The engineer chuckled. "Not so far off. A Chirrn drive can do nearly a parsec a pop in empty space—less if there's a dense interstellar medium, even less if there's a star or planet nearby. Any mass or energy increases the instability."

"How do they get wormhole mouths positioned dozens of parsecs apart without time dilation?" Tarik asked.

Haim shrugged. "Lots of small hops."

"But that means there's a wormhole metric… inside the warp metric. And if the warp ship passes *through* a wormhole en route…"

"Please, Tarik. I have enough of a headache already."

Yonchon had sent a pair of drones out to assist in loading a cargo module into a nearby warp cage, whose twin spheres had irised back into an equatorial ring surrounding the ship components within. Since each cage totally encased its ship while in use, generating the warp bubble right along its surface, the interior contents were modular and interchangeable as needed for a particular mission. This installation seemed to have reached a delicate phase demanding the Ryohoch engineer's full attention, so Tarik took the opportunity to drift closer to his old friend and speak softly. "It seems that Yonchon's sharing information with you pretty freely."

"I think so," the grizzled engineer replied. "I mean, look. Yonchon let us come here today."

"True," Tarik agreed. It was a rare opportunity to visit such an important part of Shilirrlal without needing to sneak around with R'nilinnath as Diana Thorne insisted on doing. Tarik shared the Vanguardian's eagerness to learn more of what the Chirrn hid from them, since one never knew what secrets might prove harmful to the crew (as Tarik still thought of them). Yet he was reluctant to take the kind of risks Diana did, and he took his oaths too seriously to bend them as far as she did. So he had welcomed this opportunity to gain knowledge more overtly.

"Still," he went on, "this is the first time you've actually been allowed to see the ships, isn't it?"

Silbermann tilted his head. "Yonchon thought I'd reached the point in my training where I needed to. I guess. Hard to know what's going on in that… hmm, honestly I don't know where Ryohoch keep their brains."

"So you don't feel you're being held back?"

"What do you mean?"

Tarik spoke softly. "I've heard complaints from some of the crew. Ravinder, Sita, others who feel we're being kept from asking certain questions. Larger questions about the galaxy."

"The galaxy?" Haim echoed with a frown.

"The Chirrn's place in the larger scheme of things. What lies beyond local space. What lies on the far end of those wormholes. Who built them, come to that."

"Well, I've been more concerned with the mechanics of it all. That demands pretty much all my attention right there." Haim studied him. "Where's this mistrust coming from, my friend? I thought you were fitting in rather well." He chuckled, looking the younger man over approvingly. "You certainly wear that Chirrn-style vest better than I ever could. Especially now all your chest hair's grown back in."

"Careful," Tarik said, grinning. "I appreciate the compliment, but I'm a married man now. A father-to-be."

"Well, impending fatherhood looks very good on you."

"It feels even better. To finally have a wife who shares my goals in life… and to have a son I know I will be there for."

His friend's grizzled head took on a skeptical tilt. "Except you still have divided loyalties, don't you?"

Tarik struck his palm with his fist. "I still can't get in to see the Unrenounced. I've asked time and again for permission to visit the captain, but they refuse. They assure me she and the others are in good health, but all I have is their word."

The older man nodded. "And you're wondering how much you can trust their word."

"Yes."

"Well, I haven't felt like they're hiding anything. I think Yonchon and Yonchon's staff have been pretty open about the theory and the engineering, at least up to the point I'm able to understand."

"As you said, we already had the theory. So they haven't opened any completely new doors for you."

"No, not yet. But there's still so much we have to learn. And that could be the work of a lifetime." He gestured to the warp cages outside the port. "And I'm gonna love getting to know these babies as much as you and Kweli will love getting to know yours."

Tarik turned back to contemplate the expanse of the shipyard and all the potentials it implied. What would it be like to take one of those ships on a jaunt around the galaxy with his wife and son by his side? If what Haim said about wormholes was right, even a small warp cage could take them practically anywhere. So many adventures awaiting, just a few hops away. It was frustrating to be kept from that, to be dependent on the Chirrn's judgments about when and how quickly knowledge should be dribbled out.

Seeing his frustration, Haim squeezed his shoulder. "Take it easy, my friend. Remember — we're still on parole. It's not about whether we can trust the Chirrn—it's about whether they can trust us. And we have to be on our best behavior to earn that trust."

The reminder was sobering. Still, Tarik had to wonder if Haim was being overly optimistic. "Given how our relationship began, it's hard to believe the Chirrn will ever completely forgive us."

Haim shrugged. "We used to think Jews, Muslims, and Christians would never forgive each other in the Middle East. Look what we have now. It just took a generation that got fed up with their parents' and grandparents' excuses for continuing the chaos, so they reached out to each other to end it. It took time, but it happened."

"It also happened because the most unrepentant militants and fanatics were exiled to the Belt and the Trojans. Which just made them the Striders' problem. We never truly ended the conflict, we just exported it.

"But what happens if the Chirrn never truly forgive us or accept us?" Tarik turned his gaze back to the array of starships beyond the window. "If we can't earn a place in their society… then where else can we possibly go?"

The dreams came to Cecilia again, as they had the past few nights. She was back with Stephen, Tarik, Kazuko, and the others, watching as they went about their daily lives, seemingly without a care. Many of them had paired off in couples—Stephen and Sita, Kweli and Tarik, Justine and Diana—and most of the women were just starting to show their pregnancies, with Kweli and Kazuko the furthest along. Sometimes they were working in the gardens of cozy dwellings stacked above each other in terraces, casually chatting with their neighbors. Sometimes they were meeting in bright, large-windowed offices to discuss community planning or medical updates on the progress of the women's pregnancies. Once they gathered together in a tree-lined square to listen to a song recital by Kweli and Andrea, with several Chirrn and a Zenith present in the audience. Once they were in a roomy auditorium playing an unfamiliar ball game that involved jumping and climbing on frames and lattices and making swooping, athletic kicks that seemed to emulate the sweep of a Chirrn tail.

Yet in all these scenes, Cecilia was only a watcher, never acknowledged or invited to participate. None of the other loyalists were present.

She was out of practice at this, but in time, she began to sense that these were no mere dreams.

The next morning at breakfast, Cecilia questioned the others about their own dreams. All of them described similar experiences, and the truth quickly dawned on them. "No," Shuai Bingbing moaned. "It's all real! Justine… she left me for Diana! That biǎozi! Gōng gòng qì chē!"

"We can't be sure of that," Cecilia cautioned her, wondering how much of Bingbing's anger was a cover for her lingering guilt at her own reluctant infidelity — or perhaps a gesture of liberation from it. "Just because they fed us all the same dreams doesn't mean they're real."

"Of course it's not real," James said. "They want to tempt us into losing our resolve, by showing us the others being happy and content. For all we know, they're even worse off than we are."

"If it's real, they *are* worse off," Diego replied. "Think of what we saw. Humans dressed in Chirrn clothes. Speaking their language. Playing their sports. They're surrendering their humanity more and more every day. Losing their human souls."

"Do they even remember us?" Bingbing wondered. "Do they even still care?"

Ichiba Nobuo had been sitting thoughtfully, reflecting. "They didn't seem soulless to me," he said. "They seemed content. Free to work, to create, to learn…"

"To have families," Sergei Mazunov put in softly, clasping Hannah Errgang's hand and trading a wistful look with her.

"No," Diego urged. "No, don't fall for it. Don't let the sirens' song lure us onto the rocks. We have to hold on to what we are."

"Can we do that," Hannah asked, "without children?"

The doubts Cecilia saw in so many of the loyalists over the course of the day filled her with alarm. None of the tricks and tactics their jailers had used over the months had undermined the group's unified resolve like this. The next time she was summoned to meet Churrlaya, she confronted him about it. "How dare you show us those scenes of the others when we were asleep, at our most vulnerable?"

The Frog Footman was unmoved by her anger. "We only took advantage of the dream communication you equipped yourselves to employ."

"Those dreams came from each other, and from a cyber we trusted. Invading our minds without consent is a violation! It's obscene!"

"It is unfamiliar to you because you have only learned to share thoughts to a limited extent. But all we did was allow you to witness your own crewmates' experiences. To see that they are safe and well. It was a more generous act than I believe you have earned, but I was overruled."

"Then why not just show us when we were awake? Why sneak it into our subconscious minds?"

"To allow you to feel its reality directly, beyond what mere images would convey. And to observe your reactions in their purest, most unfiltered form, in order to assess how deeply rooted your resistance to renunciation truly is."

"So you can brainwash us into losing that resistance! What's to stop you from reprogramming us outright? Plugging us into one of your consensus minds, changing our values and beliefs while we sleep?"

That got a rise out of Churrlaya. "Even if your brains had the neural architecture to permit it, that would be unconscionable," he insisted. "Forcing a new identity structure onto an unwilling subject is as traumatic as… as forcibly ripping away parts of their existing psyche. No *civilized* being would ever do such a thing."

His mention of his own trauma gave Cecilia pause, but she resisted showing it. "It's what you're doing to us bit by bit with every piece of our freedom and our dignity you strip away! Now you're even invading our very minds!"

Churrlaya hissed. "Why do you persist in seeing yourselves as the victims? How can you compare the moderate restrictions imposed on sixteen convicted felons to the permanent deaths of ninety thousand innocents?"

"What happened to them was an accident—and the result of your own bad choices. What you do to us is purposeful."

"And yet far less destructive in the absolute. It takes a special arrogance to see your suffering as greater."

Cecilia stepped closer, holding his gaze. "I don't. I recognize the magnitude of your loss. I hate that it happened, that it brought so much pain to all of us. I do not accept the blame for it, but if I could undo it somehow, I would. But all I *can* do is look out for the people who need me in the here and now."

"Does that not include the people we showed you in your dreams? Would their community not benefit from your presence? Would yours not benefit from reunion with them?"

"We absolutely would — if it were on *our* terms."

"That must be earned."

"By giving up what we are? Playacting as Chirrn, wearing your clothes?"

"Adding something new to your culture does not destroy it."

"It does when it's imposed. When there's a power imbalance. If you've studied Earth's history, you should know that."

A snort ruffled his snout cilia. "Earth's history is an undisciplined mess, with no healthy structure for cultural mediation and transition. That is why you have had so many wars and ethnic conflicts. It is hardly a model for civilized behavior."

Cecilia laughed. "'Civilized.' Honestly, Churrlaya, civilization is probably the greatest force of injustice in Earth history. Cities brought power hierarchies, concentration of wealth, the exploitation of the many for the good of the few. And that brought contempt for those deemed less 'civilized,' less worthy of consideration and rights. Being civilized is nothing to be proud of."

The ringlet-coiffed Chirrn tilted his head and studied her curiously. "Then why is it, Cecilia, that you take such pride in the city of your birth?"

She wouldn't let him trip her up that way. "Because it's *mine*. And nobody will ever take that away from me."

He held her gaze for a moment before answering. "That is what I used to believe. Yet here we are."

9

It all started so innocuously. Just another of Diana and R'nilinnath's secret excursions out of the compound. The two clandestine explorers had gotten away with it so often that others had begun going along with them on occasion.

And this time, Sita decided to join them. She'd grown tired of staying in the Arachnen compound, a prisoner of her own fear. She was a scientist, a xenobiologist in the midst of the xeno-est biology in human history, and she was wasting the opportunity because her instincts were overriding her intellect. Not to mention her growing concern that her fear would cost her Stephen. Oh yes, he was faithful, even more than she asked him to be. It didn't bother her—much—that so many of the unattached women kept coming on to Stephen, and she'd let him know he was allowed to respond. They'd all need to take multiple mates in the long term for the sake of genetic diversity; and besides, it was just the nature of a band of great apes like themselves for the females to gravitate around their alpha male. But Stephen, ever kind and generous, had so far declined to take advantage of the freedom she'd granted, insisting he was totally devoted to her and their baby. Still, Sita figured it was inevitable that he'd accept some of the other offers eventually, so the sensible thing to do was to define their relationship in a way that made allowances for it. That way, it wouldn't come down to a choice between her and someone else. She'd rather share him than lose him.

But she had become afraid that she would prove unworthy of keeping him. Stephen was so enthralled by the Chirrn, so excited to learn about their rich, ancient civilization and the broader galaxy they occupied, that she felt she could only keep growing apart from him so long as her fear paralyzed her. They'd maintained an uneasy peace since their big argument the week before (or rather, the one she'd tried unsuccessfully to get him to participate in), but things didn't seem to be getting any better. So Sita had realized it was time to make a choice. She had to decide once and for all whether to overcome her fear and stand by Stephen's side… or to step aside in favor of a worthier woman.

R'nilinnath's latest invitation had seemed to Sita like such a harmless first step. It was basically the equivalent of sneaking out to watch an adult movie. Or rather, a live sex show, for they would be attending a Chirrn "kiss dance" performance—as Arachne euphemistically translated it, since "oral sex dance" lacked the same elegance. Of course, intruding on the sexual customs of another culture could be a minefield, but R'nilinnath had assured her there would be no problem, and Sita's own studies and Kweli Ndege's backed that up. With their genitalia literally in their faces, Chirrn didn't exactly have the option of sexual modesty. And given how they metaphorically associated sex and speech, the two provinces of the tongue, a public sexual performance was considered effectively a form of public speaking: something that could be disquieting or annoying when performed extemporaneously in inappropriate contexts, but accepted and celebrated in the proper place and time. The kiss dance was apparently a popular form of entertainment, not some great secret they would be intruding upon— and it was too fascinating a scientific opportunity to pass up.

So it was that Sita now accompanied R'nilinnath, Diana, and Kweli ("What," the vivacious doctor had asked, "you think I'm gonna pass up a chance to watch alien porn?") in sneaking through the tunnels and back channels of Shilirrlal to reach the kiss dance venue. It was held at the hub, within the filligreed cylinder of shining strands that provided the habitat's light. Although the cylinder was nearly four hundred meters in radius and rotating with the rest of Shilirrlal, the air inside was somehow kept still (she'd heard Haim muttering something about a utility fog being involved) so that no Coriolis winds acted to push things outward, allowing everything within to hover in free fall. It was a popular center for recreation and exercise among the Shilirrlaln; Diana liked to call it "Coaxial Park." Many Seekers of the Zenith could also be found here at any given time; as their name for themselves suggested, the silvery avians were instinctively motivated to seek the high ground, their whole civilization being largely defined by the competition for physical and social altitude.

Sita was out of practice at freefall maneuvering, so she needed help from Diana and sometimes Nilly to move in the right direction through the vast open space as they dodged around the many Chirrn and Zenith engaged in various sports and performances, as well as the various free-floating structures that contained them—including a massive globular "swimming pool" held together purely by its own surface tension.

Sita was surprised when R'nilinnath led the three women right into the free-floating spherical lattice that was the arena for the dance, making no effort at concealment. "Won't they see us?" she asked.

"No harm if they do," Nilly told her. "It's been four *narrenn* since the trial. People have gotten used to seeing Arachnen around by now." Arachne no longer rendered Chirrn units into Earth equivalents, since by now the Arachnen should have memorized the new system and let go of their old planet-based measurements. But Sita still needed to remind herself that a *narrenn* was a Chirrn "month," just over five weeks.

"With Shilirrlaln supervisors," Diana countered. "Adult ones—no offense."

"No matter. If they see you here, they'll assume you're allowed. Just act like you belong. They'll have other things to watch anyway."

The dance was already in progress as they wended their way through the lattice to an open perch. The two performers, nude aside from mane jewelry, were joined open mouth to open mouth, their heads at right angles. Their mouths were adapted to fit together perfectly, their lips forming a watertight seal to contain the seminal fluid secreted from the male's tongue pores and absorbed through the female's. A Chirrn always had the same, essentially hermaphroditic anatomy throughout its life; only the hormonal expression and the size and activity of internal glands determined maleness or femaleness. Outwardly, a Chirrn's current sex was indicated by pheromonal cues no human could detect and by subtle differences in vocal timbre, body language, and dress that Sita was still learning to recognize. In modern times, with lives so long and procreation so rare, shifting sex was a voluntary, individual choice rather than part of a synchronized, group-wide cycle, but it was still a routine practice—something you did when you took a new lover and changed sex to match theirs, or simply when you felt like a change in your life, akin to getting a new job, or even just a makeover and a new wardrobe.

Sita wondered what sex or sexes the kiss dancers currently were, and if the spectators knew or cared. Their non-procreative relationships were usually same-sex by tradition, but there was no serious taboo against the alternative, and sex as performance could go either way—

although the show would be essentially the same for the spectators regardless of the performers' sexes. The pair wheeled slowly in freefall, held together only by their surprisingly strong labial seal and inter-locking side teeth while they performed elaborate, graceful motions with their arms, legs, and tails. Often they caressed one another or brought their bodies together into close embraces, only to swing apart again and rotate into a new joined position. Yet throughout it all, the seal between their mouths remained. Sita could only imagine what the subtle motions of their lips and jaws suggested about what their tongues were doing within. In its own way, the kiss dance was as private as it was explicit, the actual genital contact remaining unseen even though this was as overt as Chirrn sex could get. Sita found that rather wonderful.

"You guys are lucky," Kweli joked. "Get to first base and you've already made it home."

"Naw, that makes it too easy," Diana replied. "Where's the challenge?"

Nilly questioned the metaphor, and the conversation became a comic yet informative analysis of what constituted first, second, and third base among the Chirrn. It didn't help much that none of the women were American; while the metaphor had spread more globally than the sport it was derived from, they all had different understand-ings of what the "bases" meant in human intimate relations. But they finally decided that among the Chirrn, brushing the mane and neck with the muzzle was first base, brushing muzzles together was second, and caressing the body with lips and tongue was third. Entwining tails was like holding hands. "That's being at bat," Kweli declared.

"So, Nilly," Diana asked, "how many bases have you rounded with your boyfriend so far?"

R'nilinnath snorted and rolled her eyes in a way that somehow seemed closer to the human use of that gesture than the Chirrn. "Djayrulu is not my 'boyfriend.' He's just someone I've conducted some sexual experiments with. He let me get as far as 'third base' just once before I realized it wasn't as enjoyable as I'd hoped."

Diana pouted, disappointed that her effort to get her young friend shagged had stalled out. "Oh, it's not because he's a male, is it?"

"No, I actually somewhat enjoyed that part. It's a bit naughty." She hissed and waggled her tongue lewdly, and the women laughed. "But we weren't really connecting. I don't think he's as excited by novelty or difference as I am. He did make a sincere effort, really. He asked a lot of questions about my life, my work with the guild and the Arachnen. But he never seemed comfortable with it, or with me as a partner in sex play. So I broke it off. I guess I can wait a while longer to score a run to my home."

"Aw, that's a shame," Diana said, stroking R'nilinnath's mane. "Don't you have other options? Sex providers? Soligram porn?" She gestured toward the performers who were still writhing together in midair. "Dance classes?"

"Yes, of course. But that would feel like school, not play. I want to learn sex, but I want it to be for fun, with my friends. But most of my friends are human." Nilly looked Diana over. "I suppose I could take you up on that offer to experiment with interspecies sex. Your mouth is way too small to do it the normal way, but there must be some way to put our bodies together that feels good."

Sita could only listen in wonder and amusement as R'nilinnath, Diana, and Kweli began speculating about how Chirrn and human sexual anatomy could interact—clinically at first, but with increasing hilarity as they realized how absurd many of the proposed interactions would be. All three women were intrigued by what a Chirrn's tongue or tail tip could do for them, though some of their proposals for using both at once pushed the limits of the spinal flexibility that the kiss dancers were demonstrating. And Nilly could think of few ways that a human could pleasure a Chirrn in return, in the absence of any adequate counterpart for a Chirrn tongue. "I suppose a penis is close, but it's just so small and inanimate. Sucking one of my thumbs would be livelier." The women roared, grateful that their men weren't around to hear that. "Maybe a breast, if it were lactating. At least that's flexible." That made them whoop even louder.

It was all such harmless fun... until the women's laughter drew the attention of the crowd, many of whom did not react well. Sita had been so preoccupied by the actions of the performers that she'd failed to notice their coloration and build, or that of the majority of spectators.

They were Lesshchin.

The building anger of the Chirrn, their raised voices as they moved to surround her, triggered a flashback to terror and shock and agony. When Sita came back to reality, she found herself being pulled out of the arena at some speed, her wrist held gently but firmly in R'nilinnath's prehensile toes. Diana and Kweli were flanking her, watching the crowd. Protecting her in case they became violent.

And it had all been such harmless fun…

Djayrulu let the righteous outrage of the crowd surge through his mind, letting it amplify his own, which he then gladly fed back into the surge. How dare the murderers of Lesshchi come here to mock something beautiful and sacred? Could they not tolerate the idea of letting the survivors rebuild in peace? Must they continue to intrude on the life of the Chirrn and defile everything with their planetary filth?

What disgusted Djayrulu even more was the sight of R'nilinnath joining the humans in their mockery. He had known from their first meeting that she had been dirtied by her long association with the well-digging ferals, even seeking to emulate their reckless and corrupt sexuality by mating with the opposite sex for pleasure. Granted, he had felt an attraction to R'nilinnath, an excitement at meeting another Chirrn his own age and a prospective sex partner, but only at the potential she would have for eventually becoming male. He knew opposite-sex pleasure pairings had never been excluded among Chirrn in the past, but in the wake of Lesshchi's murder, Djayrulu could no longer see them as anything but human, anything but obscene. Any Chirrn who still practiced sex that way — let alone any Chirrn who eagerly invited a Lesshchin to partake in the obscenity — was committing an affront against the Lesshchin community, a betrayal of their grief and their anger.

Yet R'nilinnath's stupidity had granted Djayrulu a possible outlet for his rage, and now he was grateful for the foresight that had enabled him to seize it when it was offered. Pretending to play along with her sexual interest had given him access to the back channels R'nilinnath had used to circumvent the security on the Arachnen compound. The apprentice herself, supposedly one of the well-diggers' protectors, had led him right to their threshold, where he had been able to watch the filthy primitives as they had acted out the daily perversions that R'nilinnath found so entrancing. It had shocked him to see so many of their females gestating at once; at that rate of breeding, they would overrun Shilirrlal like vermin, ruining it more slowly, but just as thoroughly, as they had ruined Lesshchi.

At first, Djayrulu had lacked any specific plan for what to do with this access—only a recognition that it gave the Lesshchin an opportunity to exact the justice the Shilirrlaln mediators' guild had denied them. So he had contained his disgust and used the opportunity to watch and learn. He had pretended to enjoy his sex play with R'nilinnath (of course he hadn't *really* enjoyed it, he reassured himself), until she had sensed his aversion on some level and called it off. But he had learned enough, and then it was simply a matter of waiting for the right opportunity to take action.

Now, as he felt the fury of the kiss dance audience flow through him, a storm of anger and affront seeking a way to direct itself into action, Djayrulu knew his opportunity had come. Searching through the voices in his mind and ears for the ones calling most vehemently for direct and decisive action against the humans, he found them congregating around Vhehhal, a former guard aboard *Zhemhal*, the exploration craft that had hunted down and captured the human spacecraft following its assault on Lesshchi. Vhehhal had become something of a folk hero among those Lesshchin who refused to accept the Shilirrlaln's lenient verdict, for he had been the first to turn his people's righteous anger into direct action against the humans—more violent action than most Chirrn were comfortable with, perhaps, but surely a proportionate response to the unimaginable violence the well-diggers had inflicted on his home. Yet Captain Rillial had prevented him from solving the human problem then and there, and Vhehhal and his followers had been penalized and reassigned for their heroic action.

Ever since, Vhehhal had been quietly agitating in the more secluded channels of consensus—sharing his tale with those who believed he had been wronged for trying to do the right thing, making the case that all humans must be excluded from Chirrn society, and discussing possible ways to achieve that goal, legally or otherwise. Their discussions heretofore had been theoretical, but now Vhehhal was loudly rallying his followers, demanding immediate retaliation against the humans for their latest grievous assault on the Lesshchin community. Yet his rhetoric was disappointingly lacking in specifics. He and his followers were clear on what they wanted to do to the human childbearers, but without a means to circumvent the Shilirrlaln's protection of the Arachnen, there was little chance of turning their will into action.

It brought Djayrulu great satisfaction to be the one who could offer them a solution. "I know a way in to the Arachnen compound," he told Vhehhal once he made contact. "They think they can disrupt our precious speech with their own misbegotten words? Then let us echo their intrusion and silence every one of them."

Back in the safety of the Arachnen compound, L'chellin listened patiently as R'nilinnath and the women related their side of the story. Stephen and Diana sat with Sita, holding her hands, and Tarik Bahar did the same with Kweli. "They shouldn't have reacted that way," R'nilinnath insisted. "It was just a silly kiss dance."

L'chellin sighed through her nares. Her eyes swept across the humans as she chose her words. "I should have anticipated this. No Shilirrlaln has conceived a child in the three *narrayth* since you were born, R'nilinnath." Sita unthinkingly did the math, and smiled when she realized that Nilly wasn't so different from how she'd been at nineteen. "So your experience does not include the fact that kiss dances are not always recreational. The Lesshchin have lost so many. So they, like the Arachnen, have begun procreating." L'chellin's gaze took in the Arachnen as well as Nilly as she continued. "When actual procreation is involved, especially in a case like this, the dance becomes a solemn ritual, an affirmation of what human literature would call 'the Word made flesh.' The Lesshchin were in the process of restoring their diminished life. So when they felt that process was being mocked by some of the very ones who…"

"Who had taken it from them," Stephen finished.

"Yes."

R'nilinnath snorted in confusion. "I don't understand. The Arachnen completed their ordeal. They earned inclusion. Don't the Lesshchin know the rules?"

Nilly fell silent under a sharp glare from L'chellin. Tarik caught the exchange and focused his gaze on the mediator. "L'chellin? What is she talking about?"

L'chellin tapped her brow ridges several times, slowly. "You were supposed to deduce this on your own, as part of your transition," she said once her hands fell, one eye swiveling to glare at R'nilinnath. "To unlearn your human assumptions about the events of our contact and come to understand them from a Chirrn perspective. I only hope you are sufficiently included by now to understand."

The whitish-maned mediator proceeded to explain. A migratory people throughout their history, the Chirrn had always seen their identity and group affiliation as mutable, even before they had extended their minds into cyberspace. Most transitions were voluntary, and the system had been designed for millennia to accommodate them. But even so, it was not a simple matter to give up one consensus psychology and adopt a new one. The old psyche had to be deconstructed, its old affinities and habits of thought broken down, leaving it open to assimilate new ones. This bore added significance when the old identity was guilty of criminal acts. For the humans—the Arachnen—adoption into Chirrn society had been their required compensation for the lives they had inadvertently taken. That wasn't as callous as it sounded; lives were no mere commodity to the Chirrn, but as a society inclined by nature and tradition to dwell in modest-sized space habitats, they placed a premium on equilibrium. For anything that was taken, something must be given in return to preserve the delicate balance of existence. Those who took lives must pay by giving their own—ritually ending their old lives and adopting new lives dedicated to the community their old selves had wronged. The trial had not been a means of determining punishment, but the actual ordeal itself, the ritual by which the Arachnen had been cleansed of their sins, their old, tainted identity broken down so they could be prepared for their new, pristine identity as Shilirrlaln.

Stephen stared at L'chellin, looking betrayed. "You lied to us. Misrepresented the whole purpose of what you put us through."

"We tested you," L'chellin replied. "Please understand: it was always our intention to grant you adoption into our community once you had demonstrated true repentance. But your acceptance of your culpability and your commitment to making amends had to come from yourselves. You could not know the truth of the ordeal until you had transcended it through your own will and insight."

In the awkward silence that followed, Diana said, "I get it. Some of my mother's ancestors were Algonquians. Before the Europeans came and imposed their notion of 'tribes,' they were organized in bands and villages. Identity wasn't about lineage or ancestry, but only about where you lived, what community you identified with. Anyone could be adopted into any community." She flushed. "And not always by choice.

A band that lost members to disease or raids could raid a rival band to abduct replacements. And they'd be put through humiliating rituals, even torture, to break down their old sense of identity. But once they were adopted," Diana stressed, "even former mortal enemies were accepted freely as members of your own people. Sometimes they even took the names and identities of the dead they'd been abducted to replace."

"You do understand," L'chellin said. "Inclusion must be earned. Especially by those whose inclusion is repayment for lives they have taken."

"That's why you and Broadwing were involved in the trial," Sita went on. "Not lawyers or jurists, but mediators." They were the guild of Chirrn society responsible for negotiating between other guilds and estates, between habitats, between Chirrn and aliens. They managed the elaborate patterns of inclusion and exclusion that governed Chirrn psychology, derived from the interaction and competition of the small roving bands of their prehistoric ancestors. The modern Chirrn had modified it, civilized it, removed it from its origins in the planetary dirt, but the core of it remained.

"Yes. We oversaw your ordeal and adoption. Now we oversee your education, until you have matured enough to apply for membership in the guilds of your choice and contribute to society as fully integrated adults."

"But why didn't the Lesshchin see that?" R'nilinnath asked. "They saw the whole ordeal. They know the Arachnen passed."

"They passed the Shilirrlaln's test. But to many Lesshchin, the initial contact itself was the test."

Stephen lowered his head. "A test we failed."

"True. Many of the survivors, I fear, will never accept the Arachnen as their kith." Sita knew what that meant. They were Untouchables, to be shunned as totally as the overall Chirrn civilization shunned planet-dwellers.

R'nilinnath was deeply repentant, bending her knees so deeply that her elbows rested on the floor. "Sita... my failure has brought this suffering upon you."

Sita was touched. She reached down gingerly and patted Nilly's mane. "No, no, it wasn't your fault. You couldn't have known."

"But I could! I cleared it with Broadwing... I must have misunderstood his instructions about how to proceed."

"What?" Kweli asked. "I thought we were sneaking out."

Diana laughed loud and long. Untroubled by the others' scandalized glares, she controlled herself enough to say, "I knew it! Nilly, you and your 'secret' expeditions. You were working for the mediators the whole time!"

Chastened, R'nilinnath confirmed that the excursions had been authorized, a way of helping the Arachnen learn about their new world on their own terms, free of direct supervision, while still in a controlled enough way to keep them safe and within the limits of propriety. "But I should've realized there were still things *I* didn't know. And because I didn't, I offended the Lesshchin at the worst possible time. And I put you in danger, Sita. Now you'll never grant me inclusion!"

"No, Nilly, no." Moved by her sadness, Sita took the young Chirrn into her arms and held her for some time, assuring her that no harm had been done. For the first time, Sita felt no revulsion at being so close to a Chirrn. She was elated that she had finally conquered her fears.

That night, Sita was shocked awake by a loud crash and the familiar, terrifying sound of enraged Chirrn voices. This time, it was no nightmare. She was seized and pulled bodily from her bed, where she'd lain in Stephen's arms after an intense night of confident, newly energized lovemaking. The intruders knocked Stephen down with a shock stick before he could muster any resistance.

Bound hand and foot and dragged into the artificial night of the Arachnen compound, Sita saw dozens of Lesshchin, recognizable from their greenish hues and loose manes, dragging the other women from their homes as well. Some women were putting up good fights, particularly Diana, who unleashed all her Vanguardian strength in defense of her neighbors, single-handedly felling three of the Lesshchin until she was struck down from behind by vicious tail-swipes from two others. Sita could hear the crack of bone even from a distance.

As the assailants dragged all the bound women to the public square, Sita wondered where Arachne was. The Lesshchin must have found some way to shut down her avatar, just as they'd shut down the security drones and utility fog clouds that should have protected the community. Soon, all twenty women plus Rosario were in the square, and all eleven men, their arms and legs bound, were carried to the edges of the park and dropped there, facing the women, futilely screaming their names. Sita locked eyes with Stephen, feeling an incongruous need to comfort him with her gaze, to reassure him that this was not his fault.

The attackers gathered under the lights of the square, looming over the women, and Sita realized she recognized some of them. Their leader was Vhehhal, the azure-skinned, golden-maned guard who had nearly beaten her to death aboard *Zhemhal*. That did not surprise her or add much to her existing level of terror, since his was the face she still saw in nightmares like this. One or two were survivors who had testified at the trial. One had the mottled skin of a youth and a vivid pink mane — it could only be Djayrulu, the boy R'nilinnath had courted. Sita realized that must be how the Lesshchin had gained entry. Yet she felt no anger toward Nilly — only toward the Lesshchin youth for exploiting her innocence.

Vhehhal paced before the other Lesshchin and made a speech, but Sita's translation software wasn't activating and she hadn't studied the Lesshamh dialect. As far as she could tell, it was something about how those who had taken Chirrn lives had no right to fill the void with new, outsider lives.

Oh, Krishna… save my baby…

Maybe Krishna heard her, for Broadwing let out a mighty polyphonic shriek and soared into view overhead with silver wings spread wide, a resplendent sight even in the darkness. He had launched himself from his rooftop office in the administration complex. The Zenith mediator could only glide so far in this gravity and air density, but it was enough to paralyze the Lesshchin with fear. That was a justified response, for the Zenith were raptors.

Broadwing folded his wings and stooped on the Lesshchin who stood over the women, sending them scattering for safety. Vhehhal and Djayrulu both got away, but razor-sharp claws slashed the flesh of others who were too slow to retreat.

But Broadwing was outnumbered, and all too soon he sank low enough for the Lesshchin to snarl him in a utility-fog cloud that they sprayed around him, its spiderweb strands binding his wings and sending him tumbling down to the terraces below.

After that, there was no rescue. The Lesshchin closed in around her and the other women, ignoring the pleas in English and Portuguese and Chinese and Hindi and other languages they didn't want to understand. To the Chirrn, words were children of the mind, precious gifts yet grave responsibilities. But to the Lesshchin, the humans' words were bastards, as unworthy of inclusion in their minds as the humans were of inclusion in their world. The attackers allowed the women's words to die, unheard, unsustained.

And then they began to do the same to their other offspring.

Afterward, in the hospital, Sita wished this beating had been like the last. She wished that Vhehhal and the others had once again broken her arms, her legs, her skull. She wished they had simply killed her again. That would have been kinder than this. Instead, their kicks had been aimed entirely at one place. She had tried to curl up, to shield her womb with her limbs, but they had forced her body straight and then they had kicked and she could only weep and scream for her baby, for Stephen's baby…

For all the babies.

The Shilirrlaln police had arrived in force moments later, the security systems coming back online and restraining the Lesshchin en masse. Sita had prayed they were in time to save the others' fetuses. But she had felt no joy, no relief. Because she knew. She had felt the kicks crushing her insides. She had known nothing could survive that.

The doctors were able to save all but four of the sixteen pregnancies. Kweli Ndege, Justine Nguyen, and Oyama Kazuko had lost theirs as well as Sita. Justine's had been a frozen embryo, so only Stephen, Tarik, and Ravinder had to share their grief.

But Sita could take no comfort in that. As she lay in her hospital bed with Stephen weeping by her side, she wondered if she'd ever feel happy — or safe — again.

And she wondered if she would lose him now. If he would blame her for triggering the attack. She knew it was irrational, but she would understand if he blamed her.

After all, she blamed herself.

10

"IT IS THE JUDGMENT OF THIS TRIBUNAL," HEAD TRIBUNE DJ'VHERETH announced to the attackers who stood before him, "that you shall hereby be summarily excluded from all estates, leagues, and guilds, whether Lesshchin or Shilirrlaln, effective immediately. Your current mental states are toxic to the community and to yourselves, and thus you must be quarantined from consensus until such time as you regain the ability to function as constructive members of society. To that end, the tribunal instructs that you be remanded to the remedial crèche on the Vhethil habitat, where you shall receive psychological therapy and re-education until you are ready to assume adult identities and allegiances once more."

R'nilinnath was gratified that the verdict had been reached so quickly, without the need for a lengthy trial that would force the grieving Arachnen to relive the horrifying trauma they had endured. The Lesshchin attackers, Djayrulu included, had made no attempt to deny their action; indeed, they had boasted of it proudly as an act of justice, even recorded their firsthand experiences of the assault for later upload to the Lesshchin consensus. With no dispute over the facts of the case, no trial had been necessary, only the determination of how to deal with the criminals.

She drummed her feet in vindictive satisfaction as she watched Djayrulu's reaction to his fate being sealed—along with the rest of the fetus-killing mob that he had led into the Arachnen compound thanks to R'nilinnath's inability to keep her tongue in her mouth. It would be a long time before she stopped blaming herself for that; someone had to, since everyone else was so determined to reassure her and pretend it wasn't her fault. But she knew she would atone in time by continuing to fulfill her responsibilities to the Arachnen—just doing it better from now on.

And she did agree with Sita, L'chellin, and the others that the greater part of the blame lay with Djayrulu for using and manipulating her. That was why this verdict was so satisfying to hear. Djayrulu had latched onto the humans' different sexuality as the excuse for his hatred, the perceived affront against Lesshchin procreation as the excuse for his assault on human procreation. Now, sentenced to a remedial crèche in a habitat parsecs from Shilirrlal, he would be reset into an asexual juvenile, losing his maleness before he'd even had a chance to do much of anything with it. It was a case of what her Arachnen friends would call "poetic justice."

Still, just watching the verdict handed down was not enough. She needed to confront Djayrulu eye to eye. Fortunately, her status as a mediator for the wronged parties enabled her to request a private meeting with the Lesshchin youth before he was taken away to Vhethil.

"How could you do it?" she asked the pink-maned male once they were alone in a conference room. "How could you kill babies?"

Djayrulu glared at her sullenly. "They weren't even people yet. Just clumps of cells."

"It was for their mothers to decide when they were people. Not you. Their mothers wanted them, loved them for the people they would become. You had no right to take that away from them."

"And they had no right to take my friends, my guildmates, my home away from me!"

"They didn't do that on purpose! You did! You *chose* to become a murderer!" She opened her mouth and gave a loud, aggressive hiss. "You call them savages, but you're much worse than they are. At least they have the excuse of being feral." She snorted. "Maybe the Unrenounced are right and we're no better after all."

"The humans made us this way! They tore away pieces of us, left us broken and scarred. Whatever we did to them, they brought it on themselves. They deserved it! No matter how much of my Lesshchin voice they strip away, no matter how much they rebuild my identity, I will strive to cling to that certainty. I will never let it change."

R'nilinnath's gaze rolled outward, away from his smug face. Her anger faded, replaced only by sadness and pity as she realized how immature he truly was. All things changed. A Chirrn who did not grow and evolve from lifetime to lifetime might as well not be alive. Djayrulu was too young to understand that. R'nilinnath should have been too, but shepherding the Arachnen through their transition had taught her the lesson early. She hoped that the experts at Vhethil could help him learn it as well—that he would not become as stagnant and trapped as the Unrenounced.

She gave a slow, wistful sigh through her nares. "I used to find tales of violence and death so thrilling. The excitement of the taboo. Now I know how horrible they really are. I owe that to you, and I'm glad you'll be punished for it."

Djayrulu turned away. "Go wallow in the dirt with your disgusting human friends. Maybe you'll find a way to have sex with them after all. I can't see any true Chirrn ever wanting you."

With a frustrated hiss, R'nilinnath turned to go. But she paused in the doorway. "A bit of advice: When they let you be an adult again, go female. Maybe if you learn what it's like to be different things, you won't be so afraid of difference anymore."

The Lesshchin youth was puzzled. "But… changing sex is what Chirrn are supposed to do."

"Yes. That's exactly what I mean."

Stephen was still numb when he met with the mediators and Shilirrlaln officials half a *narruvh* after the attack. Two nights had passed in the Arachnen compound in that time, but Stephen had gotten no sleep, afraid of further attacks, afraid of his dreams. He wasn't sure if he was numb now because he'd run out of grief and rage or because he'd simply shut his emotions down, unable to bear them anymore.

He surveyed the scene clinically, as well as he could through his haze of fatigue. The meeting was held in the conference room of the Arachnen compound's administration center, for the Shilirrlaln government had doubts about the humans' safety if they were allowed out. The windows, normally looking out upon the recreation center and residential terraces below, had been opaqued to spare the occupants from the visual reminder of the attack site. Within the room was a low, clear-surfaced table flanked by perches for Chirrn and seats for humans. Broadwing had his own V-shaped perch on which he rested his ventral keel. L'chellin was there as well; the mediators flanked Stephen, perhaps feeling they were protecting him. Beyond them were two Shilirrlaln officials, Ch'millin and Mh'resshelel, who were hard to tell apart; one was stocky and deep purple, the other rounder and midnight blue, but both had similarly coiffed white manes, perhaps a symbol of their position. Stephen wasn't completely certain which was which.

On the opposite side of the table sat Rillial. It was the first time Stephen had seen the Lesshchin representative since the trial. Rillial had become a leading voice in the adopted Lesshchin community, due to her past roles as a starship captain and the prosecutor in the humans' trial/ordeal. Apparently, spaceship command crews were a collegium of the Mediators' guild, necessarily since they must deal with outsiders, which was why Rillial had played the key role for the Lesshchin in the trial. Now, she spoke for her people in this instance as well. (And she was still a she. According to Broadwing, she was now pregnant, though with no outward sign Stephen could detect. She had participated in an earlier kiss dance a *narrenn* before, and her embryo was developing quite well. Distantly, with cold detachment, Stephen hated her for it.)

"The guilty parties have been summarily excluded from society," Rillial reported to the white-manes, her eyes rolling to take in every sight but that of the human opposite her. "They have been remanded to the remedial crèche on Vhethil, and will undergo psychological examination and evaluation to determine the best course of treatment."

"Treatment?" Stephen asked. "Then you propose this atrocity was the result of mental illness?"

Rillial's eyes finally came to focus on him. Her posture remained nonconfrontational, even apologetic. "You humans speak of 'losing one's mind.' These Lesshchin actually did lose portions of their minds in the cataclysm—instantly, traumatically, with no transitional process. They are indeed mentally damaged.

"Even beyond that, the circumstances my people face are... extraordinary. We are an orderly species. We have a clear sense of propriety. But deprive us of order, of balance, of consensus... place us in a situation that robs us of every anchor we rely on... and definitions of propriety can become... aberrant."

"Propriety." Stephen spoke slowly, his throat tight. "You suggest that this act of infanticide can somehow be defined as... proper."

Rillial fidgeted. "No one here disputes the immorality of what was done to your offspring. But we are not a feral race. We—" Under the sharp glares from the administrators, Rillial clamped down on herself. After a moment, she started again. "My people's—the assailants' actions were not an act of unthinking rage like the initial assault. In its own way, this was a calculated choice, one that the assailants were able to rationalize as a necessary one. In the minds of many Lesshchin, the crew of *Arachne* earned automatic and irrevocable exclusion by destroying our habitat, killing our kith and our shared mentalities. To them, allowing the humans inclusion in Chirrn society is a gross impropriety. Allowing them to procreate is an even greater one. They saw this as an injustice that the authorities refused to address. And so they deemed it necessary to address it themselves."

"By murdering defenseless babies."

Rillial sighed slowly through her nares. "In their calculations, it was not murder. Most of your gestating embryos have not yet developed significant brain activity. By your own laws, termination is still a permissible option before that benchmark."

"Not by force. Not by beating them in the belly."

"Naturally not. I merely attempt to account for their rationalization."

Stephen stared hard at her. "Six decades ago, on Earth, my little brother was shot down in the street by people who did not believe he had the right to have been born. The authorities had no shortage of rationalizations for that act."

L'chellin leaned toward him. "It was not the authorities who attacked you."

"Not this time," he said, still keeping his gaze on Rillial. "I really want to believe you intend to treat us justly, L'chellin, but you have to prove it through your actions, not just your words."

"Then let me suggest an action," Rillial said. Her eyes rolled outward to focus independently on the administrators flanking her. "It may take a lifetime or more for many of the Lesshchin to heal from this trauma. All of the assailants lost nearly their entire kith groups. All have lost portions of who they were before, whether through consensus-memory loss or organic brain damage. And there are many more who have endured as much." Her eyes rolled back to Stephen. "You may not be aware… since Shilirrlal is the closest habitat to Lesshchi, the worst cases were relocated here, while most of the rest migrated to more distant habitats such as Vhethil. No other population of relocated Lesshchin has suffered worse trauma and psychological damage than those here."

Again she took in the whole room. "So I cannot guarantee that there will be no more incidents like this. I do not believe it will ever be possible for Lesshchin and Arachnen to interact peacefully as equal members of Shilirrlaln society."

"Segregation?" Stephen asked. "That's never worked that well in human history."

"But quarantine has. Both our peoples have much healing to do before we can attempt to interact in a healthy way."

He realized he could not refute Rillial's point. At the moment, he never wanted to see a Lesshchin again. "Then do you propose that we leave, or you do?"

"Is either even feasible?" L'chellin asked, tilting her head quizzically.

Ch'millin (or was it Mh'resshelel?) leaned forward. "Too many Lesshchin have come too far in their transitions already. Psychological factors aside, they have already become increasingly integrated into Shilirrlaln guilds and sectors."

"But the Arachnen are still under the probationary custody of the Mediators' guild," L'chellin countered. "We are responsible for their care and socialization. We cannot simply abrogate that duty, and it would disrupt the process of inclusion if the Arachnen were forced to start again under another guild's care."

"There is a way to surmount this." Broadwing raised his head on its long, flexible neck, calling for the floor by gaining height over the others. "Given that Shilirrlal's population has abruptly increased by more than an eighth, some groups have put forth the possibility of a migration to ease the pressure. I propose that the guild spearhead such a migration, accompanied by the Arachnen."

"Migration?" Stephen asked.

"To found a new habitat," Broadwing explained. "If Chirrn habitats grow too crowded, they may build a second habitat that splits from the first, as Lesshchi did from Shilirrlal three yanarredj ago. But such branched communities remain close for yanarr as they slowly drift apart. Sometimes, this is not enough to satisfy the Chirrn's desire for change or separation. Their ancient instinct is for a splinter group to travel far from its birth community and start fresh in a new territory. With superluminal travel, they are able to do this. Periodically they will split off smaller groups that migrate elsewhere in the galaxy to found new habitats. It is a valve for population pressures, or a result of social schisms. In this instance, both parameters would apply."

"I think that having the Arachnen join a migration is a well-born proposal," the midnight-blue administrator said. "It would allow them to repay their debt directly by contributing to the construction of a new habitat."

"As a balance for their role in destroying one," the purple one agreed.

"Let us not deliver our words prematurely," L'chellin cautioned. "Do not forget that the Arachnen are the wronged party now. They should not be made to feel like exiles in response to a crime of which they were the victims."

"But this is not a punishment," Broadwing said. "It is protection. More, it is an opportunity!" Broadwing began to shake his head subtly, enough to make his diffraction-grating crests shimmer with colors—a Zenith gesture for drawing attention or asserting dominance. Rainbow reflections danced across the opaqued windows. "Stephen, you formed your expedition to establish a colony on a new planet. I know that many of your kith have felt frustrated at being unable to fulfill this purpose. So now I offer the opportunity to establish a whole new world! You would not only be fulfilling your debt to Chirrn society; you would be fulfilling your own ambition as well! What leader could resist?"

Stephen closed his eyes, letting the Zenith mediator's enthusiasm wash over him until the words trailed off. After a silence, he spoke. "There's no need to convince me. L'chellin, I appreciate your defense. You've been a good friend to the Arachnen. But it's not necessary. After… what happened here… I think we would all be glad to leave this place forever. I will need to discuss it with the others, though."

"Of course," L'chellin said.

"One other thing. The Unrenounced should come too." The others were silent, surprised. "Rillial said it herself—she can't guarantee their safety so long as they're on the same habitat with Lesshchin. And they deserve the opportunity to complete their ordeal and join the rest of the Arachnen. Surely it's not your intention to leave them confined forever."

"Indeed not," Purple assured him. "Mh'resshelel?"

"Indeed not," Midnight Blue affirmed. "However, ensuring security during the migration would be challenging."

"Bullshit." The others stared at the untranslated term, though L'chellin's tail quivered a bit in mild amusement. "You've had us easily at your mercy from the beginning. Except for the initial incident, my people have always been on the receiving end, helpless to resist." He sighed, gathering himself. "Apologies. I don't… blame the Shilirrlaln for what happened. I… don't blame most of the Lesshchin either," he added, though he couldn't meet Rillial's eyes. "But it would be dishonest to pretend my people are anything but powerless next to yours. There's no chance the Unrenounced could pose a security risk." To be perfectly honest with himself, he couldn't even blame the assailants. Rillial was right; they would never have been driven to this act if Stephen himself hadn't brought *Arachne* out here. If he'd never brought Sita into space, never put her in this situation, then she wouldn't be huddled in their home right now, grieving for their daughter, too terrified to walk out the door.

"My reference," Mh'resshelel said pointedly, "was to the risk of renounced Arachnen communicating with the Unrenounced. And perhaps allowing certain ill-conceived words to be spoken to them."

"Giving away the truth about the ordeal, you mean. Invalidating their own repentance."

"Yes."

"All this time and you still don't trust us."

"Stephen," Rillial said, catching his gaze and holding it. "After what occurred this *narruvh*… I can no longer fully trust my own kith. We are all capable of abandoning civilized rules in extreme circumstances. We are all capable… of tragic error.

"You should join the migration, and the Unrenounced should join you." Rillial's breath ruffled her nares. "I had contemplated migrating myself, but now I know I will not. I cannot leave my people, and they need stability now. As for you…" She was silent for a moment. "The Chirrn have always understood the value of starting a new life, letting go of the past. This is your chance to do the same. Not as passive beings assimilated into a vaster, overpowering society… but as founders of a new civilization, one whose form you may help to define."

Stephen contemplated her words for a long moment. To put his past behind him… to start anew and try to forget… he wanted nothing more. But how could he trust himself to make the right choice for everyone else?

He missed Cecilia more than he had in months. He would give much to have her strength and clarity to draw on again. But he feared she would only say that she'd warned him of something like this. Then again, maybe he should have listened to her all along. Maybe if they'd listened to each other, they could have found a better option at the beginning.

As it was, though, circumstances seemed to be making the choice for him. Stephen could see no alternative but to trust the Chirrn. He had felt betrayed at first by the revelation of the secrets they had kept during the ordeal, but he'd come to understand the cultural reasons behind them and to recognize that the ultimate intent was constructive. And L'chellin had done right by him these past four *narrenn*. Now even Rillial seemed to be offering him new hope. For the second time, the Chirrn were showing him more mercy than he deserved.

"Where would we be going?" he finally asked.

"To a new life," L'chellin said. "Far away from your past. Beyond that, does it really matter where?"

After Stephen left to bring the proposal to his kith, Mh'resshelel turned to Broadwing. "Do you suggest a migration to the Antispinward Void, as has been mooted in the cloud?"

"Yes," the Zenith replied. "The Alliance needs a stronger presence there."

"Agreed," Ch'millin said. "But is it wise to send the Arachnen to a frontier zone? A migration party there will be far less able to ward off… outside interest… than we are here. If the humans are included in that migration, it will make it far more difficult to regulate their access to… certain historical information. We are still unsure how they might react to that information. Despite their renunciation, they still have sentimental ties to Earth. If they should learn the whole truth…"

"They will no doubt spy that truth once they gain sufficient height in society," Broadwing countered. "If they do not gain that perspective from outside parties, then they will from our own historical records. I say it is better to relocate them much farther from Earth, to reduce the chances of any form of contact with their larger population. In the interim, we can direct their learning process, shape how they interpret the information we cannot avoid having them discover."

L'chellin's tail twitched angrily. "I must point out," she said, "that the Arachnen have made their transition in good faith. They have renounced their planetary ties. They are our kith now. Is it right to hide the truths of history from our kith?"

"They are still young," Mh'resshelel said. "The young can be impetuous, unwise. And as Captain Rillial pointed out, even the best of us can behave unpredictably in extreme times such as these."

"Indeed," Ch'millin added, supporting his mate as always. "At least, we should let the event come in its own time and not deliberately hasten its gestation."

"Agreed," Mh'resshelel predictably affirmed.

L'chellin found it a fair conclusion in principle. Still, she had her doubts. The Lesshchin's actions had undermined the trust that L'chellin had worked carefully to build in the Arachnen. Without that trust, Stephen and his kith might have trouble understanding or accepting certain historical truths. If they perceived those truths as secrets the Chirrn had deliberately concealed, it could trigger a backlash, a reassertion of their Earthly identity.

L'chellin would just have to do what she could to prepare them. Maybe creating a new world would sufficiently diminish their loyalty to their old one. Or maybe, once they learned enough of galactic history, they would understand why the Chirrn's ancient choice had been necessary — regardless of its consequences to humanity.

11

CHURRLAYA HAD BEEN AFRAID TO APPROACH R'HHENEVH WITH HIS request, for he knew how it would wrench at his womb to see her look at him with disappointment, with betrayal. He could only hope to get through it as quickly as possible and try to make her understand. Still, the alpha's reaction was just as painful as he'd feared. "You would leave us, Churrlaya? You would leave me?"

"My alpha." He placed his hands upon hers. "I only hope you can smell how much I long to stay with you. I would not ask this if it were not something I profoundly needed."

She did not reject his touch, but did not reciprocate it either. "To continue overseeing the Unrenounced? To continue seeking retribution? You would do this after what happened? Do you think they would allow a Lesshchin to join the Arachnen now?"

His eyes reflexively jerked away. He forced them back inward to meet hers. "It is because of what happened that I must do this. It made me listen to what I had done before… and made me ashamed. I allowed Cecilia… I allowed the humans to provoke me into descending to their level. Just as they provoked… the others."

Churrlaya turned aside, paced across the room in small hops. "I thought we were so far beyond the ferals. That we had transcended our animal drives and could never sink to savagery."

"The ones who assaulted the Arachnen did not think it was savagery. Their actions were calculated."

"That is exactly what distresses me. That Chirrn could think themselves civilized and responsible, yet still prove no better than a ground-dweller… a feral…"

"They were damaged, incomplete."

"So am I!" He gave a low, bitter snuffle, shaking his head. The ringlets of his mane brushed across his shoulders. "We cannot allow this of ourselves. We cannot let ourselves be dragged down by these humans."

R'hhenevh hopped forward, placing her hands on his forearms. "Then you should not go with them. Do not let them continue to entrap you. Not while you remain incomplete and vulnerable."

"No, Nevh. That cannot be the solution. I cannot conquer this by retreating from it! The hate, the violence—the potential is in *me*. Here in my own skull," he added, tapping his head. "I cannot resolve it simply by merging with your consensus. I would contaminate it with my own weakness.

"No, I must face them—just my own inner self, alone. I must prove to them—and to myself—that no matter how they provoke me, I will remain proper and dutiful, and I will not succumb to animal aggression. I must show them, Nevh. The actions of… the excluded ones… will make it too easy for them to believe that we are beasts after all, that they need have no shame at killing us. I must show them we are better than that. I must show them what the Lesshchin truly are, in our innermost selves, and what we are not." He moved closer, placing his hands on her knees. "Please, Nevh. It is the only way I can find balance."

R'hhenevh pondered for a time, then sighed and rubbed her neck against his. "It will not be easy to convince them to let a Lesshchin retain power over the humans."

His left eye swiveled to gaze closely into hers as they rubbed necks. "I *was* a Lesshchin. Maybe I still am. But now I am your kith. You are my alpha. And my duty is to you. I swear I will not give you any reason for shame."

"Oh, but I will miss you, Laya! If only I were not alpha and could come with you."

He cherished the fantasy, but he said, "No. You have too many other kith to love. You have your duties too."

With a long, shaky tongue-hiss, R'hhenevh pulled his head down by the ridges and ground her muzzle against his. He inhaled her scent as deeply as he could, hoping he could hold it within him forever.

"Come," she said, pulling him aside to a quiet corner and giving a seductive yawn. "Let us speak sweet words before we part."

The sight of *Arachne*'s habitat and cargo modules being maneuvered inside the outer ring of a Chirrn space vessel gave Stephen an uneasy sense of *déjà vu*. Of course, it was different this time; Stephen was not inside a module but watching from the shipyard observation gallery, and the ring was actually a warp cage in retracted configuration. The modules were being connected with pressurized tubes for easy passage between them, making the whole thing look something like a gerbil habitat.

This particular design of warp cage was not equipped with AG generation as a standard feature, for it was a small, relatively low-powered cage designed for short intrasystem hops (though still requiring substantial Hawking radiation from the artificial microsingularity that powered it). The Chirrn had little use for intrasystem travel as a rule, but they sometimes used this design for conducting mining and research expeditions to the star systems or rogue planets that their habitats occasionally drifted past. "The lack of gravity should not be a concern," L'chellin explained to the watching Arachnen, "for the trip should take slightly less than two *narruvh*."

"So eight, nine days?" Diana Thorne interpreted. The statuesque engineer was here to assist in the reinstallation of Arachne's brain inside her erstwhile body, a procedure that several other Arachnen were here to observe along with L'chellin, Broadwing, and R'nilinnath. "About how far will we be traveling in that time?"

"Initially, less than two hundred parsecs. Before we can build the new habitat, we will need to obtain a supply of programmable quark matter."

Diana shook her bronze-haired head. "Playing around with degenerate matter. I still don't trust that stuff. If anything goes wrong and it breaks free of containment, it could tear through anything."

"Galactic civilization has used PQM safely for many millennia, Diana."

"But there is a nonzero risk of failure."

The mediator gave Diana what Haim called her "Jewish mother" look. "And travel aboard *Arachne* in her sailship form carried a nonzero risk of collision or lethal irradiation. Nonzero risks can still be manageable risks."

"And we all know how well that kind of thinking turns out," Stephen said. The bitterness of his tone put a damper on the conversation.

There had been a time when Stephen would have never made such a conversational *faux pas*. He had always chosen his words so carefully, used them so deftly to befriend, to appeal, to inspire, to persuade, to reassure, to romance. The key had been to empathize with others, to understand their needs and outlooks, then tailor his words to fit. But these days, he lacked the strength to face his own emotions, let alone take on the burdens of others.

And he knew he was letting Sita down. Just when she had been mastering her fear and beginning to live her life again, she had been the victim of yet another Lesshchin assault, one that had taken the life within her. He wasn't sure whether she was more unwilling to face the Chirrn or herself at this point; she seemed to have equal blame and anger for both. Her prayers and meditations brought her no comfort. Stephen wanted to find that perfect thing to say that would reach through the new walls she'd built around herself and let him connect with her. But he had no idea how to begin.

It wasn't just that he lacked the words within himself. He'd come to realize that, although he loved Sita Bhatiani ardently, he didn't really know her very well. Their love was based on a shared dream, one of which he remembered nothing but emotion and vivid erotic sensation. Their time together had been defined by passion, as they'd done their best to recreate the intensity of those dream experiences, and by awkward distance, as he urged her to join him in embracing Shilirrlal and she urged him to spend more time in the compound with her. The passion had remained strong, but the awkwardness had been increasing over time. He had striven to commit to her more fully, refusing the advances of other women, but she had reacted to it as misguided symbolism, a sidebar to the deeper commitment that she truly sought and he could not give her.

So now, in their time of mutual need, he had too little insight into what Sita needed now. She had retreated more and more within herself, and all that his attempts at comfort had evoked was the request to be left by herself. Never permanently; she still shared his table and his bed, had fierce, wordless sex with him as a mutual distraction, and sometimes wept on his shoulder through the night. But if he tried to talk to her about her grief, about their relationship, about anything substantial and emotional, she pulled away. So he had learned to stop trying, closing himself off just as much.

Trapped in a cage, he thought, staring out the gallery window at his transformed ship. *Sita and I are in nested cages, bound together but held apart.* The hell of it was, at the moment, he was comfortable with that. There was less chance of either of them being hurt still more… even if the tradeoff was that they were slower to heal.

One of Yonchon's drones fluttered back from an errand and settled in its perch on Yonchon's back. After a moment to process the report it beamed into Yonchon's receptor cilia, the Ryohoch spoke. "Preparations have been completed for the brain."

Haim nodded to Diana, who carefully took hold of the shoebox-sized unit that held Arachne's consciousness—along with the shielding, cooling systems, energy collectors, backup memory, and diagnostic and repair interfaces for the centimeters-wide wisp of optical tendrils and Bose-Einstein condensate that housed the thoughts, dreams, and desires of the expedition's youngest but wisest member. "Don't worry, honey," Diana whispered to the unit, cradling it like a child in her muscular arms. "I'll take good care of you." Stephen quashed the uncharitable wish that Diana could have been as diligent in protecting his own baby. He knew she'd only recently regained her full mobility after the injuries she'd sustained while attempting to do just that, so his resentment was undeserved. But that didn't change the fact that she'd failed.

"Come on, Stephen, let's get out there," the chief engineer said.

Stephen stared out the window. "You go on, Haim. I'd just be in the way."

"What?" Haim floated over and touched his shoulder, turning Stephen to face him. "Stephen, you have to be there. You were there when we first put her in. When we christened her. Even when the Chirrn took her out and put her in the compound."

"Nothing but symbolic gestures."

"Well, that's the point! This is a big moment. *Arachne*'s going to be whole again, and better than ever. You *have* to be there!"

After a moment, Stephen sighed. "All right. Lead the way."

Haim was displeased at his lack of enthusiasm, but took what he could get. As he and Diana glided out, though, L'chellin intercepted Stephen and said, "May I share words with you?"

Stephen quirked a brow. "That's a flattering invitation, Chell, but I don't think they've sorted out the logistics yet."

"Do not deflect. It confuses me when you use humor at times when you are clearly not amused."

Stephen almost replied, *If you thought that was funny, no wonder you're confused.* But his friend's stern gaze stopped him. L'chellin's sex change may have mellowed her, but she was still the stern, fastidious Chirrn he remembered from the Arachnen's ordeal. Why the Chirrn thought that quality made her a good cross-cultural mediator was one of the enduring mysteries of their psychology. On the other hand, it seemed to work for L'chellin. Stephen had come to value her frank, no-nonsense attitude, just as he had once valued Cecilia's more rough-hewn, big-sister version of same. So Stephen just spread his hands receptively and waited for her to continue.

"I appreciate the depth of your grief, my friend," L'chellin told him. "A child is a rare and precious thing to a Chirrn. I once thought, given how often you procreate, that humans would take them for granted. But in you, in Sita, in the others, I see that any words to that effect would be stillborn." She flicked her eyes away and back at Stephen's wince. "Forgive my choice of words. The idiomatic sense is more clearly distinct in Shilirramh."

"It's all right. It's not as though I wouldn't have been thinking about it without a reminder."

"And that is the problem," L'chellin said. "I understand your preoccupation, but you must think of other things as well. This ceremony is important to your community. You should show them it is important to you."

"That presupposes that it *is* important to me. It's sticking a box into a hole."

"No. I only said you should show them that it is. Yours is a hierarchical species, not unlike ours. Your kith group resonates with its alpha. Your mood influences their mood. Even without sharing external processors, you have your own form of gestalt thinking.

"The Arachnen are about to undertake a challenging transition. They are about to travel farther than any human has ever travelled, into regions where they will face life forms, technologies, and phenomena far beyond their experience. It is a daunting prospect. They need to begin this transition with a spirit of optimism. As the word begets the deed, as the tongue begets the life, so the onset of a transition begets its outcome. The Arachnen must be motivated to embrace the challenge and adventure that lie ahead. They must believe they can and will succeed.

"And it will be your words that beget their deeds. So you must go to them, Stephen Jacobs-Wong of *Arachne*, and you must give them words well-conceived and well-born, words they will embrace and nurture into strong, noble deeds."

L'chellin clasped his shoulder. "I know it is hard for you to find the seed for such words within your tongue. Your first issue fell unspoken, and so you fear to take responsibility for siring further speech. But if your words are well-formed, then it does not matter if they have true seed within them. If your auditors believe in your words, they will give them substance and be self-fertilized."

Stephen parsed the metaphors, which were growing increasingly disgusting the more L'chellin piled them on. "The key is sincerity," he interpreted. "If you can fake that, you've got it made."

L'chellin's brow furrowed. "You humans have a knack for paradox."

"We'd better. We need it often enough." He let L'chellin lead him out, committing himself to the task of delivering an inspiring speech for the Arachnen. But he wasn't sure how many noble words he could muster.

On top of which, he realized there was one other speech he would soon have to make.

After Stephen finished speaking to the loyalists, Cecilia stared at him in shock for a time before stepping forward to confront him. "How can you even propose such a thing after what they did to your child? You should be joining us, not the other way around!" Her gaze, and her words, took in Tarik Bahar, who stood silently at Stephen's side.

She could see the haunted, agonized look in Stephen's eyes, and it hurt her to rage against him on his own behalf. But he stayed calm and faced her squarely, maintaining that air of levelheaded, accessible reasonability that had made him so good at persuading others to sign on for his wild schemes. "Believe me, Cecilia, I've already had this argument with myself. I've already thought of everything you could say to me—and other things you mercifully have no context for imagining.

"But there's no us and them here. *Some* Lesshchin did terrible things to my wife, my daughter, my neighbors. But it's because of the quick response of Shilirrlaln security and the tireless efforts of Shilirrlaln doctors that my wife and most of our unborn children are still alive."

"Alive to serve their purposes," Diego Narvaez spat, pushing forward. "Alive to labor as slaves building their plantations!" Tarik shifted his weight forward and threw Diego a warning look, his commanding presence sufficing to halt Diego's advance. On Stephen's other side, the Chirrn arbiter L'chellin, apparently still responsible for handling the human prisoners' case, observed warily. At a faint gesture from Cecilia, Diego sullenly retreated. Not that the utility fog would have let him get away with anything anyway. Even so, Churrlaya's reptilian gaze took everything in from the corner where he stood, and Cecilia wondered what punishment he would cook up for Diego.

"Don't, Diego," Stephen warned. "That's just rhetoric to you, but it's family history to me. If I thought this were anything like that, I'd be with you already.

"What I see instead is an opportunity. A chance to do the thing we dedicated our lives to doing: building a new world, a new home. We'll be building it with new partners, in a new way, true. But can any of us truly say that we knew what to expect, what the rest of our lives would be like, when we set out on this expedition?"

"Pretty words, Stephen," Cecilia said. "But they gloss over what you were *forced* to give up. What you're now asking us to give up."

"A symbolic allegiance."

"A symbol of submission! A surrender of our humanity!"

"An admission of remorse. A commitment to make amends for our mistakes."

"We made no mistakes! It was the Chirrn who chose to hide themselves."

"Does that mean it's all right to walk away from a disaster of such magnitude? To do nothing to help its victims rebuild?" He shook his head. "The Cecilia LoCarno I knew would never have looked for excuses to avoid responsibility."

He turned to address the rest. "And that's the key. Responsibility isn't a burden to be avoided, a penalty to be shied from. It's a choice we make for ourselves, and a commitment we make to others. We are all here because we felt a responsibility to humanity, to future generations. We welcomed that responsibility. We embraced it.

"And along the way, we made every possible effort to take responsibility for other living things as well. We planned our colonization in a way that would be responsible to the indigenous life of Cybele. We designed our ship with our responsibility to other starfaring civilizations in mind, even though we had no reason to expect we'd encounter any."

His voice still addressed the group, but his eyes came back to Cecilia. "So isn't it paradoxical to say that our choice to take responsibility for the well-being of other life forms gives us an excuse to renounce any responsibility to them now? If we had come across the Chirrn as victims of a natural disaster, say, would we walk away because it wasn't our problem? Or would we try to help, as a way of being good neighbors in the galactic community, and simply because it was the right thing to do?"

"If they hadn't forced us," Amrita Dhillon said. "If they hadn't put us through torture and humiliation and a mockery of a trial. If they hadn't—" She broke off, seeing the look in Stephen's eyes. He knew perfectly well what they had done. *What a few of them did,* a small voice in Cecilia's head corrected her. It sounded a lot like Stephen's.

"Look," her former partner said after a long moment. "Nobody denies that what's happened here is tragic for everyone involved. Nobody wanted any of this to happen. But this is the reality we have to live with. What matters is what we decide to do with it next.

"Whether you renounce or not, you'll be taken with us to found the new colony. There will no longer be any realistic chance of seeing Solsys or Cybele again. I don't deny the cost of that. But you wouldn't be safe here with the Lesshchin, and you deserve the chance to join the rest of us again.

"But I see no reason to force you to wait. And I'd prefer to have all of you by my side once again." He looked around. "You heard the offer. If you want to join us, if you want to help us build a new world and new families, just step up here beside me."

Beside him, L'chellin stepped forward. "And by so doing, you will be officially recognized as renouncing all ties to any planetary civilization."

Cecilia was grateful to the supercilious kangaroo for the reminder of what was at stake. Sometimes Stephen's tongue could be too golden for others' good. Not that she would have needed any reminder. She knew where her roots were planted.

Diego's hardliners stood firm as well. But most of the others were lost in thought, contemplating the offer. Amrita stared at them in disbelief. "You're not actually considering this?"

Cecilia touched her arm, caught her gaze. "Amrita… don't. This has to be everyone's own choice, or our loyalty means nothing." She noted Churrlaya's gaze upon her, wondering why he suddenly seemed so curious.

No one moved for a moment. But then Shuai Bingbing stepped forward, stopping briefly by Cecilia. "I'm sorry, Captain," she said. "But Justine needs me now. Whatever mistakes we've both made… she's still my wife. I need to be with her more than I need to live on a planet."

Sergei Mazunov and Hannah Errgang were the next to step forward. "Sorry, Captain," the grizzled Russian said. "But we know the dreams were real now. The life they're living—it's better than this. They do have freedom… because they have family."

"That's all Sergei and I ever needed," Hannah added. "I don't know what we're clinging to anymore." They moved away, hand in hand as always.

Then Ichiba Nobuo faced her with apology in his eyes. "You can come with us, Cecilia," he said. "There's no point in this anymore. It's time to let go of our illusions and submit to the inevitable."

"You're asking me to give up who I am," she told him.

The look of disappointment in his eyes was palpable. "I stayed with you before because I believed in you. Now… I see you getting in deeper with Diego and his group, indulging their hate… and I think you've already lost who you are."

She slapped his face. The fog only impeded them from attacking Chirrn, not each other. "That is the one thing they will never take from me."

Nobuo walked away sadly, and three more soon followed him in turn. Cecilia closed her eyes to compose herself, afraid to open them again for fear that when she did, her group would be reduced to just her and Diego's band. She had to believe there were more reasons than their petty xenophobia for remaining loyal to Earth and humanity. There had to be.

Then she heard a welcome voice, soft and close at hand. "Captain?"

She smiled and opened her eyes. "Tarik. Good to see you." She hugged him, whispered urgently in his ear. "Do you have an escape plan?"

He pulled back to stare at her, confused. "Captain?"

"Come on," she hissed. "We'll be in ships again. There'll be confusion, chaos. We may never have a better chance."

"Captain… I'm sorry, but this is our best chance. Not to try to flee; that's not an option. Their ships are… amazing, but I'm years from comprehending how they work. I wouldn't want to anyway. This is what we wanted, Cecilia. To build a new home for our children. Not to become fugitives in an alien galaxy."

She stared at him, devastated. "You swore to me you would never renounce your duty."

"And I haven't. My duty is to our crew, Captain. *All* of it. And the best decision for our crew is to reunite, to join the Chirrn migration as partners."

"Tarik, they *killed* your son."

He winced, but stood firm in his resolve. "All the more reason I can't leave Kweli now. She needs us — all of us — to help her through this."

"Then we need to fight them together."

"We can't! Violence only breeds more violence. History has taught us all that, if we don't let ourselves forget. And if we take arms against the Chirrn, we're guaranteed to lose. Kweli is barely coping as it is. I can't put her through any more loss. She needs peace if she's to heal."

"So you've sold out like the rest. Renounced your allegiance to Earth."

"My only allegiances are to Allah, my wife, and my crew."

"What about Allah, then? If you've forsworn all ties to Earth, how can you pray to Mecca? How can you honor Allah's will?"

"Facing Mecca is only a way to focus thought and devotion. When we cannot face Mecca, we simply focus within, where Allah truly resides." He clasped her shoulder. "And Allah asks nothing more from us than we are able to give."

She glared daggers at him. "Then for your sake, I'm glad your god has such low standards."

He turned his back on her and stalked away, and she hated herself for her words.

Mercifully, no one else defected to the Chirrn side. In addition to Diego's foursome, she still had Nik Zacharias, Kahina Amrouche, Ibrahim al-Bakri, and Zhao Changkun. She belatedly hoped Ibrahim hadn't heard her final words to Tarik; the geneticist's faith was the only thing that kept him a loyalist, since he, unlike Tarik, saw submission to the Chirrn as a betrayal of his submission to Allah. At this point, she needed to keep every ally she had.

And things would be tense in the remaining group. Only nine loyalists now remained; from an even third of the colonists (not counting Arachne), they were down to under a fifth. And the offer to defect was still open. What if Nik switched sides and left the loyalists without a human doctor? What if Kahina left and six men had only two women to compete for? Cecilia would have to work harder to hold the group together — to keep them strong.

So she ignored the sound of Stephen calling her name. Maybe he hoped to make one more attempt to persuade her; maybe he just wanted to say goodbye, or even that he understood. She would welcome that, if they could be alone and have one of their classic knockdown, epic, cappuccino-fueled arguments. Maybe then he could actually make her understand what the hell was going through his head, so that maybe, for once, she could talk him out of it. But they were not alone, and she had obligations to the remaining loyalists. So she turned toward her group, away from Stephen, and stood firm until he and the other defectors finally left.

"What is wrong with them?" Amrita exclaimed after Churrlaya and the other Chirrn had left them alone. "With Bingbing? She wants to have children? Didn't she hear what they said? They're killing our children in the womb!"

"We cannot let that sin go unpunished," Diego said with quiet, ferocious resolve. "We have to find those murderous animals and make them pay."

"You heard Stephen," Nik Zacharias said. "They've already been sentenced and sent away. They're long gone."

"You think the other Lesshchin are any less to blame? We'll exact justice from any of them we can find! Starting with the Frog Footman!"

Nik scoffed. "You think we could possibly manage such a thing? There's the small matter of escaping first."

"That may be doable." Cecilia's firm, simple statement captured the whole group's attention. "Despite what Tarik believes, I still think the confusion of the move will be our best chance to seize a ship. If we make a break and offer the others a chance, some of them will probably come back to us. Possibly some who have knowledge of Chirrn technology and could help us operate the ship."

"And then just flee?" Diego challenged. "No, we have to avenge our unborn."

"As Nik says, escaping comes first. The rest will follow, once we know what our options are." She placed a supportive hand on Diego's shoulder, another on Amrita's. "Trust me—I'm as full of rage as you are. But we have to aim it wisely if we want it to have the greatest effect."

After holding her eyes for a moment, Diego nodded. The nine remaining loyalists then began to make their plans. They all knew escape would be a long shot, even with the opening offered by the move. Given the Chirrn's proven capacity for deadly violence, they knew they might not all survive it. But they had never had a more powerful incentive than they had now.

12

"I SHOULD BE GLAD TO BE LEAVING THIS PLACE," SITA BHATIANI SAID AS she stared out the window of Oyama Kazuko's residence. The dwelling was on the highest terrace, affording a fine view of the entire Arachnen compound — including portions of the public square. Even after weeks of therapy, it was still painful to catch even a glimpse of that place.

"I *am* glad that I'll be away from the Lesshchin at last," she went on. "Dozens of parsecs away, where none of them can ever hurt us again. But still…"

Kazuko spoke gently, knowing what Sita wanted to say. "But even away from the Lesshchin, we'll still be surrounded by Chirrn, by aliens. It's hard not to be afraid."

Sita winced. "But that's just it. I'm a xenobiologist! I'm about to go out into a vast universe filled with aliens, the very thing I've dreamt of my whole life… and now they're just a reminder of what… what happened."

She turned to take in the other three women's faces, seeking what understanding she could find in their eyes. These past few weeks, while the bulk of the Arachnen had focused on the ongoing preparations for the migration, Sita had closed herself off from the outside world, accepting visits only from other humans, and spending most of her time in the company of Kweli, Kazuko, and Justine, bonding through their mutual grief. As the four of them had talked and commiserated, though, Sita had come to realize that each of them had been affected differently by their loss. Justine was angry at herself and wracked with guilt, blaming herself for coming on the expedition or for not staying with Bingbing among the Unrenounced — when she wasn't furious at Diana Thorne for failing to protect her baby, at the Lesshchin for their brutality, or at Arachne for destroying Lesshchi in the first place.

Having Bingbing by her side again helped her sometimes, but they'd had their share of angry dust-ups over their reciprocal infidelities—which, in an odd way, seemed to be doing Justine some good.

Kweli, conversely, was grief-stricken and devastated by her bereavement. She had been well into her second trimester, farther along than any of the others, and she and Tarik had already decided on a name for their son and built an elaborate nursery for little Mehmet. The couple loved each other and their son deeply, and their sorrow was wrenching to behold—although at least they found comfort in each other, the tragedy binding them closer than ever.

Kazuko was the one who had held them all together. The fiftyish administrator had miscarried before, as a member of a Martian group marriage. Though she did not feel sexual arousal, Kazuko had valued her duty as a colonist to procreate, and had borne the group three children; yet the effects of Martian gravity and environmental chemistry on fetal development were still not fully understood, so she had lost two more. While that didn't make her current tragedy any easier to bear, it gave her an enviable confidence that she would work through it and move on. She had been a bastion of strength for the other three, and for her platonic co-parent Ravinder.

Now, though, Kazuko sharpened her gaze upon Sita. "You still avoid talking about it. 'What happened.' Sita, you need to be able to face it to get through it." Sita was reminded that the older woman was not just a grieving mother, but an experienced lawyer as well.

With a sigh, Sita returned to her armchair. "It's not that I'm not willing to talk about my feelings. At least, I'm willing with you." She could not yet bring herself to talk about it with Stephen, for some part of her blamed him for bringing her here in the first place. She knew how irrational that was, and she knew he grieved as much as she did; but her pain was just too difficult to bring under control.

And she was starting to realize why. "The thing is... I'm not even sure how to describe what my feelings are. I've been through them all at least briefly—despair, guilt, anger, hate, denial, panic, the whole lot. But it all feels... unfocused. Directionless."

Kweli stared at her in shock. "Unfocused? There's only one thing to focus on. The life you lost. The baby inside you."

Bristling at the doctor's tone, feeling judged, Sita snapped, "Well, it's easy for you, innit? Mehmet was already a person to you and Tarik. You had his whole life planned out." Tears filled Kweli's eyes, making Sita feel ashamed. "Look, I'm sorry. I didn't mean to—oh, it's daft."

"Go on," Kazuko said. "This sounds like something you need to get off your chest."

"It's just… Stephen and I hadn't even picked a name for our girl. It seems like a trivial thing, but somehow, it matters. It's like… like I'm not sure who it is I'm grieving for. The more time passes, the more the baby feels like, like some abstract ideal rather than a person. And I feel awful for thinking that way about her."

Kweli reached out to take her hand, the tension past. "No, honey, it's okay. You… you should feel grateful you have that distance."

"There's nothing for you to be ashamed of," Kazuko assured her. "Every woman's experience with miscarriage is unique. We all react in our own ways, and there's no wrong thing to feel."

"Isn't there? What about…" She swallowed. "Sometimes… I almost feel relieved that my pregnancy is over. Not that I—I mean, I cherished her, that little life growing inside me. But… but it didn't bring me and Stephen closer, like I hoped it would. It just seemed to drive a wedge between us. I was afraid his preoccupation with the Chirrn, with the community and helping us adjust, would keep him from sharing in the whole parenting experience with me.

"No, more than that—I was afraid I wasn't ready to be a wife and mother. That I let Stephen rush me into it because he was so eager to begin building the community. Not that I blame him for any of it, not really," she insisted. "It just caused me as much bother as joy. Sometimes more. I don't really know if I would've been any good as a mum, or how our marriage would've weathered it."

"Have you tried talking to Stephen about this?" Kazuko asked. "Maybe if you heard his side of it—"

"Oh, I've heard it, all right. Our Stephen, he's not one to keep his thoughts to himself, is he now? I've been there for him, listened to him. I know how much the burden weighs on him. But it… it doesn't feel like *our* burden. It's just part of his larger burden of guilt about everything that's happened in the past seven months. And I just can't bring myself to pile my own troubles on top of his." She gave a humorless laugh. "I'm afraid losing our baby didn't bring us any closer than conceiving her did."

She shot to her feet again and began pacing. "Arrh, it's just so bloody frustrating! I don't bloody know what to feel or what to do about what I'm feeling. I don't know where to direct my thoughts or my emotions. It's all just such a jumble."

"Just tell me what you're feeling right now," Kazuko said, watching her pinball around the living room. "What do you want to do?"

"I just want to get away!" she cried. "To bloody go somewhere. Get away from all this emptiness inside me. But I can't very well get away from that, now can I?"

Kazuko rose and intercepted Sita, clasping her shoulders and bringing her to a halt. "Then maybe you need something to fill it with. Some new goal or purpose. Maybe what you need is something to head *toward*, not to run from." She smiled. "You've been keeping your distance from the migration preparations because of all the Chirrn you'd have to deal with. But maybe you should think about what else is out there waiting for us at the other end of the trip."

After the session, Sita strolled through the compound, pondering what Kazuko had said. The more she considered it, the more right it sounded. The overwhelming pain and guilt of her loss had crowded out the questions that had filled her mind before, questions about the knowledge the Chirrn were still holding back. Once she began to contemplate those questions again, the fervor to find the answers began to enter her mind once more. Where had the Chirrn come from? How had they allied with the Zenith and the Ryohoch? What greater galactic civilization lay beyond Shilirrlal, beyond the other Chirrn habitats in local space? Did most sophonts abandon planetary living, and if so, how many other ways had they found to adapt to space?

Finding the answers to those questions would require coming out of her self-enforced seclusion. It would mean having to interact with Chirrn and other large, scary aliens, but it seemed likely that her interactions would continue to be primarily with L'chellin, R'nilinnath, and Broadwing, and she could cope with them. She was even grateful to Broadwing for his valiant attempt to save her, and she found it easy to admire his iridescent beauty.

Most of all, Sita simply needed to gain a sense of movement. Engaging with the fleet preparations would help her feel that she was making progress toward leaving the ordeals of Shilirrlal behind her at last. Ordeals like…

With a start, Sita realized that her distracted stroll through the compound had brought her unerringly to the central square—nearly to the very spot where she and the other mothers had been dragged that horrible night. Her throat tightened at the sight… but no panic attack came. She stared at the grass and soil that must still have some of her blood soaked into it… and it did not reach out and grab her. It was just there. Just a place, like any other place.

Perhaps it was the knowledge that she would soon be leaving this place behind forever that made it bearable to face it. Or perhaps she simply needed to know she could face it and not be harmed. If she could stand up to the worst memory of her life without being broken any further, then she could stand up to anything the future threw at her.

Sita turned away from the square and began to climb the stairs toward the admin center, where the plans for the Arachnen's departure were being finalized. It was long past time she started pulling her weight around here.

At last, the wait was over. The assembly of the migration fleet was complete and the crews were beginning to board. Yet Churrlaya was more anxious than ever when the time came to move the remaining Unrenounced to the ship that would be transporting them—a separate ship from *Arachne*, for their sentence still kept them apart. Shilirrlal's shipyard/dock complex was not conducive to the use of security fog; its wide-open construction left insufficient anchor points for the fog's restraining filaments, and the high-intensity fields and discharges emitted by the dockworkers' tools and apparatus could disrupt the fog's internal signals. Thus, if the Unrenounced intended to attempt an escape, this would be their prime opportunity.

The Shilirrlaln security personnel insisted his concern was unwarranted, pointing out that the Unrenounced were still enswathed in restraint garments and under careful guard. They dismissed his fear as a vestige of his Lesshchin reflex of exclusion and hostility toward the Arachnen. But Churrlaya's fear of an escape came from a very different attitude toward the Unrenounced: respect. Now that he had recognized how his anger toward the humans had blinded him, he had begun to reassess his conversations with them over the past months. The more he thought about their words—at least those of Cecilia and other relatively rational ones such as Nikolos and Nobuo—the more appreciation he gained for the raw intelligence, shrewdness, and determination that had allowed the human species to survive its own excesses and reach the stars with no outside assistance. He could never forget nor entirely forgive their recklessness in doing so, for it had taken Simisshen, Marellel, and so many others from him, along with a sizeable piece of himself. But he saw so much potential in them to learn from their mistakes and embrace the strengths that had brought them so far on their own. He was optimistic that he could win many of them over in time.

Still, so long as the humans remained Unrenounced, their drive and ingenuity posed sufficient danger to set Churrlaya's bristles aquiver. He had urged Cecilia to keep her people in line for their own protection (and that of the dock workers, though he didn't mention that), but she had made no promises.

As it turned out, Churrlaya's fears were warranted. The escape attempt occurred while the Unrenounced, clad in their restraint coveralls, were being escorted into the freefall shipyard where the migration fleet was undergoing final preparations for launch. Their guards and accompanying security drones led them down a wide, lattice-framed tubular gangway toward the warp vessel where they would be confined during the journey, while Stephen Jacobs-Wong and a few other Arachnen, along with their Shilirrlaln mediators, watched from the nearby gangway leading to the newly warp-caged *Arachne*. This was the closest contact the Unrenounced would be allowed to have with their fellow humans until they chose to renounce planetary allegiance.

The attempt began with the most unlikely person—Evan, who was usually petrified with fear at the very sight of a nonterrestrial sophont. As the prisoners were escorted past a refitting team consisting of three Zenith, two Chirrn, and two Ryohoch, Evan gaped at them in shock and soon appeared to succumb to a panic attack. The vitals feed from the young human's coveralls verified that the attack was genuine. He began to struggle, attempting to break from the group, and naturally his coverall locked to restrict his movement. But Evan continued to struggle, forcing the coverall to tighten still further until he had difficulty breathing. He bounced off the gangway framework and back toward the refitting team that so terrified him, his pulse continuing to race to a dangerous degree.

Nikolos, the Unrenounced physician, demanded to be escorted to Evan's side. "You've got to get him out of there, he's dying!" Churrlaya granted it, aware that it would take too long to summon one of the

Arachnen's doctors, let alone to waive the restrictions on contact between the groups. Nik hastened to pull his arms and torso free of his coverall as soon as it was unlocked. Upon reaching Evan, the physician began to strip off that human's coverall as well. Churrlaya took hold of Evan and gripped the gangway's framework with his feet for leverage. Rolling one eye, he saw that Stephen was drifting closer out of concern.

Once Nik had Evan fully stripped, he swiftly examined the younger male. "Tachycardia, borderline asphyxia… this isn't good. I need more help. *Human* help, you're not trained for this. I need James."

Churrlaya stared. "You ask me to trust—"

"He's the only other one with paramedic training! Without equipment, we have to do this just right or we'll lose Evan!"

After a moment's thought, Churrlaya acceded, releasing James's coverall as well.

That was his mistake. Moments after James had shed his upper coverall and reached their position, he struck out at Churrlaya, dazing him. For a moment, Churrlaya only perceived consensus, and he sent an alert into it. When his sensory awareness cleared several moments later, he saw that James had stolen a plasma torch from the work crew and was brandishing it as a weapon, waving it madly at the crew to force them into retreat. Nik had seized a bladed tool and was using it to cut the others free of their coveralls. As tools, not weapons, the implements were not security-coded for their owners' use only.

Through the active consensus link, Churrlaya could see through Mediator L'chellin's eyes that Stephen had launched himself from the edge of *Arachne*'s gangway, crying "No! Stop!" as he flew toward the site of the struggle. L'chellin and the others had been too surprised to restrain him in time. "James Oates, stand down!"

It was fortunate that these humans could only look in one direction at a time. Once James's attention was diverted by Stephen's cries, Churrlaya began to swing around, preparing to club James with his tail. Defense guild Shilirrlaln were already offering to share awareness with him, to let him draw on their physical-combat training so they could guide his body to defend itself. But before he had the opportunity, he was tackled by another human, one so massive it had to be Diego. The impact knocked the breath from him.

"You don't order us anymore!" James cried at Stephen, struggling free of the rest of his coverall to prepare for the larger male's approach. He turned up the plasma torch and thrust it toward Stephen as he drew near, forcing the Arachnen leader to twist desperately and cover his face with his arms, even though he had no way of altering his trajectory. Fortunately, James was either not trying to damage Stephen or too clumsy with the torch to succeed. But Stephen's defensive position left him helpless to avoid a collision with the gangway's frame. The pain incapacitated him long enough for James to get a firm grip around the taller man's torso with one hand and brandish the torch before him with the other, guaranteeing his passivity.

Through L'chellin's senses, Churrlaya could see Sita Bhatiani crying out for Stephen and attempting to launch herself after him. Tarik Bahar and Broadwing held her arms to restrain her, but she fought against them so fiercely that even those two large individuals had difficulty maintaining a grip on her diminutive frame. "Oates! Fuck you, you wanker! Don't you dare hurt him, you sodding…" She carried on in terminology that the translation protocols struggled to interpret.

Before long, all nine Unrenounced had shed their coveralls and floated naked in the gangway. Several now brandished cutting tools, and others were using the remains of their coveralls to bind Churrlaya and their other guards, stretching their legs back to tie them to their tails. Ibrahim al-Bakri assisted James in binding Stephen's limbs as well. Evan was recovered now, hanging behind an armed Amrita Dhillon rather than participating actively in the escape, but grinning nonetheless. Livid bruises were starting to form across his body from his struggles against the coverall. Churrlaya realized that he had deliberately given into his impulse to panic, fighting the coverall and forcing it to tighten dangerously to create a convincing appearance of a medical crisis. The rest had been lies to get the Chirrn off their guard. Churrlaya felt much disappointment in Nikolos; he had always seemed one of the more reasonable Unrenounced until now.

But his disappointment in Cecilia was greater, for she was at the head of the pack, brandishing a plasma torch of her own. "Tell them to take us to *Arachne*," she told Churrlaya. "You were crew, right? You probably know how to fly one of these things."

"It won't work," Churrlaya told her. Even as he spoke, the guild defenders floated into view, readying their restraint-gel sprayers. Amrita began searching through the work crew's abandoned equipment, no doubt seeking potential countermeasures. This was a matter of some concern; while the mining engineer was no doubt unfamiliar with the more advanced aspects of Chirrn technology, much of it relied on universal physical and chemical principles that were well within human comprehension.

Churrlaya felt Diego's forearm tighten around his neck, and a cutting tool pressed against his flesh. "Back off or this one dies!" the human cried. Through consensus, Churrlaya advised them to hold off for the moment.

"Don't do this, Cecilia," Stephen said. "We're not prisoners. We *want* this."

"You've just lost the will to fight back," Cecilia countered. "Once we offer the crew *real* freedom, they'll come back to us."

"Freedom to do what? To be fugitives?"

"To avenge our unborn, for one thing!" Diego cried. "To punish the beasts that killed them!"

"They've already faced justice, Diego. At Chirrn hands."

"A travesty, like the rest of their justice! We'll exact real retribution!"

"Against whom? The killers are parsecs away. You'll never find them."

Diego pressed the cutting tool harder against Churrlaya's throat. "We have one of their kind right here. If you want it to live so much, then tell it to take us to *Arachne*. Tell the others to stand down."

"Do you really think you can end my life with that, Diego?" Churrlaya strove to bear only calm words, though there was little calm within him to spawn them from. "I have taken extra precautions since the disaster. Even if you did enough damage to halt the oxygen supply to my brain, what memories I do not have stored in the cloud are backed up in genetic-medium storage throughout my bloodstream. Any damage could be repaired and I would be whole again. At worst, you could spill enough of my blood to leave my memories incomplete. But it would be no worse than the losses I have already sustained, and there are many things — things you humans are responsible for — that I would happily forget. So you have nothing to threaten me with."

The blade dug in, and globules of blood spilled out into the air. The pain was startlingly intense, and his biofeedback systems seemed to take forever to dull it to a bearable level. "How about pain? You creatures have no comprehension of the cruelty the human imagination is capable of." Nearby, Amrita looked up from her inventory and grinned, fingers tightening against her own cutting blade as if imagining she were the one cutting Churrlaya's throat. He doubted she would be able to exercise as much restraint as Diego had.

Churrlaya strove for calm. "I can simply transfer the focus of my awareness into the network — cut off sensory input from my body. You can do nothing with lasting consequences." He spoke to convince himself as much as Diego. "So I will not tell the guards to back down. My duty is to ensure that you remain within your proscribed bounds."

Cecilia looked indecisive. Amrita did not. "It wants to bleed, then let it bleed! We can fight our way to the ship!" She brandished a container from the work crew's supplies. "Look here. Graphene polymer. Seven cases of it. And there's a solvent here I can use to break it down into graphene oxide. How about that, Frog?" she asked Churrlaya. "You think you can survive a firebomb?"

"That's insanely dangerous, Amrita," Cecilia warned. "There are ships all around us. There's no telling what kind of high-energy systems or power cells they have. It could start a chain reaction. Not to mention the overpressure hazard in an enclosed space! You could kill us all!"

"It's worth the risk," Diego said. "I bet even their medicine can only reverse death if it's caught soon enough — and if the body isn't blown to bits. We do enough damage to this place and they'll have to make saving lives their priority. It will give us a chance to get away in the confusion. And damage these ships enough to prevent them from following us." Amrita nodded and went to work. Churrlaya hoped she knew what she was doing well enough to avoid immolating herself — or the people around her.

"And if we go down, we at least get revenge on a few hundred of them!" James cried, waving his plasma torch recklessly.

"Does that include me, James?" Stephen gasped as the torch waved dangerously near his face. "Does that include *Arachne*, and all the humans that are aboard her? The people who only want to get away from the cycle of violence and raise their families in peace? You talk about revenge — but *we're* the ones who are grieving! Not you! You don't get to use our loss as an excuse for killing more people!"

"James, take it easy!" Cecilia ordered. "Remember, he's as much a wronged party here as we are." Catching Stephen's gaze, she went on. "Don't you get it, Stephen? Your loss is our loss. We're still in this together. Or we should be. Don't you see? This is our one chance at a life on our own terms. Just help us get aboard *Arachne* and we won't have to hurt anyone. The threat should be enough."

"Not everyone gets a life on their own terms, Cecilia. People like you and James, you were born to privilege. You take your entitlement for granted, kick and scream at any compromise. Me, I grew up under *real* oppression. I had to learn to adapt and compromise, to make the most of the limited degrees of freedom I had. Even once I got out, even once I built my empire, I was always aware that there were still limits I had to live under."

"Are you kidding? You became one of the richest people on Earth!"

"By learning how to work within the limits. The limits of economic reality, of what law and politics made possible… and most of all, the limits on what I could do without hurting other people, or imposing unfair limits on them. One advantage of growing up the way I did was that I never learned to feel entitled. I never assumed that what I wanted gave me an excuse to mistreat others. Because I never forgot how that felt from the other end.

"Cecilia, we are living under limitations, yes. But that's the compromise we have to make to be responsible members of a larger community and to repay our enormous debt to it. That's not slavery or oppression — it's just a lack of unfettered entitlement. I guarantee you I can tell the difference.

"What a few damaged, hateful Lesshchin did to our women, our babies — it was intolerable. But it has been dealt with. Their hate has been contained. But if you do this — if you repay their violence with more violence — then you're just unleashing that hate again, and giving them more reason to turn it back on us again.

"That's the part people never seem to think of when they want revenge — that the other side is no different. What I see in your faces now is the same thing I saw in the faces of the Lesshchin who killed my baby. The same sense that their revenge was justified, that they were the only victims." He locked eyes with Cecilia, Amrita, and Diego in turn. "The same mistaken belief that their action would end the cycle instead of perpetuating it."

"It's not about hate or revenge, Stephen!" Cecilia insisted. "It's about doing what's necessary for the freedom of our crew. Maybe you're right, maybe we do owe the Chirrn something, but this is not the way to repay it. The fact that you can tell me you don't feel oppressed so soon after they killed your baby is inconceivable to me. You say these Chirrn aren't responsible for the crimes of those others, but they enforce the conditions that leave us vulnerable to that kind of attack. And as long as they define us as criminals, there *will* be more attacks. Maybe you're just too deep in grief to see it, but we have hope now. We have one shot, however slim, of getting away from those unsafe conditions."

"That is exactly what we are doing," Churrlaya told her. "Starting again, building a new community of Shilirrlaln and Arachnen, with the past left behind."

"Shut up!" Diego's blade cut into Churrlaya's flesh once again, reopening the nearly-closed wound. Even with pain suppression engaged, the violation of his bodily integrity was a shocking indignity. "We won't let you animals decide our fate for us anymore!"

"Do it, Diego!" Amrita cried. She held up a pair of completed incendiary devices, which would require only a spark to set them off. "No more talk — let's start doing damage!"

Stephen kept his eyes locked on Cecilia's. "Are you really so sure this isn't about hate?"

James brought the torch flame closer to Stephen's face again. "Shut up! You're no better than the other animals!"

"Stop!" Cecilia cried. Visibly reaching a decision, she released her own torch, which deactivated itself. "Stand down, all of you! I won't have a bloodbath."

"But Captain—"

"You heard me! This is not who we are!"

"Cecilia, we must," Diego said. "Don't lose your resolve now. We have to make them fear us!"

"And what good would that do us, when they have so much more power?"

"Guerrillas have toppled the powerful before."

"When they've had support! When they've been on their home turf and known the lay of the land. We make them hate and fear us and we just make things worse for ourselves. A clean escape is one thing, but we give them a massacre and they'll hunt us down like dogs." She locked eyes with Diego. "This isn't the way. There's no strategy behind it, only rage and wounded pride. That's not who we're supposed to be. That's not who we'll ever become so long as I'm captain. So stand... down."

For a disturbingly long moment, Churrlaya wasn't sure Diego would still heed her authority. More of the Unrenounced seemed to be in his favor than hers at the moment. James even looked as if he was willing to cut his own captain down after first killing Stephen — though Churrlaya knew he would act only if Diego gave the word.

But with a heavy sigh, Diego finally released his grip on Churrlaya. At his signal—not Cecilia's—the others lowered their weapons and allowed the security team to move in and restrain them. Amrita was the last to back down, staring at Cecilia with hatred as she finally released her grip on the makeshift explosives, which the security personnel hastened to take in hand.

Once Stephen recovered his breath, he made his way to Cecilia's side and clasped her shoulders. "Thank you, my friend. I knew there was still hope for you."

His words only made her tense, resisting a further embrace. "I've never lost sight of my humanity and I never will. I won't sink to the level of the monsters who took your baby from you. I'm grateful to you for reminding us all how important that is. I still admire you for that integrity. And I am truly sorry for your loss, and Tarik's, and the others'." She pushed his hands away. "But I still think you've lost your way, Stephen. You've let guilt and grief overcome you, and you've surrendered to a punishment you think you deserve, without seeing how much it costs you. It may not be like the atrocities you grew up with in Florida, but there are subtler forms of oppression. And I hope that, someday, for your future children's sake, you will recognize that."

Seeing that there was nothing more he could say to change her mind, Stephen turned away, blinking moisture from his eyes, and grabbed hold of the gangway frame, giving an angry thrust to push himself back toward *Arachne*. The guards moved in to secure Cecilia's arms behind her back and guide her toward the confinement ship along with the other Unrenounced. A medic took Churrlaya in hand and began to administer regen gel to his neck, asking questions to assess his physical and emotional state. Churrlaya assigned a portion of his mind to go through the motions of responding. Yet he remained preoccupied with the realization that winning over the rest of the Unrenounced would be a greater challenge than he had hoped.

Few of the other loyalists would meet Cecilia's eyes as they were escorted into the prison ship and given new confinement coveralls. Even Nik and Kahina only gave her ambivalent glances, as if relieved that violence had been avoided but embittered at her decision to abort their escape attempt. Cecilia was sure, though, that the others would all see the wisdom of her decision once they'd had time to calm down.

Well, fairly sure. Hopeful, at least.

She stared at the coverall, reluctant to put it back on and resume a life where her every movement was confined and monitored. It had felt so good to float completely free for a brief while.

"May I assist you?" Startled out of her reverie, she turned to see Churrlaya waiting behind her.

"Not on your life," she answered, crouching in the prison ship's artificial gravity to pull on the garment. If she had to wear the damn thing, at least she would retain the dignity of dressing herself.

"I intended no affront," the blue-maned Chirrn went on. "Rather, I hoped to offer my gratitude. You saved many of us, including myself, from pointless hardship and pain."

She stared at him. "I didn't do it for you. I knew it wouldn't work… and I didn't trust you not to retaliate. You're good at that."

The charge actually seemed to embarrass him. "Your anger toward me is warranted—not as a Lesshchin, but for my role in how you have been treated in captivity. But surely you see now that this fierce resistance is misguided, destructive."

"No. What's destructive is your demand that we abandon who we are. Your intolerance is what killed our babies and provoked us to fight back."

"All that is being asked of you is to leave your planetary past behind. Is that past so critical to your existence that it is worth continued confinement, humiliation, and isolation from your community to cling to it? Even though it will never be an active part of your life again no matter what you do?"

She shook her head. "I suppose a nomadic people can't understand what it means to have roots. To have your very existence defined by the soil in which you were raised."

Churrlaya's brow ridges furrowed. "I struggle to understand why you would value an upbringing in which you were constantly soiled. I thought you lived near the water; was bathing not customary?"

Cecilia laughed out loud for some time, welcoming the release. As long as she had her precious human idioms, quirks of a distinctly human neurology and social training, she'd always have something these aliens couldn't master, something she could use to confound them. "Yes, we were dirty all the time and we loved it," she extemporized. "Playing in the mud, running barefoot through the streets, rough-housing and getting scuffed and scraped… filthy little urchins, that was the life. In that soil, in that dust, was the skin and hair and blood and shit of our ancestors, anointing us, caking us in history that stretches back to the Renaissance, to the merchant princes, to the might of Rome itself. We dug that history into our nails and our teeth until it became part of our very bones!"

The Lesshchin studied her for a long moment. He almost seemed contemplative, but more likely she'd simply overloaded his brain with metaphors. "Then it is not the place," he finally said. "It is your kith and your forebears you feel connected to. Thank you; this clarifies much." Cecilia stared at him, stunned.

"And yet," Churrlaya went on after a moment, "it also creates a paradox."

"And how's that?"

"If being in the place of your ancestors bears such meaning for you, then why did you choose to leave it forever to colonize another world?"

She opened her mouth, but checked herself. Thinking for a moment, she found herself giving him an honest reply. Somehow she felt he was entitled to one—or maybe she felt for the first time that there was something to gain by giving one. "As I said, Venezia is in my bones. I take it with me wherever I go. I miss it terribly, but... I left my home because it helped my home. Because the world needs new places to send its people so they won't overrun it and destroy every last trace of its beauty."

"That is a sensible purpose. But it does not answer my question. Why did it have to be *you* who left?"

She held his gaze. "You don't get that answer. Suffice to say I had my reasons."

Churrlaya gave a slight knee bend. "It will suffice until you are ready to say more," he said, continuing to startle her. "But a question still lingers."

She hesitated, but had to ask. "What question?"

"You were willing to leave behind the world you love in order to help your people. Why, then, are you unable to make the same choice now?"

She had no answer for him. But Churrlaya didn't wait for one. He turned and hopped away, leaving her alone with the question echoing in her mind.

EPILOGUE

"I STILL DON'T BELIEVE IT," SAID SHUAI BINGBING. "THERE'S NO WAY we've actually traveled faster than light!"

Sita laughed at Bingbing's skepticism, trading an amused look with Stephen as they floated arm-in-arm. They and several others were crowded into one of Arachne's habitat modules to view the vista outside.

Next to them, Justine Nguyen laughed, wrapping an arm around Bingbing's dainty shoulders and drawing her closer to the port. "Come on, silly, you can see for yourself!"

"Yes, okay," the recently renounced economist told her wife. "The starscape's different. And that's definitely not the same Chirrn habitat we were at before." This habitat was undergoing expansion, with smaller cylinders being constructed at either end, aligned with it coaxially but not yet rotating with it. Sita thought it looked like a fat rolling pin. Unlike Shilirrlal, which had floated free in interstellar space a parsec and a half from the binary red dwarf Gliese 257, this habitat orbited a large cometary-belt object that the Chirrn were mining for construction material, with a yellow-orange dwarf called HR 4523 dimly visible in the background. This, Sita knew, was a preview of what lay ahead for the migration fleet. Their target destination was a young rogue dwarf planet on the outskirts of the central Scorpius-Centaurus Association, one that Chirrn surveys had identified as a good source of materials for colony-building: uninhabited, with a good mix of carbon, volatiles, and metals close to the surface, low gravity to facilitate their extraction, and plenty of residual core heat to provide a geothermal power source—with the bonus that it was a short warp hop from an unclaimed young blue dwarf that could be tapped as a power source for the Chirrn's antimatter plants.

None of which Bingbing was yet willing to take seriously. "But we didn't actually see the ship move," she insisted. "How convenient that the warp cage totally surrounds the ship when it's engaged." Renounced or not, her loyalist suspicions toward the Chirrn died hard.

To be fair (Stephen thought), while faster-than-light travel may have been mind-boggling in concept, the actual view left much to be desired. The activation of the warp cage had been an impressive sight, at least: the latticework had unfolded elegantly to encase *Arachne*'s modules in two nested spheres, whereupon the programmable quark matter superfluid had flowed into the gaps like a living thing until they were completely encased within. Yet after that, there had been no visible change until the process reversed itself at the end of the wormhole passage. So the only sign of motion aside from the subtle change in the star patterns when they emerged—which was difficult for a human without astronomical training to recognize—had been the different appearance of the local habitat and the different number and configuration of the local cluster of wormhole portals in their Casimir cages.

"You wouldn't have been able to see anything anyway," Justine insisted. "The outer warp shell is so tiny that it would be like looking through a microscopic pinhole. That's why we need to be in a warp bubble to dive through one of the Chirrn's wormholes—it's the only way we're small enough to pass through."

"If you can't see outside the ship, then how do you avoid hitting stuff?" a skeptical Bingbing asked her.

"A spacetime metric is shaped by the mass and energy around it. If the warp bubble comes near a massive object, it changes the shape of the metric. The warp bubble itself serves as a proximity sensor."

"How convenient. Look, for all we know, this entire 'warp cage' could be nothing more than a simulator ride."

While the lovers' serious but playful argument continued, Sita drew Stephen away into the module's central passage until they could speak privately. "What's on your mind?" he asked.

She answered by kissing him deeply but gently. As he returned the kiss, he sensed its importance. This wasn't hunger for erotic distraction from her pain—it was a quieter, gentler, deeper connection than she'd been able to offer him since the attack, if not earlier. "I've missed that," he said at length.

"So have I. Seeing those two lovebirds reunited… it made me think about how I almost lost you. Ooh, if that pasty, microphallic… *American* had hurt you, I'd have…"

He stroked her hair. "I saw you trying to come to my rescue. Fighting with two people twice your mass and almost winning. You can be one scary pixie."

She laughed. "It… clarified some things for me. I've been so afraid of the Chirrn, of aliens. But… seeing you endangered by one of our own… I realized it wasn't about aliens anymore. We're as dangerous as they are." She smirked. "I guess I had my own privilege growing up in London. A dainty bird like me—for a lot of history, I'd never have felt safe walking those streets by myself. I was lucky to be born in an age when I didn't have to feel that kind of fear. But now I've known it, and I thought it was aliens I had to fear, but now I see—it's just life, innit? And you can let it control you, you can let it beat you down and make you scared or hateful… or you can stand the bloody hell up and live your bloody life on your own terms. And when I thought I might have to live that life without you… I just wouldn't bloody stand for it."

This time he initiated the kiss, and it was all the communication they needed for a while. "So… are we okay?" he finally asked.

She thought it over. "It still hurts. A lot. And I'm sure I'll still be scared from time to time—at whatever we may find out there. But… I'm ready to face it. We fear because we have something to lose. And that means we have something to gain too. Something to hope for. Out there… in all that infinite universe… I figure there's got to be more hope than fear."

Stephen clasped her hand. "I've… been afraid too. But I've been trying so hard to be strong for you… I see now I didn't need to be. I should've been more open about my own fear, my own pain. I should've shared everything with you. From now on…"

She kissed him again. "I know. It's a new beginning. The Chirrn have the right idea—if your old life doesn't work anymore, just bung it in the bin and build yourself a new one. Shilirrlal, Lesshchi, Earth—they're all in the past now. They're not who we are anymore." She clasped Stephen's hands and gazed into his eyes, seeing in them the endless optimism and sense of wonder that had made her love him in the first place.

"Like you said at the start of our last new life: We're star people now."

To Be Continued in
Arachne's Exile

ABOUT THE AUTHOR

Christopher L. Bennett is a lifelong resident of Cincinnati, Ohio, with a B.S. in Physics and a B.A. in History from the University of Cincinnati. A fan of science and science fiction since age five, he has spent the past two decades selling original short fiction to magazines such as *Analog Science Fiction and Fact* and *BuzzyMag*. For the past dozen years, he has been one of Pocket Books' most prolific and popular authors of Star Trek tie-in fiction, including the epic Next Generation prequel *The Buried Age*, the *Star Trek: Department of Temporal Investigations* series, and the *Star Trek: Enterprise — Rise of the Federation* series. His original novel *Only Superhuman*, perhaps the first hard science fiction superhero novel, was voted Library Journal's SF/Fantasy Debut of the Month for October 2012. His short story collections *Hub Space: Tales from the Greater Galaxy* and *Crimes of the Hub* are available in e-book and print formats from Mystique Press.

Christopher's homepage, fiction annotations, and blog can be found at christopherlbennett.wordpress.com, and his Facebook author page is at www.facebook.com/ChristopherLBennettAuthor.

APPENDIX 1: DRAMATIS PERSONAE

Arachne **senior personnel**
Arachne: shipmind
Bahar, Tarik Hüseyin: first officer
Bhatiani, Sita: biologist, behaviorist
Jacobs-Wong, Stephen: expedition leader
LoCarno, Cecilia: ship commander
Narvaez Duarte, Diego Felipe: assistant chief engineer, pilot
Ndege, Kweli: chief surgeon
Oyama Kazuko: political scientist, legal scholar
Pritam, Ravinder: senior cyberneticist, programmer
Silbermann, Haim: chief engineer

Arachne **junior personnel (incomplete list)**
al-Bakri, Ibrahim: geneticist, ecologist
Amrouche, Kahina: mathematician, programmer
Bhadra, Vijay: pilot, engineer
Brentwood, Jason: climatologist, meteorologist
Caravalho, Joana: physician, neurologist
Dhillon, Amrita: geologist, mining engineer
Errgang, Hannah: climatologist, oceanographer
Ichiba Nobuo: physical therapist, builder
Jiang Erfan, Evan: planetologist, meteorologist
Marcoe, Renata: political scientist, historian
Mazunov, Sergei: sociologist, economist
Nguyen, Justine: astrophysicist, mathematician
Nguyen, Marc: teacher, child psychologist
Oates, James: industrial engineer, cyberneticist
Olatunji, Scott: geneticist, botanist

Oliveira-York, Andrea: biologist, ecologist
Shuai Bingbing: economist, political scientist
Soares, Rosario: nurse, therapeutic sex provider
Thorne, Diana: construction engineer
Vidmar, Joshua: climatologist, environmental engineer
Zacharias, Nikolos: physician, psychologist
Zhao Changkun: programmer, systems analyst

Lesshchin (Chirrn)
Churrlaya: *Zhemhal* biologist, later Shilirrlaln xenopsychologist
Rillial: *Zhemhal* commander, prosecution advocate
Vhehhal: *Zhemhal* security officer, radical agitator
Djayrulu: youngest intact survivor
Simisshen: Churrlaya's lover
Marellel, Ruzhalu: friends of Churrlaya

Shilirrlaln (Chirrn unless otherwise specified)
L'chellin: trial advocate; senior mediator, Intersocietal guild
Broadwing (Zenith male): trial arbiter; junior mediator
Dj'vhereth: head tribune
R'nilinnath: apprentice mediator
R'hhenevh: alpha of Xenopsychology guild
Yonchon (Ryohoch): starship engineer
Mh'lellissh: physician assigned to Arachnen
Ch'millin, Mh'resshelel: Shilirrlal administrators

APPENDIX 2:
ARACHNE EXPEDITION PROFILE

Destination: Cybele (Gamma Leporis Ad), distance 29.3 ly

Microsail probe launch: 2083
Microsail probe arrival: 2113
Telemetry received at Earth, Cybele confirmed viable for colonization: 2142
Arachne launch: August 4, 2147
Stage 1: Particle-beam acceleration (40 g) to 0.84*c*: August 4-11, 2147 (5.9 dy shipboard due to time dilation; crew cushioned against acceleration by hibernation gel)

Projected:
Stage 2: Coast at 0.84*c* for 28.45 ly: August 2147-June 2181 (18.4 yrs shipboard)
Stage 3: Magnetic braking against interstellar medium (c. 0.4 g) to system insertion: June 2181-June 2183 (1.6 yrs shipboard)

Actual:
Stage 2: Coast interrupted at 24.1 ly: April 18, 2176 (15.6 yrs shipboard)
Gravitic deceleration by *Zhemhal* capture field (3993 g): 107 minutes (85 min shipboard)

APPENDIX 3: CHIRRN TIME UNITS

THE BASIC UNIT OF CHIRRN TIME MEASUREMENT, THE NARR, IS ONE STANDARD habitat rotation, equal to 96.64 seconds. Chirrn employ base 8 mathematics, so their time units are derived as follows:

1/64 narr	=	*narrat*	=	1.51 seconds	
1/8 narr	=	*narreth*	=	12.08 s	
1 narr	=	*narr*	=	96.64 s	=	1.61 minutes
8 narr	=	*narredj*	=	12.89 min	
64 narr	=	*narrach*	=	103.08 min	=	1.72 hours
512 narr	=	*narrissh*	=	13.74 h	
4096 narr	=	*narruvh*	=	109.95 h	=	4.58 days
8^5 narr	=	*narrenn*	=	36.65 d	
8^6 narr	=	*narranl*	=	293.21 d	
8^7 narr	=	*narrayth*	=	2345 d	=	6.42 years
8^8 narr	=	*yanarr*	=	51.38 y	
8^9 narr	=	*yanarredj*	=	411.03 y	
8^{10} narr	=	*yanarrach*	=	3288.2 y	
8^{11} narr	=	*yanarrissh*	=	26,306 y	

APPENDIX 4: SHILIRRLAL PARAMETERS

A TYPICAL CHIRRN HABITAT IS CONSTRUCTED ON MUCH THE SAME LINES AS a classical O'Neill cylinder, a rotating habitat of the type proposed by physicist Gerard K. O'Neill in the 1976 book *The High Frontier: Human Colonies in Space*, and commonly used by the Strider civilization of Sol's Main Belt and Trojan asteroids in the 21st and 22nd centuries. However, Chirrn habitats are single cylinders rather than the tethered, counterrotating pairs used in Solsys, since deep-space habitats have no need to precess to keep their mirrors pointed at a star as they orbit it.

Centripetal acceleration a (equal to the effective gravity) equals the square of the linear velocity of rotation v divided by the radius r, or:

$$a = v^2/r$$

The velocity equals the circumference of the cylinder over its rotational period:

$$v = 2\pi r/T$$

Thus

$$a = 4\pi^2 r/T^2$$

The habitat section is a cylinder with hemispherical endcaps, equal in length to 8 times the radius. Thus, its volume can be computed as that of a cylinder 6 radii in length ($\pi r^2 \times 6r = 6\pi r^3$) plus a sphere of 1 radius ($4/3 \times \pi r^3$).

Results:

Rotational period:	1.00 narr = 96.64 s
Gravity at outer shell:	1.302 g = 12.76 m/s^2
Rotational velocity:	196.25 m/s
Total radius:	3.018 km
Length of main habitat section:	24.144 km
Total length:	30.18 km
Volume of main habitat section:	633.30 km^3

AFTERWORD

PART ONE OF THIS NOVEL IS BASED ON THE NOVELETTE "AGGRAVATED Vehicular Genocide," initially published in *Analog Science Fiction and Fact* in November 1998 and reprinted and revised in my 2018 collection *Among the Wild Cybers: Tales Beyond the Superhuman*. In that story, *Arachne* was an interstellar ramjet traveling at 99 percent of lightspeed, using high-energy lasers to ionize the interstellar medium so that it could be magnetically channeled into the ship's fusion drive. These lasers could be concentrated to pinpoint focus to deflect oncoming debris. This was what inspired the story in the first place, when I wondered what would happen if such defense lasers struck an alien ship by mistake. In the original version, the Lesshchi habitat, housing roughly 8700 Chirrn, was struck by such a pinpoint beam which melted through its southern end in milliseconds, superheating the air and rupturing the hull from the sudden pressure increase, blowing the end completely away and killing all but some 350 of the habitat's population.

I subsequently learned that the ramjet concept has serious practical flaws. The magnetic field would create drag against the interstellar medium, which would be too thin anyway to provide an adequate fuel source, particularly here in the Local Bubble—unless the lasers and magnetic field were powerful enough to ionize an immense volume of interstellar hydrogen and drag it in to the centerline of the ship at sufficient speed. When I republished the story on my website in 2004, I tweaked some technical details and added some hand waves in an effort to make it more plausible. But the more I studied interstellar propulsion techniques, the more I realized that ramjets were an outmoded idea. So for this novel, I abandoned the ramjet concept altogether in favor of a modified form of magnetic sail propulsion. The concept of a magnetic sail accelerated by pellets rather than a particle beam was developed by

Dana G. Andrews and Robert Zubrin, and the sailbeam concept was proposed by Jordan Kare. They were brought to my attention by Paul Gilster in his book *Centauri Dreams* and his blog of the same name. Adam Crowl's *Crowlspace* blog article "Magnetic Sail as a Star-Brake" (crowlspace.com, February 10, 2007) provided additional details.

This decision led me to re-examine the entire work, and I discovered other flaws. For instance, I greatly underestimated the interior volume and population capacity of the Chirrn habitats as described. Also, a laser defense system would be unlikely to have the required power unless it were far too immense for a ship as light as the new *Arachne* had to be. I quickly realized that at relativistic speed, a simple sailbeam propelled ahead of the ship would be more than sufficient as a defensive weapon. The nature of the impact would have to be different than I had described, and even if the habitat was less thoroughly devastated, its population, and thus the death toll, would have to be far higher. I'm deeply indebted to the Jet Propulsion Laboratory's Paul Woodmansee and "Orpheus" of the Ex Isle BBS for helping me work out the physical details of the revised Lesshchi incident. Robert Zubrin's 1993 paper "Detection of Extraterrestrial Civilizations via the Spectral Signature of Advanced Interstellar Spacecraft" in *Astronomical Society of the Pacific Conference Series*, Volume 74, p.487 helped me address the critical question of *Arachne*'s bow shock and its detectability.

Thanks also to Marco Palmieri and David Mack, whose advice on story structure helped me improve this tale immensely. Thanks to Sam Morgan and Greg Cox for their advice on earlier drafts, which helped me strengthen the plot and characters. Thanks to Michael A. Burstein for helping me realize that my crazy idea to rework my really long epic novel into a duology was actually worth doing. And thanks to Stanley Schmidt for buying the original story and offering me the guidance that helped me become good enough to sell my work at last.

Finally, a particular thanks to the fans who came through for me with their generous donations at a point when my financial situation was desperate. My deep gratitude to Vasilios Arabatzis II, Byron Bailey, Matthew Buck, Scott Crick, Michael Evans, Shawn Fox, David Gian-Cursio, Adam Czarnecki, Justin Hilyard, Mari Johnson, Ronald Mallory, Cody Lee Martin, Daniel Nicholls, Bernd Perplies, Troy Rodgers, Johanna Schliemann, Clive Viagas, Christian Zenker, Mark Zieba, and everyone else who helped.

COLONY SPONSORS

A. Parsons
Allyn Gibson
Amy Laurens
Andrew Corvin
Andrew Glazier
Andrew Timson
Andy Hunter
Anonymous
Ashli Tingle
Barb and Carl Kesner
beardedzilla
Bradij
Brenda Cooper
Brendan Lonehawk
Brian D Lambert
Brian Griffin
C. Frost
C.A. Rowland
Caleb Monroe
Carol Gyzander
Carol Jones
Carol Mammano
Charname
Chelsea Provencher
Cheri Kannarr
Chris Matthews
Christopher D. Abbott
Christopher J. Burke
Christopher J. Ford
Christopher Thompson
Chuck Wilson
Cody Steinman
Craig "Stevo" Stephenson

Dale A. Russell
Daniel Lin
Danielle Ackley-McPhail
Danny Chamberlin
David Holden
Dawfydd Kelly
Diánna Martin
Dominic
Donald J. Bingle
Dr Douglas Vaughan
Dr. Karen
Eli Berg-Maas
Eli Mellen
Emily Weed Baisch
Eron Wyngarde
Evan Ladouceur
Frankie B
Gary Vandegrift
Gavin
GraceAnne DeCandido
Håkon Gaut
Hiram G Wells
Howard J. Bampton
Ian Harvey
Idran
Isaac 'Will It Work' Dansicker
J Paulus
J. B. Burbidge
Jakub Narebski
James Flux
James Goetsch
Jaq Greenspon
Jeff Metzner

Jeff Singer
Jennifer L. Pierce
Jeremy Bottroff
Johanna Rothman
John Green
John Idlor
Joseph Charpak
Josh Vidmar
Josh Ward
Judith Waidlich
Keith R.A. DeCandido
Keith West, Future Potentate of the Solar System
Kelly Pierce
Kerry aka Trouble
Kierin Fox
Kyle Franklin
Lark Cunningham
Larry
Leon W. Fairley
Lewis Phillips
Lisa Hawkridge
Lisa Kruse
Lorraine J. Anderson
MaGnUs
Malcolm Eckel
Margaret M. St. John
Maria T
Mark Beaulieu
Mary Catelynn Cunningham
mdtommyd
me@edmondkoo.com
Michael Brooker
Michael Doyle
Mike M.
Ms. Dyane Stillman
Nathan Turner
Norman Jaffe
Pam DeLuca
Patrick Foster

Paul van Oven
Peter D Engebos
Phillip Thorne
PJ Kimbell
Pulse Publishing
Ralph M.Seibel
Richard P Clark
Richard Todd
RKBookman
Robert C Flipse
Robert Claney
Robert M. Sutton
Samara N. Lipman
Scott Crick
Scott DeRuby
Scott Mantooth
Scott Schaper
Serge Broom
Shane "Asharon" Sylvia
Sharon Abdel-Malek
Shervyn
Sheryl R. Hayes
Stacy Butcher
Stephanie Souders
Stephen Ballentine
Stephen Lesnik
Steven Callen
Stoney
The Amazing Maurice
The Creative Fund
Thierry Millié
Tim DuBois
Tom B.
ToniAnn Marini
Tony Hernandez
V Hartman DiSanto
Vince Kindfuller
Wayne Garmil
William C. Tracy
Zeb Berryman